NEWSTAR
ONE

NEWSTAR ONE

PAUL BROWER

This book is a work of fiction. All names and events described in this work comes from the author's imagination. Any resembalnce to real life names or events is purely coincidental and not intentional.

Copyright © 2022 by Paul Brower

Library of Congress Control Number: 2022908027

Gravity Assist Publishing
Gainesville, VA
www.gravityassistpublishing.com

For Brayden, Eliana, Alex and of course my dear Sonia.
May your dreams always reach to the stars and beyond.

NEWSTAR
ONE

PROLOGUE

"T minus twenty minutes to launch."

Nine-year old Alex Stone listened to the booming voice as he sat on hard metal bleachers in Florida air as thick as soup. The setting sun cast an orange glow across the marshes and bays of the Kennedy Space Center. The shadows slowly lengthened as Alex watched the numbers on the huge digital clock tick backwards, seeming like they would never reach their destination.

His mother's face appeared on the giant projection screen set out by the water, and her head, enlarged on the monitor and enclosed in an astronaut's helmet, was the size of a whole person. Alex's mother was smiling the way she always did when she was excited about something, her bright white teeth sparkling and the skin at the corners of her blue eyes wrinkling like cat whiskers. She reached up and flipped a switch on the control panel with her gloved hand. Alex waved at her image, even though he knew she couldn't see him.

As far as Alex was concerned, his mother was perfect. Everyone said how smart she was, and Alex knew it was true. He loved to hear her talk about her work as a geneticist. She would explain in ways Alex could understand how all life was made up of tiny cells that contained plans called DNA. These plans decided what every living thing looked like, what colors it had and what its capabilities were. By studying these plans, his mom explained, we could help fix problems that sometimes happen when the plans are written a little wrong. That was why she had to go back into space for the next five months, to help figure these things out.

A calm female voice came over the loudspeaker. "Orion crew, lock your visors and verify positive O2 flow."

"Copy that, Houston," replied a deep baritone voice that Alex vaguely recognized.

"Grandma, what's oh-two?" he asked, looking up at her in the seat next to his.

"It's an abbreviation for oxygen, dear," said his grandmother with a smile. She put her hand on his knee and patted it gently.

Alex squinted to try to see the rocket better. From this distance it was a blurry pillar of light against the darkening sky. His mother was somewhere in that distant bright tower. A warm gentle breeze washed over the bleachers.

Alex was starting to grow restless. He stood up on his seat and looked down at the dirt path that ran alongside the bleachers. A thin line of people trickled into the viewing area, while a sparse few headed in the other direction towards the smelly, plastic portable toilets that bordered the parking lot. Alex spotted his dad in the crowd that was coming towards the bleachers. He jumped up and down and shouted for him as he made his way up the crowded metal steps.

"Hey there, kiddo." His dad smiled and gave Alex a high five. He was wearing his blue flight suit and he looked every bit the part of a military pilot and astronaut. His sandy brown hair was cut short, and his chiseled jaw, well-built upper body and tall posture emanated a relaxed confidence. Alex loved his father, but not in the same way as he loved his mother. Sometimes daddy was too serious and bossy. Mom was always warm and loving.

His dad sat down next to Alex.

"How was the press briefing, Mike?" asked Grandma.

"It was great until they asked me to explain Barbara's science experiments. I really had to pull that answer out of my..." His father stopped and looked at Alex. "...behind. It was pretty bad. Wish they could just stick to questions about how to go to the bathroom in space." His dad chuckled.

"I could explain her experiments," Alex piped up. "She's studying how to fix DNA when it gets broken. It messes up the plans for our cells."

"Well, aren't you the smart little scientist. Now we just have to teach you how to fly an F-35 and you'll be ready to be a super-astronaut when you grow up." His dad ruffled Alex's hair and Alex smiled.

The countdown was nearing the last few minutes. As the last stragglers began to settle into their seats, a silence fell over the crowd. The last light of day faded as the clock ticked down the final sixty seconds. A booming voice began to count with the clock. "Five...four...three...two...one."

The sky exploded in light, and the crowd let out a collective gasp. The sound took a few seconds to reach them but then it shook the bleachers. Alex began to clap as he watched the light climb the sky up towards the stars. The last launch he had seen was for his father's last mission two years ago. This was even better than he remembered. The light seemed to be getting brighter and then as it crossed a cloud, it seemed to explode like a firework.

Alex was overjoyed and began to clap even more furiously. His hands hurt from the clapping; they felt like they might bleed but he wanted to clap louder than the booming sound hitting his ears. He kept clapping as bits of light fell, just like a fireworks show.

Then he suddenly became aware of the fact that nobody else was clapping anymore. The booms had stopped. He looked up at his father who was standing. His face looked ghost white in the evening twilight.

"Daddy, why aren't you clapping?"

Alex slowly looked around. The entire crowd was still. Then he heard a sob from within the mass of bodies. In the distant sky, it was raining sparks.

Something was wrong.

His grandmother gathered him in her arms as she began to cry.

Seven years later...

CHAPTER 1

ALEX PULLED THE TEST TUBE FROM THE CENTRIFUGE AND SET IT on a stand at the lab table. Using a pipette, he carefully extracted the liquid at the top of the tube. Moving slowly, he squeezed out the contents into a tall glass filtration column, and watched it dribble down past the filter and into the beaker. He tried to control the slight shaking in his hand, but the excitement was building inside of him as it had the past two times he had done this.

Maybe this time it will work.

As he always did when he was nearing the end of an experiment, he thought of his mother. It was getting harder to remember her voice and what her face looked like in real life, not in frozen snapshots of time he kept on his wall. He thought about how proud she would be of him when he was on the cover of a magazine or casually telling a news reporter how he had discovered a cure for a deadly genetic disease and it had all been because of his mother. In these moments, he could just about see her smile and feel the warmth of her hug.

Alex's thoughts were interrupted when Mr. Bromley walked over and sat on a stool. "I'm pretty sure this is not the lab assignment you're supposed to be working on," he said. Alex sighed at the unwelcome interruption from his dimwitted teacher.

"I already finished it during class." Alex didn't bother to look up from the test tube from which he was sucking more liquid into his pipette.

"I figured as much. This is becoming a bit of a habit lately."

"Sorry." What else was he supposed to say?

Mr. Bromley's button-down shirt had sweat marks by the armpits. His large chest heaved in and out, as if the walk over to the stool had been too much exertion for his two-hundred pound figure. He sat quietly, and Alex ignored him, continuing to transfer liquid from the test tube into the filtration column.

"Look, Alex," he finally said. "I don't get a lot of extra supplies. I'm happy you want to try some of your own experiments in open lab time, but you need to tell me what you're doing. These chemicals can be dangerous. You're one of my best students, but that doesn't mean you know everything. So what are we working on today?"

"I'm trying to synthesize a protein."

"What kind of protein?"

"It's a capsid protein made by modifying several base pairs of an adenovirus." Alex smiled at the confused silence that followed. He decided one of his frequent requests for needed scientific equipment might end this conversation, so he added, "Do you think we could get some mice to experiment on? Especially if we can get mice with cystic fibrosis, that would be good."

Mr. Bromley laughed out loud. His belly shook like Santa Claus. "I don't think that you're going to find a mouse with cystic fibrosis anywhere."

"No, you can. There was a lab in the nineties that figured out how to insert a mutated gene into mouse embryos and create a line of mice with cystic fibrosis. You can buy them for research."

"So is that what your experiment is about? Curing cystic fibrosis in mice?"

Alex looked at Mr. Bromley like he was simple. "Um, if you can cure it in mice, then you can do the same in humans."

Bromley sighed loudly. "Look, Alex, I love your enthusiasm for biology. But I can't get you any mice to experiment on. I can't even imagine what Principal Chesterton would say about that. I shouldn't need to tell you again that after-school lab time is to make up the assignments from class. If you want to do other experiments, you need to tell me what you're doing ahead of time and I'll tell you if it's OK. Do we understand each other?"

Alex looked up at the sweaty ignoramus of a teacher. He decided he needed to play along or risk losing access to the lab equipment he needed. "Yes, sir. Does that mean if I show you what I'm working on, I can come back next week?"

The teacher let out an exaggerated breath. "Yes, of course," he said, although he didn't sound like he meant it. "For now though, clean this up. Open lab is over in ten minutes."

Alex finished filtering the liquid and poured the solution from the beaker into a test tube which he sealed with a rubber stopper. When Mr. Bromley was looking away, he slipped it into his backpack. Then he cleaned up the glassware and put away the equipment. He needed to get ready for his basketball game anyway.

*****

Two hours later, after running across the street for a hamburger and changing into his uniform, Alex sat on a wooden bench in the school gym and watched his team-mates run furiously back and forth down the basketball court. Every few minutes, his eyes wandered up to the bleachers, where a crowd of happy, smiling parents sat beneath a huge banner that read, "Creekside High Hawks Basketball – Welcome to Parents' Night." In smaller print were inscribed the words, "Your dedication makes our success possible." Alex searched the faces of the crowd and tried not to get his hopes up. Even though his father had practically forced Alex to join the team this year, he hadn't shown up for a single game. Not that it mattered since Coach Dudley had given Alex all of about ten minutes of play time so far this season.

Alex ran his hand through his sandy brown hair. It was unusually thick and long. He was trying to see how much time it would take his dad to notice and insist on him going to the barber shop for a buzz cut. So far, the answer was at least three months.

"Alex, you're up!" shouted Dudley. They were up by 12 points, which was probably the only reason he was being given play time. Alex jumped up from the bench and jogged onto the court. His sleeveless green uniform shirt emblazoned with the Hawks logo bounced around loosely on his wiry frame.

Alex took up his position just outside the three-point line on the left side of the basket. As he waited for the center to bring the ball down, he looked into the crowd. No sign of his dad, but he did spot Mackenzie Dale on the bottom row of the bleachers. His eyes lingered on her. She was wearing a light pink tank top and her blond hair fell loosely around her face and past her shoulders. She was sitting next to Heather Townsend, and the two were chatting animatedly. As Mackenzie spoke, her hands flew through the air, gesturing this way and that as her entire face seemed to glow with a smile. She looked so happy, and so pretty, and so...nice.

Suddenly, Alex heard his name and looked up just in time to see the basketball flying towards his face. Before his hands could react, the ball smashed his nose and he fell to the ground. The crowd gasped.

Alex sat up just in time to see Coach Dudley running over. He spotted Mackenzie on the sideline pointing to him as she whispered something to Heather. He wanted to disappear off the face of the earth.

Coach Dudley squatted next to Alex. "You okay, sport? That nose doesn't look so good."

Alex reached up and felt the stickiness under his nostril. When he pulled his hand away, he saw a gob of red blood stuck to his finger. *Perfect, a bloody nose in front of everybody in the eleventh minute of game time I've had all season. This was why I didn't want to play basketball.*

"I'm fine," Alex said and pulled himself up, holding his nose to try to stop the bleeding.

"Come on, you can sit out a few minutes and catch your breath," said Coach.

As Alex walked away to unenthusiastic applause from a handful of spectators, the coach handed him a tissue. He sat down on the bench and pinched his nose while staring at the ground and pretending that there weren't a dozen people staring at him and making fun of his stupidity.

After the game, Alex shuffled across the court with his

head down, but he was interrupted by his best friend, Tyler Davenger, running up to him before he reached the door to the locker room. Tyler wasn't a big fan of sports, but he often came to the games to watch Alex play. It was a gesture Alex appreciated more than he would ever admit. In truth, neither he nor Tyler had any other close friends at school besides each other, and so they stuck together as much as possible.

"Nice job, bro," Tyler said, giving him a pat on the shoulder.

"Yeah, very funny," Alex replied. "I didn't even want to be on this team in the first place. And I don't know if I should be happy or not that my dad didn't come out to see that."

"You should probably be glad he missed that performance. I'm sure he's got important space stuff to take care of anyway."

"Just like always."

"Hey, so are we still on for *Star Crusader* this weekend?" Alex and Tyler had been playing video games together since they were kids. They played together online a lot, but a lot of the time they would get together at one or the other of their houses and gorge themselves on junk food while they played. Tyler's father had been in and out of his life since Tyler was a child, and his mother worked two jobs to maintain the house, so his parents were generally as absent as Alex's dad. Playing games together was a good excuse to not be alone.

"We are definitely on," said Alex. The new game would allow players to design their own spaceship and use it to complete missions around the galaxy. Alex had always preferred games with a space theme, so he was particularly excited about this new one.

"Sweet. I will catch you later then," said Tyler. He and Alex bumped fists before Alex left to face the ridicule of his teammates in the locker room.

CHAPTER 2

STEWART LOCKE SAT IN A PLUSH RED CHAIR IN THE VIEWING AREA behind his own privately-run mission control. The forty-seven year old CEO of NewStar Space Technology looked through the glass at the rows of computer consoles that seemed like pews to an altar of space exploration. In the front of the room, a large map littered with blinking lights and data showed where over the earth Stewart's nascent space station soared.

It seemed a bit egotistical to think of it as his space station, but it would not be there were it not for him. Sure, many investors had contributed money and thousands of engineers were involved in designing, building and maintaining the orbiting complex. However, none of them would have done any of it had it not been for Stewart's vision and passion. In some ways, he felt as if he had birthed this space station through his own sheer effort. And it was nearly complete and ready to become operational.

As Stewart sat in the chair and watched the work of the engineers below, the door in the back of the room opened and a smartly dressed blond woman in her mid-forties entered carrying a brown leather portfolio. Her heels clicked on the floor as she made her way to the chair next to Stewart's.

"I thought I'd find you here." Stewart looked over at Melanie Howell, the company's marketing director. He had rescued her two years ago from a monotonous career as a public affairs officer for NASA.

"What can I do for you, Melanie?"

"You can give me a big bonus this year," she said.

"Oh yeah, why is that?"

Melanie smiled. "Because I just got you a booking for the first customers who will stay in our hotel."

"What are you talking about? We already have a waiting list 38 people long."

"Yes, we do," said Melanie. "And we are going to bump every one of them down the list."

"Like hell we are!" shouted Stewart. "These people have contracts with us!"

Stewart's infamous angry outbursts stopped most people dead in their tracks and left them groveling for forgiveness. But Melanie did not fear Stewart like others in the company, and she simply smiled a little wider. "I think you'll be willing to buy them out in any way you can. Because I just got John Fritzer, his wife, and his daughter to agree to fly if we put them at the top of the list."

Stewart's scowl vanished in a flash. "You're kidding me!" he said with a huge, almost childish grin on his face. "You mean THE John Fritzer?"

"The one and only – actor, producer, owner of Real Life Media. This is the big one."

Stewart shook his head. He couldn't believe his luck. John Fritzer was probably one of the most beloved personalities in the country. Who couldn't like a handsome, well-spoken thirty-eight year old who starred in big films and then took vacations in Africa volunteering at refugee camps? If John Fritzer wanted to vacation at the NewStar One space station, everybody in the country would want to go too.

This was exactly the kind of breakthrough Stewart needed. The truth was, without a serious change of course, the company was going to come crashing down in flames. The space station that NewStar Space Technology had privately built was over budget, behind schedule and not forecast to generate even half the revenue it would need to stay operating. NewStar One was designed to be a sprawling complex, consisting of a space tourist hotel and a science lab that received funding from universities and governments. The stingy science grants wouldn't be nearly enough to justify the cost of the orbital station, but the hotel had the potential to bring in huge revenues. By launching on reusable rockets, ultra-wealthy families could shell out a few million bucks per week at the hotel and bring in a cash stream that would allow NewStar to stay afloat.

Unfortunately, bookings for the hotel had been slow. Stewart and the company were discovering trepidation among all but the most adventurous of the wealthy public. The rocket technology wasn't proven well enough yet. They needed some ambassadors to go experience the hotel for themselves. That would get the ball rolling. And it looked like John Fritzer was going to be that ambassador.

"There's just one little catch," said Melanie.

"What's that?" asked Stewart.

"The Fritzer family doctor has apparently advised them against bringing their daughter, Elodie. They say the radiation in orbit could be damaging to a younger person."

"That's a load of crap!" said Stewart. Before founding

NewStar, he had worked for NASA on the International Space Station program, and he had lived through several seemingly endless meetings with the flight surgeons where they discussed radiation risks to the astronauts. It was true that the doctors assigned a higher risk factor to younger astronauts, but it wasn't by much. He remembered them discussing numbers along the lines of an extra 40 or 50 cancer cases out of 10,000 people when the subjects were exposed at a younger age versus an older one. That didn't seem like a big risk to Stewart.

"Well, the doctors don't think it's crap," said Melanie. "The Fritzers are torn. John and his daughter are very close, and he insists that they do this as a family. But nobody has ever sent someone as young as a teenager to orbit before."

"Damn," said Stewart. "We need to find a way to convince them that it's safe. We can send out the radiation data from our sensors to the medical community."

"We could and we should do that. But I was thinking maybe we should be even a little more bold than that."

"What did you have in mind?"

"Let's send a teenager up ahead of the Fritzers to show them it's safe."

"But I thought the Fritzers wanted to be the first hotel guests," said Stewart.

"Exactly," said Melanie. "So we send a teenager not as a guest. We send one up as crew."

Stewart sat back and thought.

A teenage crewmember on the space station? Would a teenager be able to handle the demands and avoid damaging anything? Could a teenager represent the company well? Then again, we are paying the crewmembers a lot and some of them will have to tend to the hotel, clean the rooms, and make food for the guests.

Teenagers are great at jobs like that, and you can pay them so much less.

"I was thinking we could have a public competition. Just think about it – an open call for the first teenage crewmember on NewStar One. The publicity would be ridiculous. We could even make it into a competition-style reality show."

Stewart paused and thought for a minute more. "I don't know," he said. "First of all, I'm not sure that John Fritzer would want the attention taken away from his family. And second of all, I'm not sure how much I trust an arbitrarily selected teenager onboard NewStar One. It's a pretty damn expensive station, Melanie."

Melanie looked disappointed. "Well, what if we limit it just to the children of our own employees? We could maintain discretion about the selection process and can have a bit more assurance that we are selecting someone we know."

Stewart leaned back and rested his head on the soft padding of the chair. "That's not a bad idea. Do you think sending a crewmember will really be enough to convince the Fritzers to sign on?"

"From my discussions with some of his people, I think this would seal the deal for us."

"Hmmm, interesting. Doesn't Mike Stone have a teenage kid?"

Melanie winced. "I feel like that would be a delicate situation."

"What do you mean?"

"Well, it's just that since the accident with Barbara..."

Stewart abruptly sat up straight and looked at Melanie with dagger eyes. "Give me a break! Mike wants to fly again. That's why we hired him. Our reliability numbers beat anything NASA ever built. If Mike is going to fly, there's no reason he shouldn't want to take his kid. And since he's the first one up there, he can supervise the boy. Then it's easy and we don't have to change around flight crew assignments."

"Alright," Melanie said reluctantly. "We can certainly try that."

"I'll go talk with Mike. Meanwhile, see what other crew have kids in the right age range and bring them in as well. Make sure they sign a non-disclosure and threaten them with some serious consequences if they break it."

Melanie agreed to Stewart's demands. Sensing the deal was done, she stood and clicked her way towards the door.

"Hey, Melanie," Stewart said. She stopped and turned around. "Nice work."

She nodded and turned back to the door. She smiled to herself as she left the office, already planning how she would spend her bonus check.

*****

Mike Stone sat at the curved grey desk in his spacious office at NewStar Space Technologies headquarters on Bay Area Blvd in southeast Houston. The sun had set hours ago, but Mike had barely noticed. His eyes were glued to the computer monitor as he flipped through pages and pages of space station procedures, making notes and comments as he went. The knock on the door startled him and he jolted upright. Stewart Locke did not wait for an invitation before strutting across the room.

"You're here pretty late," he said to Mike.

"I've got a lot of procedures to go through before the

operations review next week."

"Well, I'm sorry to interrupt, but I need to talk to you about something important."

"Of course, have a seat." Mike gestured at the blue chair in front of his desk, and Stewart fell into the chair, leaned back comfortably and extended his arms outward in both directions, resting them on adjacent guest chairs.

"I think we might have had a breakthrough in our bookings problem," Stewart began.

"Oh yeah?"

"Quite possibly. This is not public information yet, but John Fritzer has shown some interest in making a trip."

Mike's eyes widened. "Wow, that would be a big win. Great for publicity."

"Exactly. The only problem is that he wants to bring his family and their idiot doctor is recommending against flying their teenage daughter. John won't go unless she comes along. They're very close."

"What are they worried about? Radiation?"

"Yes. Mainly, the increased lifetime cancer risk."

"Well, I mean, that's an understandable concern, but is it really that high of a risk?"

"Not really. I had the biomedical folks look into it and they would be looking at about a 0.7% lifetime cancer risk increase."

"Well, shit, you've got a better chance of dying in a car accident."

"Exactly. It seems like you agree with me on this, which is good. We can't have the world thinking that teenagers and children can't fly in space. It would eliminate a lot of clientele. There are lots of wealthy folks with families."

"Yeah, it's hard to educate people about the realities of these things."

"That's because people don't respond well to numbers and statistics. They respond well to demonstrations. Which is why we're going to send a clear message. I'm planning to fly a teenager up with the first crew, to prove that we have no concerns. And I want that kid supervised by parents."

Mike's eyes widened as he realized what Stewart was asking. He stood up abruptly. "No way."

"And why not?" Stewart remained relaxed in the chair. "You just told me how safe our system is. And you've promised me that what happened to Barbara will not affect your judgment in this job."

"Don't be an asshole," Mike said sharply. Stewart leaned forward in his chair and raised his eyebrows as if to say, *are you really going to talk to me like that?* Mike glared at Stewart in his expensive black suit and perfectly starched white shirt.

Stewart could be difficult to deal with, but Mike owed him a great debt for bringing him to NewStar Space Technologies. After Barbara's death, it had become clear very quickly that NASA would never let him fly again. It was only three months after her death when they made him talk to the psychologists. They had asked pointed questions about his desire to continue taking risks, how he was handling the grief, did he ever feel like hurting himself. Mike had been more determined than ever to continue exploring space because he knew that was what Barbara would have wanted. She shared his passion for exploration, for seeking out the unknown, and if he stopped because of her death then it meant that her sacrifice was meaningless.

After just a few sessions, though, the psychologists declared that he was not fit to fly in space again. They cited his grief as a risk to other crew members, saying his performance would likely suffer from the traumatic event. Mike had been furious, but luckily Stewart had rescued him from the death throes of his career and brought him onto the NewStar One project just as it was beginning. Now, Mike was the director of operations for the company and would have a chance to fly in space again and keep alive his dreams and those of his lost wife. He just had to put up with the whims and demands of his powerful and temperamental boss, which was usually a small price to pay. But this request...this was more than Stewart's usual ask. He took a deep breath. "Look, Stewart, I can't take on that responsibility. I've got enough going on with this mission. I'm not bringing Alex into it. He'd be a distraction."

"I think it would be helpful to have some low-cost labor onboard to take care of the hotel guests. Are you really thinking about having yourself and the science crew clean up their rooms and make their food? This space station is half hotel after all. And the hotel part is the part that brings in the money."

"We have a good plan to divide up those duties among the crew. We don't need extra help."

"Well, you do now because I say you do."

"Why Alex?"

"I thought I made it clear. I don't want a random teenager running around on the station without a parent. And right now, you're scheduled to go to NewStar One first. None of the other two on the first flight have kids, at least not at the right ages. And the next scheduled crewmember who has a teenager is Jim Abbott. Of course, if you don't want to bring Alex along, I could easily send Jim up on the first flight instead of you."

Mike felt his face flush red and he unconsciously balled his hands into fists. His nails dug into his palms. "I'm the director of operations for this company and the chief astronaut. You can't tell me how to make crew assignments."

"Well, excuse me, Mr. Chief Astronaut," said Stewart, standing up and waving his hands dramatically. "Oh, but wait a minute. I just remembered. I'm the CEO of the goddamn company. So I can do whatever I want to crew assignments or anything else." Stewart turned and headed for the door. As he left, he said, "Just think about it, Mike. I'll give you until tomorrow to get me an answer."

Mike stood up and watched Stewart disappear around the corner. He remained behind his desk looking dumbfounded, as his fatigued mind tried to process the complexity of what he was being asked to go along with. As a fighter pilot, Mike was used to making snap decisions, and his instinct was to say "hell, no" to Stewart's request, to protect his son. This was a dangerous business, and Barbara had lost her life in it.

But the implication of losing what might be his last opportunity to fly in space hung heavy in the air. Mike sank deeply into his chair and swiveled it so that he was looking out the window. Was he being hypocritical by promoting a hotel in space to other families but being unwilling to trust it enough to bring his own family? He had to admit, the reliability and safety numbers Stewart had shown him certainly seemed robust on paper, and while Barbara had lost her life in the Orion mission explosion, that accident had been a rarity in the past several decades of spaceflight. In fact, there had been no other fatal accidents since hers.

Then there was Alex. They had grown apart since Barbara's death. Mike couldn't be sure what Alex would think about this opportunity. He had made offhand comments about wanting to be an astronaut one day, and he was really smart. He wasn't that athletic, but this wasn't like the astronaut training program Mike had gone through that required top-notch physical fitness ability. Alex could do this. But should he?

As he often did when facing difficult decisions, Mike tried to imagine what Barbara would do. He could almost see her face in front of him, framed by the glass window that allowed the light of a few visible stars to touch his face. As Mike stared outward, the stars transformed into Barbara's icy blue eyes. He was taken back to a time before the accident. Barbara was frowning at something Mike had done wrong. Alex was a baby and Mike had let him crawl along the couch, but he had fallen to the floor, crying loudly. Barbara had rushed over, and even though Alex was fine after a few moments, she scolded Mike for letting him roam.

"I wanted him to learn to explore on his own and discover the dangers for himself in a way he will remember," Mike had explained, but this explanation did not satisfy his protective wife. They laughed about their differences, but at the end of the day, protecting her little boy was always Barbara's first instinct. Surely that's what she would want now, even if it meant the end of Mike's career?

A breeze rustled the palm trees outside the window and Barbara's face was gone, leaving Mike unsettled and confused.

CHAPTER 3

ALEX TOSSED HIS BACKPACK ONTO HIS BED AND PULLED THE TEST tube out of its outer pocket. He placed it into a small freezer next to a desk practically buried under papers, empty soda cans, books, parts of a LEGO rocket and an empty paper plate covered in crumbs. Then he flopped down onto the bed and stared up at the ceiling, his mind carefully going over the next steps of the experiment. After a few minutes, he sat up and reached underneath the bed. His hand found the old cardboard box with its weathered edges, and he slid it out until it sat on the floor between his feet.

Alex's eyes scanned the box before he reached in and extracted a notebook. He opened it gently to avoid ripping the old, delicate paper and turned to a marked page in the middle. He stared at it for a few minutes and then ran his fingers across the diagram of letters, numbers and interconnected symbols, feeling how the pen had embossed the lines into the thinning paper. His mother's handwriting looked beautiful to him.

If she had been right, then none of Alex's experiments would work, but he needed to see for himself. If she was right, then the only way to cure one of the most destructive genetic diseases of our time was to remove the force of gravity while creating a very specific protein structure. If the chemical structure could be created the way his mother had drawn it, then it could be used to encapsulate corrected RNA in a way that it could be injected into humans. The combined protein structure and corrected RNA would effectively be a virus that could spread the correct DNA throughout the cells of a human body with the condition. It had taken Alex years to understand this meaning behind the scribbles inside the notebook, but now it seemed so simple.

Except that making the protein was not so simple. Proteins are complex structures, and even when the correct chemical chain is created, the proteins have different ways of shaping themselves by "folding" in different directions. The chemical chain that made up his mother's protein could be easily created, but the atoms within the chain could fold and twist a number of ways. And every time it was created, it always seemed to fold the wrong way.

His mother had hypothesized in her research that removing gravity might cause the structure to fold a different way – the correct way. She had been planning to try this experiment on the space station, but the accident had abruptly ended her research. Nobody had continued her line of investigation until Alex came across her notebooks as he was entering high school. At first, everything he had read seemed like gibberish written in a foreign language and then scrambled into code. Slowly, though, he had sought out books, websites, teachers and research papers that had made the purpose and method of his mother's experiments clear. He now understood the problem, but the solution remained elusive.

Alex wondered if he could find another way to influence the protein structure growth even in a gravity field. Maybe a magnetic field could force the polarized ends of the molecules to bend and twist in the right way. It was a long shot, but something he should try in his next round. Then he needed to get the mice to test the results. That part was going to be challenging.

Alex closed the notebook and put it away before sliding the box back beneath his bed. He walked down the hallway towards the kitchen. His cereal bowl and juice glass were still on the table from breakfast. His dad, who was fanatically neat, would be upset when he came home if the dishes were still there.

Good, thought Alex. *Maybe it'll help him remember that I'm alive at least, even if he can't remember to come to my basketball games. For the team that HE wanted me to join.*

Alex walked past the dishes, leaving them in place, and pulled a tall glass from the cabinet, which he filled with water from the tap. He returned to his room, turned on some music, and began a calculus assignment. He flew through the problems, quickly manipulating the equations and variables until the answers came forth. As he was finishing the last of his homework, he heard the back door of the house by the garage open and slam shut. He glanced at the clock. It was 11:18 PM.

Alex could hear his father muttering some curses about the dishes on the kitchen table and he smiled to himself. He continued working on the calculus problem, half expecting his father to enter his room any minute, even though he knew it wouldn't happen. Before the accident, his dad would come in to say goodnight to Alex every night he was in town, even when Alex was asleep. He could remember a few times being woken for just an instant as his father's stubble grazed his cheek with a kiss. But after his mother had died, he stopped seeing his father very much. Alex's grandmother had moved in with them for a while, and she told Alex that his father was just overwhelmed with grief and that he would eventually turn his attention back towards Alex. That had never happened, though. His dad had been hired by NewStar One and turned all his attention to work.

Alex finished the calculus problem just as he heard the door to his father's bedroom close. There wasn't even an apology for missing parents' night. Alex changed into shorts and lay down on his bed. Within minutes, he was fast asleep.

*****

Alex groaned at his alarm clock. He smashed it a few times with his palm until the screeching stopped and then rubbed his eyes. Orange daylight was beginning to peek past his curtains as he sat up and looked around for some clothes to wear. As he picked through the items scattered around the floor, his nose picked up the unexpected smell of bacon, which didn't make any sense on a Wednesday morning.

Alex pulled a relatively clean pair of pants off the floor and found a T-shirt in his dresser. Then he walked down the hallway and was surprised to find that his dad was still home and cooking breakfast in the kitchen. Usually, he was gone to work before Alex was even awake.

His father turned and saw Alex standing in the doorway.

"Hey there," he said. "I'm making breakfast if you

want."

"Since when do you make breakfast at home?"

"Well, let's just say it's a special treat."

"Trying to make up for missing the game?" He noticed his father wince at the reminder.

"Oh, Alex, I'm sorry about that. I was caught up with something yesterday and I completely forgot. How did it go?"

"Pretty crappy. I got smashed in the face with the ball and got a bloody nose."

"How did that happen? You've got to keep your eyes on the ball."

"I was trying. I just got distracted."

"Distracted by what? Were you staring at a girl instead of the ball?"

How could he possibly have known that!? "No, Dad, jeez," he lied.

Alex sat down at the table and watched his father scramble eggs in a pan and turn shimmering slices of bacon in another. After a few minutes, the plates were ready, and his dad came to the table and handed one to Alex.

"I have something I want to talk to you about," he said. He sat down and rested his arms on the table, his back perfectly straight. Military posture.

"OK."

His dad stared at Alex, making him feel uncomfortable. It felt like he was probing him with his eyes. After a grueling silence, his father took a deep breath and spoke. "Son, you know that the first launch to NewStar One is coming up this summer. And you know that I'm supposed to lead that mission. But the company has decided to make some changes to the crew assignments."

Alex's eyes widened. This must be bad news. "Are they taking you off the crew?"

"Not exactly. I'm volunteering to be reassigned to the next mission, later in the year."

Alex couldn't believe what he was hearing. "Why would you do that?"

"The company has asked me to do something that I just cannot do to fly on the first mission."

"What did they ask you to do?"

"I can't share that with you right now, but I will in the future. For the moment, you just need to know that I will not be participating in the first crewed mission to NewStar One. And that's not public information yet." Alex had heard the not-publicly-announced speech a million times. He knew that meant the information was a secret he was to tell no one until he read it in a newspaper. His dad was still sitting fully erect with an unreadable expression. If he was upset by this news, it didn't register in his face. Alex knew how hard he had worked and how excited he always used to be about flying in space. Surely, something was wrong.

"Dad, are you, like, are you OK with this?"

His father shook his head. "It is the way it is. I can't change that."

"But you said there was something you could do to keep your spot on the mission. Whatever it is, it can't be that bad if you really want to go."

"It's not bad, but it's something I'm not prepared to do at the moment." His father stood up and began to clear his dishes, even though he had barely touched his food. Clearly, the conversation was over. Alex shrugged and scarfed down the eggs and bacon. Then he left the kitchen to get ready for school. He felt guilty about his anger towards his dad the night before. Clearly, he had bigger things to worry about than making it to some high school basketball game. Then again, if his mission was delayed, maybe he would be around a little bit more.

Back in his room, Alex shoved a stack of books into his backpack. Then he pulled a few test tubes out of the mini-freezer and shoved them into an overflowing side pocket before slinging the bag over his shoulder. He walked back out to the kitchen to find his father wiping down the table.

"Sorry about your mission, Dad," Alex said as he walked past. "Hope today goes better for you."

"Thanks," his father replied, looking up. Alex waved good-bye, but as he did a test tube fell from the overflowing side pocket that he had failed to close completely. It hit the tile floor and shattered, spilling clear liquid everywhere. Alex cursed under his breath.

"What on earth was that?" his father asked in a booming voice.

"Sorry, Dad, it's just some science class stuff." Alex dropped his backpack and grabbed a paper towel to clean up the mess. He was angry at losing a perfectly good sample. His father came over and inspected the mess.

"What was inside of that test tube? And why did you have it at home?"

"I told you, Dad, it was for science class."

"They let you bring home test tubes from science class? With chemicals in them?"

Alex was silent and his face began to flush. How could he explain this to his dad?

His father looked concerned. "Alex, are you stealing supplies from the school?"

"No," Alex said too hastily. "I mean, it's not like that."

"What exactly is it like?"

"Dad, it's just some stuff I've been working on after school."

"Oh, God." His father clutched his head as if he were wounded. "I knew I should have paid closer attention." He grabbed Alex by the shoulders and pulled him close. "Now don't you dare lie to me. Are you making drugs?"

"Holy shit, Dad! No!"

"Then what is this!?" His father was practically screaming now. "Explain to me what science experiments you are doing that require you to sneak home samples from the lab! I've read about kids using decongestants in their school science labs to make drugs. You know I can have this stuff tested."

Alex was furious now. "Dad, I'm not making drugs! Maybe if you were home more you'd know me better than that!"

His father looked wounded, but undeterred. "So then why won't you tell me what this is?"

"Because you're screaming at me and not giving me a chance!"

"Then here's your chance. Come clean before I call the police to test this sample."

Alex took a breath. "I'm working on synthesizing proteins to insert corrected DNA into a virus. OK!? I'm working on mom's experiments!"

His father pulled back with a shocked look which quickly morphed into disbelief. "That sounds a bit ambitious for someone your age."

"Give me some credit, dad. I'm not stupid."

"Watch your attitude," he barked.

"If you don't believe me you can look at my research

notebook."

"I think I'd like to see that." Alex couldn't believe this was happening. How could his own father not have even the slightest trust in him? With a dramatic flair, Alex reached into his bag and shoved the brown notebook at his father. His dad opened it and flipped through the pages, his eyes widening with each turn.

"I don't even understand half of this," he finally admitted. Wistfully, he added, "Your mother used to do stuff like this all the time."

"Yeah, I know. I kinda got the idea from her."

"What do you mean?"

"I'm working on the experiments she had been doing, trying to finish them."

"How? I mean how do you know about her work?"

"I have her old notes."

His dad had calmed down from his freak-out and Alex was torn between anger with his father and excitement about his interest in the research. His dad asked to see the notes Alex was working from, so Alex led him to his room and slid the box out from underneath his bed. His father looked like he might cry as he picked through the notebooks and read his late wife's writing.

"I found them in the closet one day and started to read them," Alex explained. "She was working on a virus that might have allowed someone to repair DNA. She needed to create a protein cap that attaches to a virus and allows it to pass corrected RNA strands into a healthy host cell. Her idea was to use the virus to correct the defects that are caused by genetic disease. She was focused mainly on cystic fibrosis though."

"I know. It was her dream that she'd discover a cure

through her work on the International Space Station."

"Well, she was really close. She just needed the protein to fold in the right way. She thought a zero-gravity environment was the key to generating the right protein isomer. I tried the same experiments she did and I can see why you'd have a better chance of the protein folding the way she wanted by doing a protein crystal formation in zero-gravity."

His father sat in silence looking blankly over a page of a notebook for what seemed like several minutes. Finally, he looked up.

"Alex, do you think you could finish your mother's experiments if you had access to a zero-gravity environment?"

"I want to try one day. I'm going to become a scientist like her and apply to the astronaut corps."

His father nodded solemnly. "Maybe it's a sign," he muttered. "Maybe she's giving me a sign."

"What?" Alex asked.

His father stood up suddenly. "Alex, remember how I told you about that thing the company wanted me to do to fly on the first mission?"

"The thing you said you couldn't do?"

"Well, I think I might change my mind about it."

CHAPTER 4

IT WAS ALEX'S TURN TO REGISTER DISBELIEF, AS HIS FATHER explained the situation with NewStar One and the need to have a teenage crewmember fly to space. His eyes grew wide as he listened to his father describe the upcoming launch in the summer and the decision by the company CEO to use a teenager as both a demonstration and an extra laborer to handle the hotel duties. Alex had dreamed about flying to space one day, but he had always imagined it would be years and years in the future. Now there was a chance he could achieve his dream before even finishing high school!

"I didn't want to bring you," Alex's father explained, "because I thought your mother wouldn't approve of putting your life at risk. But Alex, I had no idea you were..." his voice trailed off and his eyes focused on a distant nothingness. After a heavy pause, he snapped out of it and refocused on Alex. "You're growing up quicker than I realized. This is what Mom would have wanted. For you to finish her work. And whether you take that risk this year or ten years from now, it's the right thing to do. It's what she and I both believe in – exploring the unknown, making new discoveries, even if they're risky."

Alex spotted a droplet growing in the corner of his father's eye, and he couldn't help but smile. As he leaned forward to embrace his father, he felt as if Mom was right there with them, her arms surrounding them both with warmth. It all felt as though it were meant to be.

"Well," his father said, pulling away from Alex and taking a deep breath. "I guess I'd better tell my boss that I've changed my mind. He was planning to give the assignment to Jim Abbott and his son."

"Call him now!" Alex said, giddy with excitement.

"I will, but first you'd better get to school. I think you've already missed the bus."

"Do I have to go? I want to hear more about this mission!" Alex was practically jumping up and down.

"You will, but let me go sort things out at work first."

Reluctantly, Alex let his father drive him to school. Twice, his dad made him promise not to mention the mission to anyone, and he promised that he would pick Alex up from school directly so they could talk. The day passed by in a blur, with Alex barely able to concentrate. Fortunately, the only person who usually talked to him at all was Tyler, and he was able to steer the conversation to video games and other kids. When the final bell rang at three-thirty, Alex nearly sprinted down the hallways to the line of cars for student pick-ups. As soon as he sat down in the passenger seat, his father said, "The company CEO, Stewart, wants to talk to us both in person. He was busy all day so I only left a message with him about agreeing to bring you along on the mission."

"When does he want to talk?"

"Right now." His father pulled out of the school and sped down Bay Area Boulevard weaving rapidly in and out of traffic as he always did. Before he knew it, Alex found himself seated in an expansive office with NewStar's CEO. It was immediately obvious that Stewart Locke was not pleased with Alex's dad's initial decision or his recent change of mind.

"So first you tell me to take you off the flight and give Jim the slot. And I go make all the arrangements. Now you've decided you want back on the mission," Stewart said with a frown that bordered on a scowl.

"I'm sure you can understand that I had some hesitation after what happened to Barbara."

"I thought we had agreed that that wasn't going to affect your judgment. You know we have a very different and much safer system."

Mike looked down at his hands. "I know, I know. Stewart, I'm sorry. I should have taken more time to think through my decision, but you didn't give me much time to work with."

"You're an astronaut, Mike. You should be better at making quick decisions."

Alex looked over at his father. He had never seen him put down by anyone, and he couldn't believe his dad was just sitting there and taking it! Alex wanted to jump out of his chair and scream to Mr. Locke that he would never find a better astronaut and he should be lucky to have his father at the company. But he didn't want to make things worse, so he bit his tongue and silently watched the exchange. Stewart stood and slowly walked to a model of the NewStar One space station in the center of the office, his hands clasped together behind his back.

"Well, Mike. I've already told Jim that he could bring his son on the mission," Stewart finally proclaimed.

"Stewart, please, let me talk to Jim. He'll understand."

Stewart turned to face them. "I'm not happy with this, Mike. You've been with me from the start, but this last-minute doubt really doesn't sit well." Stewart paused and the silence that hung in the air was palpable. Alex tapped his left foot nervously against the blue carpet. Stewart turned back and looked at his model which was bathed in a blue LED glow that gave the station a futuristic look.

Taking an exaggerated breath, Stewart said, "Alright, Mike, I'll tell you what. We should have a backup teenage crewmember just like we do for the regular crew. So for now I'm not going to name a prime crew just yet. Let's put both Alex and Brock through training and see how they do. Then I'll re-evaluate things closer to the mission." Then he added in a tone that dripped of sarcasm, "With your input, of course."

"OK, Stewart. That sounds reasonable," his father said. His voice betrayed nothing. Alex stared at him and waited for him to change his mind, to protest against the injustice of turning their flight to space into some kind of game show competition, to explain how Alex had research that could make NewStar One world-renown as a laboratory. But his father remained silent.

"Very good," said Stewart. "I have another meeting to get to, but I think we've come to a good agreement."

With that, Stewart left the room. Alex's father stood up slowly.

Alex burst out, "Dad, how could you let him talk to you like that?"

"He's my boss, Alex, and he makes the decisions here at this company. If you want to fly, hell, even if *I* want to fly, then I have to be respectful."

"But he didn't even make a decision! When will I know if I get to fly?"

"I don't know, Alex. But I've known Stewart for a long time now. He likes to be in charge and show he is in control, but he is also a reasonable decision-maker. I think that as long as you do well in the training, he'll put me back on the first flight with you. But he needs to feel like it's his decision, and so he's going to take his time making it."

"If we don't go on the first flight, will he send us on the second one?"

"He'll send *me* on the second one. I don't know if he's going to repeat this teenager in space thing again once John Fritzer agrees to fly. For now, let's just focus on getting us both on that first flight. Which means we have a lot of work to do."

"Like what?"

"Training. Let's head downstairs and get you signed up for training classes."

"What kind of training classes?"

"All of the flight crew has to complete a training program that includes classroom lessons, physical fitness and hands-on training. You're smart and athletic, so you should have no problem."

Alex cringed slightly. Did his dad really think he was athletic? He would know better if he'd shown up to any basketball games. Classroom lessons and hands-on training sounded easy and fun, but Alex wasn't so sure about physical fitness training. But for the chance to fly in space, he would do anything. Surely the physical fitness part wouldn't be that bad.

*****

The classroom training started two days later. The schedule was going to be challenging. It required Alex to take classes immediately after school. The trainers did their best to adjust the schedule so that Alex wouldn't miss too many basketball practices or games, to avoid raising suspicion. He'd been forced to sign agreements that he would not reveal his training or participation in the program until after a selection was announced publicly, and he was also not to divulge any technical details about the space station design or operation to anyone for something like the rest of his life. Alex didn't care - he would have given a kidney to fly in space and have a chance to try protein synthesis in zero-gravity.

Already, his father had piled stacks of manuals on the kitchen table for Alex and flooded his e-mail inbox with even more reading material. Alex had attacked the material with a vigor that surpassed even his passionate investigations into his mother's biological research. In just the past two days of study, he had already learned the layout of the space station by heart and could describe where all the major electrical, mechanical and computer components resided. He was excited to begin the in-person training and he made sure to arrive early to the NewStar building and its large training room.

When he arrived, Jim Abbott's son was already seated comfortably behind a table facing a projection screen and lectern. Brock Abbott was built like an oak tree, with a solid torso and thick limbs. He didn't hesitate to tell Alex that he was a linebacker for his Brookdale High School's football team. Alex didn't even know what a linebacker was, but he assumed this guy could probably outrun, outcompete and generally beat the crap out of Alex if he wanted to. After introducing himself, he flashed his ultra-white teeth at Alex in a goofy grin, stood up, and extended his right hand. Alex grasped it and shook reluctantly.

"Looks like we're going to be training together," Brock said, stating the obvious.

"I guess so," Alex replied dryly. He turned away from Brock and flung his backpack onto the long white classroom table. He took his seat and removed a notebook and pen. Brock appeared to have come into the room empty-handed and he sat back down in his chair and swiveled it back and forth while they waited for the instructor to arrive.

According to the company training lead whom Alex had met with his father two days earlier, both boys would need to attend twelve lectures like this one, ten hands-on training sessions, and three simulations. Near the end of the training, the boys would be scored on their skills in three categories: their ability to detect and fix anomalies during a simulation, their performance on a physical fitness test and their grade on an extensive written examination. The company had been vague about exactly how the scoring would work or what it would mean about whether or not Alex or Brock would fly on the mission. The training lead had indicated that there was a score that was required to pass; beyond that, the meaning of the scores was anyone's guess.

Written exams and simulations didn't intimidate Alex. But looking at Brock, Alex grew knots in his stomach thinking about the physical training. There was no way he would ever beat Brock in a fitness test. His only hope was to excel in the academic side and hope to obtain at least a passing score in the fitness component.

The instructor breezed into the room. She introduced herself as Emily Baker, a systems engineer who had worked at NewStar Technologies since the founding of the company. After working on designs for avionics systems, she had moved on to lead the training division when it was created and she now split her time between developing simulations and managing classroom training for astronauts and guests. Emily pulled her long brown hair into a ponytail and then wasted no time turning on a presentation that described each module of the space station in detail and spoke to the safety and emergency procedures to follow in the "unlikely event of a contingency situation."

Alex was quick to recognize the metallic structure of the space station as it flashed onto the screen. Below the field of solar arrays that were mounted to trusses sat the hotel module with its five guest rooms and the Commons, a combination galley and recreation module for hotel visitors.

"This is where you will spend most of your time working if you are selected to participate in this mission," Emily said. She moved on to next describe the Central Node, a small six-sided module that connected the hotel corridor with a long hallway which ran perpendicular to the hotel and Commons. Going "up" from inside the node would take you to the airlock, "down" was a storage module and looking forward directly across from the end of the hotel corridor was one of the two laboratories on the station.

The long hallway which extended out the port and starboard sides of the Central Node connected to the crew quarters on the port side and the docking port and a second laboratory on the starboard side. The entire design was modular and extensible, with the idea of expanding the station in the future when the company had more funds and a steady stream of business.

Alex looked over at Brock. He didn't have even a single sheet of paper for taking notes, and his head was nodding forward, his eyes only partially opened. Emily did not seem to care and continued to the next part of the presentation discussing what to do in an emergency. The Crew Transfer Vehicles, or CTVs, that carried them to the space station would remain docked the entire time they were there. Most emergencies could be handled onboard by automated systems, but in the event of a serious calamity such as a cabin leak or fire, they were to go directly to the docking port in case an evacuation became necessary.

Alex raised his hand. "If there's a leak in one module, couldn't we just close the hatch to that module?"

"Very good," said Emily. "You're already ahead of me. One of the responsibilities of the crew will be to close hatches behind you as you make your way to the docking port. That way, if the leak can be isolated, you will know. Then the Commander will have time to make a decision whether to evacuate or attempt a leak repair."

"How is a leak repaired?" asked Alex.

"We have special equipment to detect the leak and sealing chemicals that can permanently fix a small hole, generally something less than 8 millimeters in diameter. You will be trained on the use of that equipment in another class."

Alex scribbled this information in his notebook. He glanced over at Brock whose eyes seemed unnaturally wide, as if he were trying to force them to stay open. He seemed just like every other varsity-jacket athlete Alex knew at school. They could all dominate on the field but were utterly lost in the classroom.

Emily finished her lecture and asked if there were any more questions. Neither boy had anything else to ask, so the lecture was concluded and the two headed out of the room.

"That was pretty interesting," said Brock as he walked empty-handed alongside Alex. "I didn't know that you could seal a pressure leak once the module was up in space. Really awesome."

Alex was shocked that the beefy football player had absorbed any information at all from the lecture. "Yeah," he replied simply. The two walked in silence the rest of the way to the front of the building where their parents were waiting to take them home.

"Good to meet you, Alex," said Brock as he left with his father. Alex managed a polite smile which vanished as soon as Brock turned away.

"Stupid jock," Alex mumbled.

"What was that?" his father asked.

"Nothing," Alex replied. "Let's get out of here."

CHAPTER 5

THIS SUCKS, THOUGHT ALEX AS HE VOMITED FOR THE FIFTH TIME into a white plastic bag.

"You OK, kid?" asked a smiling man in a blue flight suit floating nearby. His name tag read "Dr. Robert Carpenter, Flight Surgeon."

"Yeah, fine," Alex said as he tied up the bag. He was hovering a few inches above the white padded floor of NewStar's zero-gravity trainer aircraft. The aircraft, modeled after NASA's astronaut trainer, created a temporary weightlessness for its participants by climbing to 40,000 feet and then nose-diving into a free-fall for 30 seconds. During the fall, the passengers experienced no gravity as they fell towards the earth with the plane. From inside the padded cabin, they could float around freely as if they were in space. This magical but unsettling experience was followed by a rapid shift to twice normal gravity as the aircraft reversed its fall and pulled up back to 40,000 feet. The original NASA aircraft had been nicknamed the "vomit comet" and all aircraft modeled after it, including this one, were called by the same nickname. Alex's dad told him the constant switching between zero gravity and twice normal gravity, called "2G", made most astronauts more sick than just a normal flight to space where zero-gravity persisted. Alex hoped he was right or it was going to be a long three months on the space station. They were about to finish their twentieth parabolic maneuver, out of a planned thirty.

Just ten more to go.

"Feet down, coming out!" shouted the test conductor. This was the signal to get close to the airplane's floor because the vomit comet would be pulling out of its nose-dive. Alex was already near the floor, but he put his arms down to catch himself as he drifted downwards, beginning to feel the weight of his body return. Before long, he was being pressed down into the floor, as if by an invisible hand. He leaned up against the padded wall of the airplane and closed his eyes. He could hear his dad talking and laughing with the other crew members near the front of the airplane. Brock was up there too, and from what Alex could tell he was showing no discomfort at all in this strange environment. Alex felt totally alone as he sat near the back with the doctor. He didn't care. He was going to prove that he could do this.

It was only the second week of training, and Alex was already feeling overwhelmed. The technical aspects of the training were no problem, as he had assumed, but the physical training was even more demanding than he had imagined it would be. Two days a week, an instructor led him and Brock in a series of intense exercises, many of which Alex had never even heard of. Burpees? They sounded like something that would involve drinking a lot of soda, not catapulting your body back and forth between a plank and a jump, usually being told to add a push-up in the middle. Alex could barely do four before he was out of breath. He was beginning to wonder what the physical fitness exam would involve, and whether he would even be able to pass.

"Over the top!" came the call from the blue-suited test conductor. The lights inside the aircraft brightened and Alex felt the floor falling away from him. As it had with every parabola, his stomach lurched, but he was able to keep from losing his breakfast for the sixth time.

Alex's father pushed off a bulkhead and shot towards him head-first. He grabbed a handle on the ceiling of the aircraft and stopped himself gracefully near Alex.

"How you doing, Alex?" his father asked. His eyes were glowing with excitement. Alex hadn't seen him act this way in many years; he was carefree and almost playful.

"I threw up five times."

"Don't worry, you'll get the hang of this. The vomit comet is harder on most than actually flying in space."

"I know, Dad, you told me."

"Just keep your perspective and everything will be fine." With this, his father smiled and spun himself upside down so that his feet were on the ceiling and his head faced the floor. He looked at Alex with a mischievous smile. Without gravity as a reference, seeing his dad inverted made Alex's stomach lurch again. Just then, the test conductor called for feet down, causing his father to come back to a normal orientation. They sat together on the floor for the next 2G climb. Alex kept his eyes closed and focused all his energy on not throwing up.

Over the next ten parabolas, Alex vomited three more times and was grateful when the test conductor announced the end of the training. The crew members settled into the four rows of seats at the very rear of the aircraft for the flight back to Ellington Airfield in Houston.

"Dad, that was awesome," Brock said in the row behind Alex.

"Glad you enjoyed it," came Jim Abbot's reply. Alex had met Brock's father in person for the first time today. Jim was much leaner than his son, but shared his brown eyes and deep voice. Before the flight, Jim had introduced himself to Alex with a firm handshake and wished him luck in the training. Alex couldn't stand the awkwardness of the encounter. Everyone knew what hung in the balance of this training program, and everyone knew that Alex supposedly had the upper hand since his father was the chief astronaut. Even though both Brock and Jim seemed incredibly nice and never said a mean word, Alex couldn't help but resent the fact that they might steal away his chance to fly to space and his father's chance to command the first mission to NewStar One.

The flight back to Ellington Field was uneventful, and Alex was glad to disembark onto solid asphalt under a bright Texas sun. He changed out of his flight suit in a cramped locker room with the other crew members and then went for a brief physical exam by one of the company doctors. They asked him a lot of questions about his nausea. Alex tried to sound nonchalant, as if it was not a big deal, but the probing questions produced another knot in his belly.

On the way out of the building, Alex's father put his arm on Alex's shoulder.

"Don't worry, son," he said. "No matter what happens, I know you're doing your best."

Those words hurt more than they helped.

*****

The next day, Alex was back at school, but he could hardly focus on his classes. His mind kept wandering back to the zero-gravity training. His father had told him after the flight that it didn't matter how much nausea he'd experienced, that it took some time to acclimate to zero gravity, and that nobody would be disqualified for throwing up in the trainer. Alex wasn't so sure. Why would the company not pick Brock, who seemed to be a natural in zero gravity, over the skinny kid who couldn't hold down his breakfast for even thirty seconds? He had always thought that his science knowledge would get him into space, but now he was realizing it took more.

He continued mulling over the details of the flight as he sat in world history class, barely listening to a mind-numbing lecture about the Roman Empire from Ms. Taurino, whose monotonous and scratchy voice could tranquilize even the most caffeinated history buff. When the lecture was finally over and the bell rang, he eagerly snatched his backpack and headed for the door. It was lunchtime, and he was excited to catch up with Tyler.

As he rounded the corner coming out of the classroom into the hallway, he walked straight into Mackenzie Dale. A folder full of papers fell from her hands and scattered across the floor.

"Hey!" she exclaimed.

"Oh my gosh, I'm so sorry," said Alex.

"Oh, hi Alex," she said, after she noticed who he was. "It's OK, I was just in a rush." Alex was surprised she even knew his name, and he smiled at her a little too eagerly. The sunlight coming in through the skylights seemed to catch in her hair and make it glow. Alex suddenly had an urge to reach out and touch it, but he kept his hands to himself as Mackenzie bent down to pick up her papers. Alex dropped his bag on the floor and knelt to help her gather them.

"Thanks," she said after the papers had been collected. She clutched the discombobulated stack in her arms and rushed away down the hall, as Alex's gaze followed her. He picked up his bag, but the zipper had been left open and his books spilled everywhere. He threw up his arms.

It's just going to be that kind of day.

When he finally arrived at his usual cafeteria table with a tray of mushy pasta and a wilted salad, Tyler was already halfway done with his lunch.

"What's up, bro?" Tyler asked as Alex sat down. Tyler was wearing a black hoodie that covered up his lengthening black hair which now had a blue streak running through it. In the past few months, Tyler had experimented a lot with "his look" and lately he had been trending more and more emo.

"How can you even see where you're going in that thing?" Alex teased.

"Man, you sound like my mom."

"Sorry, it's just a bit of a weird choice. I mean, it's April and it's hot out and you're wearing a sweatshirt."

"Whatever. Where have you been lately? You never texted me back about playing *Star Crusader* this weekend. I came over yesterday afternoon but nobody was home."

"Sorry, I've been a little busy lately," Alex replied.

"It's fine," Tyler said. "But I hope you're not busy this weekend. There's the spring dance on Friday night."

"You want to go to the dance? Since when do you care about that?"

"Bro, we've got to stop being these antisocial nerds.

There's a whole other world out there to explore."

"Seriously," Alex said, shaking his head. "What have you done with my best friend?"

"Come on, Alex. There's going to be food and socializing and girls, and..."

"OK, who's the girl?" Alex interrupted.

"Nobody, I just want to go be social for once. There are tons of hot girls in our class. We're never going to get girlfriends playing video games all the time."

With everything Alex was doing for NewStar, the last thing he was thinking about was finding a girlfriend. But he wouldn't mind dancing with Mackenzie. "Alright, I guess we could check it out."

"I knew you'd come around." Tyler smiled as he stuffed the rest of his cheeseburger into his mouth. Alex shook his head, wondering secretly how he would rearrange his studying schedule to fit in a few hours for the dance on Friday.

CHAPTER 6

THERE WAS NOT ENOUGH AIR TO BREATHE. ALEX FELT THIS instinctively the moment he removed his oxygen mask. He tried desperately to suppress the panic welling up inside his chest. His eyes darted around the white cylindrical walls of the hyperbaric chamber, a small and barely noticeable feature buried in the corner of NewStar's cavernous training center. The other participants in the hypoxia training seemed calm and relaxed without their masks. They must be better adapted to low oxygen levels than he was. Alex's cheeks felt hot and he tried to suck in deep breaths of the thin chamber air, but no matter how many breaths he took, it seemed that it wasn't ever enough.

The instructor, still wearing an oxygen mask, walked down the narrow length of the chamber towards him.

"Just stay calm and try to identify your symptoms on the paper," she said gently to Alex.

"I'm trying, but it's hard to breathe!" he blurted out. His head hurt. His father looked up from the paper he was writing on with a stubby pencil. His cheeks were red but he wore a relaxed expression that quickly became concerned as his eyes fell on Alex.

"Don't breathe too hard," his dad said in a calm and

steady voice. "You'll be fine. Just four minutes to go." Alex couldn't believe they made people do this. If you deprived someone of food, it was torture. Here they were depriving him of oxygen – wasn't that worse?

In the briefing, everyone had been instructed to keep their masks off for five minutes. Alex wondered if that was a requirement to fly in space. The whole point of this training was to help them recognize what was happening if the oxygen levels began to fall either due to a cabin leak or a failure of the atmospheric regulators that balanced the mix of gases in the air, and Alex felt like he was very quick to recognize his symptoms!

His mind was starting to have trouble focusing and everything around him seemed thick and slow. Alex noticed in a detached way that his heart was racing now. He wanted to control his breathing, but he couldn't decide if he needed more or less breaths, so he tried fast gulps of air. He began to feel tingling at the ends of his fingertips. He shook his hands to try and work out the sensation. His head was spinning, and now he worried that he had taken in too much air. He decided to pause and hold his breath. He began to feel dizzy and the chamber walls blurred in front of him. Quick, more breaths! He briefly saw the instructor moving in his direction. His attempts to take in more air were too late, and Alex felt his head falling forward before everything disappeared.

*****

When Alex opened his eyes, his father's face came into focus showing a mixture of concern and displeasure. Alex tried lifting his head, which felt heavy, but was held back by a tube connected to a clear plastic mask over his mouth.

"Just lay back," his father said. "Keep the mask on until the doctor says it's OK." Alex noticed a man in a white coat standing with his back to them and typing notes into a computer.

"It's fine," the man said. When he turned around, Alex recognized him as Dr. Carpenter, the flight surgeon who had helped him on the vomit comet. "You can take off the mask now. Hypoxia clears quite quickly with a return to normal oxygen levels."

Alex pulled the mask off his face and sat up on the small uncomfortable exam table. Dr. Carpenter came over and checked Alex's ears and nose.

"I guess I didn't make it all the way," Alex said dejectedly as the doctor probed him.

"One minute and forty-seven seconds," his father replied without expression.

"Your blood oxygen levels returned to normal shortly after we put your mask back on and repressurized the chamber," said the doctor in a calm and measured tone as he continued to examine Alex. "I think perhaps your body had a bit of a shock adapting to the low oxygen environment. Have you spent any time at altitude before?"

"Not really," Alex said.

"I see. Well, it also appeared you were hyperventilating which may have further disrupted your body's homeostasis. I'm not particularly concerned, but I'm going to recommend another run in the chamber just to make sure you don't have any kind of physiological condition that would put you in danger in a hypoxic environment."

"You want me to go again?" Alex asked, feeling a familiar panic return to his belly.

"Well, not today, of course. But yes, we should schedule a second training run for you. Next time try to let your body control your breathing and if you feel that you are losing control, you can put your oxygen mask back on. The company criteria for astronauts in flight is the ability to go five minutes at 25,000 foot equivalent altitude. It might take that long to get to an oxygen mask on the station in the event of a depressurization."

Alex nodded solemnly and pushed himself up off the exam table.

"Come on, kid, let's get you home," his father said. "I think we've had enough for today." Alex knew that his father was disappointed, even if he didn't say it outright. They walked slowly to the car and rode home in an uncomfortable silence.

When they arrived at the house, Alex went straight to his room and collapsed onto his bed. The training fiasco, coming after a long day of school, had left him totally exhausted. Within a few minutes, his eyes were closed. He was about to fall into a blissful sleep when his phone beeped and vibrated, shocking him awake. Groggily, he pulled it out of his pocket and read the text message from Tyler.

When should I pick you up?

Alex stared confused at the glowing screen, until his sleepy mind finally recalled the spring dance Tyler had so desperately wanted to go to. There was no way Alex was going anywhere tonight. He put down the phone, but a succession of messages followed until Alex finally sent a text saying he wasn't feeling well. The phone rang almost immediately after he sent the message. He groaned, but quickly decided the only way to stop being harassed tonight was to tell Tyler directly that he wasn't going. He answered the phone and said "Hello," trying to make his voice sound even more feeble than he felt.

"Are you dying?" Tyler asked.

"Technically, we're all dying, it just depends how long you want to wait."

"If you can think of clever lines like that, you're fine. I'll pick you up in fifteen minutes."

Tyler hung up without waiting for a reply. Alex groaned again. Tyler's level of enthusiasm for socialization was very uncharacteristic, and was more than a little annoying. Alex lay still for a while, but eventually decided there was no easy way to stop Tyler and he was too good of a friend to leave him going solo to a high school dance. Begrudgingly, Alex pulled himself up from his mattress and changed into nicer clothes.

Tyler was at least willing to stop for fast food before the dance. Alex's chamber run had left him famished, and he wolfed down a cheeseburger, chicken nuggets and fries while Tyler watched in awe and slowly picked at a fish sandwich.

When they finally arrived at the school around 7:20, the sky was turning dark and the parking lot was already packed. They merged into a throng of students heading towards the gym.

"I don't even recognize half of these people," Alex said. "Do they even go to our school?"

"Seriously? Where have you been? The spring dance is always done with another high school."

"Yeah, sorry, I don't go to many dances." Alex really wasn't in the mood for being called out on his lack of social knowledge by his equally introverted friend.

"All of Brookdale High is here, bro. Lots of new chicas

to meet."

"Yippee," Alex replied dryly.

They entered an overcrowded and dimly lit gym and forked over $10 each. Music blared from speakers set on stands in the corners of the room. A dark-skinned DJ with a shaved head stood behind a table underneath the far basketball hoop, jabbing at buttons on a large control panel as colored beams of light flashed across the room. To the right of the DJ, a long line of tables held sodas, water, bowls of popcorn, pretzels, fruit and other snack fare. Across from the food and drinks, the bleachers were overflowing with students, and even more were gathered around the tables. The middle of the gym, which was presumably the dance floor, was vacant except for two students dancing in a close embrace, even though the song was upbeat, and four girls in dresses who were facing each other and bouncing wildly to the music.

Alex watched as Tyler scanned the scene, clearly unsure of what to do next. Finally, he started walking towards the snack tables and Alex trailed behind, grumbling quietly that he wasn't hungry since they had just eaten. Still, Alex picked up a Coke and Tyler grabbed a handful of pretzels.

"OK, now what do we do?" Alex asked.

"I guess we should go hang out with people."

"Like who? We don't have any other friends."

Tyler shrugged. "I don't know." But Alex noticed that his friend's eyes were fixed on a small group of three girls who were talking to two other boys. As he followed Tyler's gaze, Alex caught a glimpse of Mackenzie standing in front of the bleachers. She was with her friend, Heather, and the two of them were talking to a large boy whose back was towards Alex. Mackenzie was smiling shyly as she tucked her hair behind her ear. She was wearing a light blue dress that hugged her upper body but fanned out around her knees. Alex watched her lips move animatedly and he could almost see the sparkle in her eyes from across the room. The boy she was talking to laughed at whatever Mackenzie was saying and reached out his hand. She took it, and the boy turned around to take her to the dance floor. As he turned, Alex finally had a good look at his face, and his jaw fell. He let go of his soda can, and it crashed to the floor, splattering brown fizzy liquid everywhere.

"Alex! You got soda on my shoes," Tyler yelled.

"Sorry, sorry," Alex said. He grabbed the can and looked back up. Mackenzie was being led onto the dance floor by the muscular boy from Brookdale who Alex now recognized as Brock Abbott.

The music turned slower, and Alex felt his muscles tense as he watched Brock wrap his tree trunk arms around Mackenzie and they began to sway back and forth. He was infuriated. Why did the school dance have to include other high schools and why of all schools did it have to be Brock's school?

"Hey, are you OK?" Tyler asked.

"Yeah, fine," Alex muttered. Then he added, "This dance sucks. We should leave."

"Bro, we just got here. What's wrong with you?"

"We're not doing anything. This is a waste of time. At least if we were home, we could play video games."

"Just give it a chance. It could be fun."

"It's not fun!" Alex blurted out, eyeing Mackenzie and Brock. "I don't want to be here anymore. I'm not a dance person, and neither are you. Let's just go."

"How do you know I'm not a dance person? How do

you know you're not if you've never even tried?"

"Tyler, come on. You and I are not the type of people who come to these things. Look at us, hanging out by the snack table after we already ate dinner. We don't have other friends. We're not going to go talk to people. I'm sorry, but I just don't see you starting up a conversation with some random girl from Brookdale. You're all talk, man."

Tyler appeared shocked at Alex's outburst but then his eyes narrowed and pierced Alex like daggers. "If you want to be a nerd your whole life, go ahead," he spit out in a low voice. "I came to have fun and be social. And not only are you being really negative, you're being kinda insulting. So why don't you go sulk in the corner while I go meet some people." With that, Tyler spun around and stormed across the gym, slowing down considerably as he approached the cluster of kids he had been eyeing earlier. After a brief hesitation, Tyler approached a girl with short black hair who Alex recognized, although he didn't know her name. Amazingly, she took Tyler's hand and walked with him to the middle of the gym. Tyler shuffled his feet as the girl put her arms on his shoulders, and Alex fumed. Mackenzie was dancing with Brock, Tyler was dancing with some girl that he obviously had been interested in but had never told Alex about, and now Alex was standing alone like some kind of diseased animal that nobody wanted to touch. And since Tyler had driven, he had no way to get home.

Disgusted, Alex turned and pounded his feet across the wooden gym floor as he headed towards the exit to the school hallway. He threw his coke can forcefully in the trash and the remaining soda splattered across the refuse in the plastic bag. Avoiding eye contact with everyone he passed, he walked straight into the bathroom, where he took his time releasing a full bladder and washing his hands. As he rubbed soap around his fingers, he looked in the mirror at his face. His eyes were puffy and looked like they were drooping. He had only run a comb through his hair briefly before leaving the house and it ran wildly in all directions around his head. His jawline, though, looked firm and strong, maybe in part because his teeth were clenched in anger and frustration at how horribly this day was going. If he cut his hair and got some more sleep, he might actually look like an astronaut – like the type of person who was brave and strong and capable and physically fit enough to fly into space. Like his father.

He left the bathroom and wandered down the dark hallway away from the gym. He came to the empty science lab and peered through the glass of the locked door. He saw the benches and the microscopes and the small PCR machine that could sequence purified samples of DNA. He remembered a day when he was small, maybe only 3 or 4 years old. His daycare had been closed for some reason he couldn't recall and his mother had taken him with her to a lab like this where she had to do some work that couldn't wait until the next day. Mom had sat him on a stool like the ones in his classroom and placed a piece of a leaf on the microscope with a low-powered lens. He remembered spinning on the stool and peering through the tube with one eye closed to see into a world that was all around him but nearly invisible. His mother had shown him how to identify individual plant cells. He'd grabbed leaves from all the windowsill plants in the office and tried them in the microscope, shouting each time, "I found the cells, Mommy!"

Shaking his head to clear the memory away, Alex's vision began to blur. He reached up and wiped the gathering tears out of his eyes. He couldn't let Brock beat him. No matter what, he had to find a way to make sure he was on that mission to the space station. He had to do it for his mother.

With newfound determination, Alex marched back to the gym. He wasn't sure what he was going to do, but he felt like he needed to do something to show up Brock. He pulled open the heavy metal door and the thumping of the music hit him like a wave. Walking into the darkened gym, he let his eyes adjust to the light for a few seconds and then looked around for Brock and Mackenzie. He spotted Mackenzie across the gym but then his jaw dropped for the second time that evening when he saw the person she was talking with. Mackenzie was standing by the bleachers talking to Tyler!

As anger welled inside him, Alex stormed across the dance floor towards them, nearly running into a boy who was flailing around the floor looking like he'd lost control of his limbs. As he approached the two, Tyler spotted him and waved with a smile on his face. Alex stared him down as he walked, but when he noticed Mackenzie looking at him funny, he softened his expression.

"Hey Alex, where've you been? I was looking for you," Tyler said.

Alex wanted to scream at Tyler, but he didn't want Mackenzie to see him angry, so he just said, in the harshest way he could, "I had to go to the bathroom."

"So Mackenzie here was just asking about what training you are doing with Brookdale High," Tyler said in an almost accusatory voice. "But I told her she must have heard wrong because you don't do anything with Brookdale kids."

Alex looked at the two of them as he tried to understand what Tyler was asking.

"Sorry, boys, I didn't mean to make a big deal," Mackenzie said sweetly. "It's just this Brookdale boy I danced with saw you and said he knew you, Alex. He said he was doing some training or something with you. But when I asked him for what he wouldn't say, so I was just curious."

Alex felt the blood rush to his cheeks. How could Brock be such an idiot! They had been told over and over that the teenager astronaut program was supposed to be a secret. Even when he was a little kid, he had carefully guarded the secrets his father had told him were not public yet. He remembered his father telling him the story about how a NASA engineer had once been talking with a colleague about a lunar probe mission that had an unexpected failure at a restaurant before the details had been made public. A waiter had overheard and told his brother, who worked for a newspaper. The next day, NASA was overwhelmed with calls from journalists asking to confirm that the probe had failed. They had planned to hold a press conference to present all the information in an orderly manner, but after the leak, rumors flew for days and made the agency look like they were hiding information. The head of the mission had been furious, his father said.

If rumors started to spread about Alex and Brock's participation and made it out to the press, the company might decide neither of them could be trusted. Even worse, if the rumors originated from Creekside High and could be traced back to Mackenzie, NewStar might assume Alex was the one who had leaked the information.

Mackenzie and Tyler were staring at Alex, and he realized he hadn't responded to Mackenzie. He tried to think of something to say quickly.

"I...uh...don't know why anyone would say I'm training with them. I did...play basketball against Brookdale once."

Mackenzie gave him a puzzled look. "I'm pretty sure this guy said training with you, not playing against you. And he said he was a football player, not a basketball player."

Alex couldn't come up with a good explanation quickly. He was exhausted and wanted to go home. He took a deep breath and looked up at the darkened ceiling of the gym. Exasperated, he pulled closer to Mackenzie and Tyler.

"Come with me outside," he said in the lowest voice he could without being drowned out by the music. "I need to tell you a secret."

CHAPTER 7

THE MOON HUNG BRIGHTLY AMONG THE FEW VISIBLE STARS AND dropped a blueish light over the pecan trees that stood proudly in the center of a grass circle in front of Creekside High School. Alex walked into the dark shadows beneath the trees as Mackenzie and Tyler trailed him curiously. They all came to a stop underneath the broad branches and Alex turned to face them, his heart beating quickly. He was still trying to think of a good lie to tell, but nothing materialized in his mind.

"Look, this is a little complicated," he began. "I'm not supposed to tell anyone about this and neither is that idiot Brock." Mackenzie smiled for some reason.

"The truth is," he continued, "I've been training for a while with my dad's company. They want to send me to work at their hotel."

"Wait, hold on a second," Tyler interrupted. "You don't mean...like onboard NewStar One?"

"What are you guys talking about?" asked Mackenzie, looking puzzled.

"You know who Alex's dad is, right?" Tyler asked.

"Yes, of course, everyone knows about Alex's dad and his...mom," Mackenzie said, trailing off at the end with a guilty expression. Alex never liked people tiptoeing around the subject of his mother.

"It's fine, Mackenzie," he said. "I don't mind talking about her. But anyway, you may not know this, but my dad quit NASA and works for NewStar One now...the company that's trying to build a private hotel and lab in space."

Mackenzie's eyes lit up. "No way! I think I heard about them, but I didn't realize they were taking kids up there."

"It's not exactly public information," said Alex. "But think about it. If they're going to allow guests up there, they will have to allow families with kids. They want someone to go as a kind of demonstration and to do extra work."

"Holy shit, bro!" Tyler screamed.

Mackenzie looked as though she might jump up and down. "That sounds amazing. You'd be like a real astronaut!"

Alex couldn't help but smile. He'd never been popular at school and definitely never had a girl so interested in something he was doing. Most of them seemed grossed out by the work he did in the lab.

"But wait," Mackenzie said. "That guy Brock said he was training with you."

Alex deflated a little. "Yeah, so that's the thing. My dad at first didn't want me to go. He thought it was too risky. So they picked another kid to take my place: Brock. Then my dad changed his mind – long story – but now they have us both training and I think it's like some kind of competition even though they don't really say that. And I don't think I'm doing so well."

Mackenzie frowned. "That Brock kid seemed like he was really full of himself. I would much rather see you fly in space."

"Yeah, me too," said Alex. Mackenzie laughed and Alex smiled at her. For a moment, their eyes locked and Alex felt better than he had in weeks.

"Yeah, great joke," Tyler said. "Now seriously, how can you, the smartest kid in the universe, not be doing so well in space training?"

"Oh man, it's not at all what I thought it would be," Alex replied. "I'll tell you but first, you guys seriously have to promise not to tell anyone about this. I mean, I could lose my chance if the company finds out I told anyone."

"I pinkie swear," said Mackenzie. She and Alex locked fingers.

"Yeah, I'm not pinkie swearing with you because we're not ten years old, but bro, you know you can trust me," added Tyler.

"Alright, let's sit down." Alex gestured to the benches beneath the trees. "This might take a while."

For the next twenty minutes, Alex whispered the story of his past several weeks while keeping a constant lookout for eavesdroppers. He told Mackenzie and Tyler about the vomit comet, the physical fitness training, the classroom instruction where Brock would doze off but still somehow retain all the knowledge he needed. He finished with the story of his hyperbaric chamber run from that afternoon that had left him passed out on a table. When he was finished, Tyler and Mackenzie were speechless and Alex felt as if his body had been released from emotional chains that he didn't even know had been restraining him.

"You know, Alex," said Mackenzie. "I don't mean this in a bad way, but it sounds like you need to get in shape."

"She's right," Tyler agreed. "You'll have no problems

with the technical stuff. It's the physical part that's killing you."

Mackenzie moved over to sit next to Alex. "My big sister is a personal trainer, and I go out with her in the morning three times a week and she does like serious boot camp type training. It's amazing for your balance and your breathing and everything. I bet it would help you with some of that stuff."

"Well, NewStar has me in a physical fitness training program, but I guess it wouldn't hurt to do some extra." Alex relished the thought of spending mornings with Mackenzie. After a terrible start, this night was turning out way better than he could have imagined.

"Awesome. We meet at El Dorado Park at 6:00 AM on Monday, Wednesday and Friday."

"OK," said Alex. "Count me in." He looked over at Tyler.

Tyler shook his head. "Yeah, forget about it. I have a policy of not waking up any sooner than fifteen minutes before the bus comes."

Alex exchanged phone numbers with Mackenzie. Then the sound of a door slamming in the distance reminded all of them where they were. Alex looked over to see clumps of students exiting the gym and heading towards the parking lot. Their loud voices and laughter echoed off the school building. Alex looked down at his watch. It was 10:14.

"I should probably get back and find Heather before she calls the police to come looking for me," said Mackenzie.

"Yeah, we should probably get going too," said Alex.

"Really?" asked Tyler. He looked disappointed, but Alex was too exhausted to do anything else. The three of them ambled slowly back to the gym doors. Mackenzie said goodbye and Alex left with Tyler for the parking lot.

"That girl totally wants your body," Tyler said once they were out of earshot.

Luckily, in the dark, nobody could see him blush. "Nah," he said. "I doubt it."

As they walked towards Tyler's beat-up Honda, Alex saw Brock standing on a curb talking to some of his friends. Brock spotted him and waved enthusiastically. Alex nodded his head back, but then felt like an idiot for even acknowledging the guy. He wanted to take back his nod, but it was too late. Still, Mackenzie had said she would rather see him fly in space than Brock. That was victory enough for him.

*****

Mackenzie was serious about her workouts, and Alex was serious about impressing Mackenzie. On Monday morning, he arrived at the park a few minutes late at 6:05 AM. He had been up until almost one o'clock the night before studying life support systems, but the thought of working out with Mackenzie made him jump vigorously out of bed when his alarm sounded off at 5:30.

Mackenzie and her sister, Emily, were stretching on the grass when Alex dropped his bike at the curb. The sun was peeking above the horizon and its heat was heavy in the already stifling humid air. Alex approached the pair of blond-haired girls. Good looks ran in the Dale family. Emily had the same long flowing hair as Mackenzie, just a shade darker. She was clearly quite fit, with a pronounced muscular structure. She smiled as Alex approached, and her bright white teeth gleamed. Just above her right lip, a dark birthmark punctuated her face.

"You must be Alex," Emily said. "I heard you needed to get in shape for baseball tryouts."

"What?" Alex asked, confused.

"Yeah, Alex," Mackenzie piped in. "You told me if you didn't get in better shape, you might not make the team." Alex looked over at Mackenzie who mimed zippering her lips shut. He nodded imperceptibly, pleased that she had kept her promise of secrecy.

"Oh, right," said Alex. "Yeah, Mackenzie said you do a pretty intense workout and that it might help me."

"Great. I'll try to go easy on you the first day. Stretch out, we're about to start with a quick mile jog."

Alex had barely stretched his legs when Emily and Mackenzie took off running down the concrete path that wound through the park. Their idea of a light jog seemed like a sprint to Alex and by the time he caught them at the end of their run, he was wheezing and felt nauseous. However, Emily didn't stop. She jogged to a nearby soccer goal, this time at a more reasonable pace, and jumped up to hang from the top. She began doing pull-ups, and Mackenzie followed. Alex had to jump up three times before he was able to maintain a grip on the thick beam that ran along the top of the goal. He managed to do two pull-ups before his arms gave out and he fell to the ground. He sat on the grass and leaned back into his hands to catch his breath.

Mackenzie finished before Emily and sauntered over to him. Her skin glistened with sweat, but she barely seemed winded. Alex had never noticed the muscular definition of her smooth arms before. He was embarrassed to be so far behind the girls in physical ability.

"Don't worry if it seems intense, rocket boy. It'll get easier the more you do it."

"I hope so. I really need to pass that test."

"Well, then stop laying around and let's get to work!" She smiled and offered her hand to help Alex up. He could feel Mackenzie's strength as she pulled him quickly to his feet and then took off in a sprint towards some nearby picnic tables with her sister by her side. Alex caught up and they began doing sets of inclined push-ups with their feet on the benches and their hands down in the grass.

After forty-five minutes, Alex's whole body felt like rubber and he was incredibly relieved when Emily said it was time to go get ready for school. Alex said good-bye and ambled slowly to his bike. Every muscle complained loudly during the ten-minute ride back to his house. His workout with Emily and Mackenzie had left him even more fatigued than the ones he had done with his father at NewStar's gym. He realized that he probably had worked himself harder in front of Mackenzie than he did at the space center.

If he kept this up, he would surely be able to get ahead on the training and secure his spot on the mission. And if he could impress Mackenzie, they might end up more than just friends. Things were finally looking up.

As Alex arrived back home, he had little time to shower before leaving for school. But he took a moment to look up into the bright blue Texas sky. He felt the warmth of the sun on his face and felt certain that his mother was smiling down on him.

CHAPTER 8

EXAMS INVIGORATED ALEX. HE LOVED THE SATISFACTION OF solving a tough problem or figuring out the secretive trick answer to a subtle multiple choice question. This was probably one of the reasons he wasn't very popular at school. Most kids assumed that the smart ones in class were kissing up to the teacher or just trying to show off their intelligence to make others feel inferior. It probably never occurred to them that the nerd who seemed boastful might just enjoy solving problems. So Alex felt great in the silence of the NewStar One conference room where he and Brock sat scribbling answers into the lines of a thick packet of questions on topics ranging from orbital mechanics to chemistry to food preparation.

This test was considered pass/fail, but both Alex and Brock assumed that the score would have some bearing on Stewart Locke's ultimate decision over which boy would fly in space. It was a closed-book test, with no access to computers, manuals or any other resources that might help them. The company wanted to really understand how much the boys knew in their heads. After all, some situations in space called for quick action where stopping to look up information simply was not an option.

Emily, the instructor Alex had met on their first day of training, sat at the end of the glass conference table working intently on a laptop computer and looking up at the boys every once in a while. Alex had learned a lot about her over the past few weeks listening to her training classes. She was passionate about space and wanted to be an astronaut herself. She was thinking of joining the Air Force Reserves to see if she could become a pilot. Alex appreciated her passion and no-nonsense attitude. He smiled at her when she looked up at him and she returned the smile.

Alex looked back down at his paper, feeling that he must be Emily's favorite, even though that probably didn't matter in the final selection. As he flipped pages, he noticed a glow coming from below the glass surface of the table. His eyes followed it until they settled on Brock's knee, visible through the transparent table surface. Alex looked up at Brock. He was looking down at his lap and his hand was below the table. He was reading something on his phone!

I knew he couldn't have memorized all that stuff without taking notes.

Alex turned his head to look at Emily. She was still intently working on her computer, not paying attention to either of them. Should he tell her? Alex hated the thought of being a snitch, but he didn't want Brock to get away with this. He faked a cough. Emily looked up, but Brock quickly returned his hands to the table and began writing on his paper. The glow of the phone was gone.

Alex shot Brock a hateful look. He knew if he said something, Brock would just deny it. He should probably just focus on his exam. Brock couldn't possibly cheat much without getting caught, and Alex felt sure he would score higher even if Brock was able to sneak a few answers on his phone. He put his head down and continued pounding out answers.

An hour later, Alex finished his exam and handed the stack of papers to Emily. He took his backpack from the corner of the room and meandered down the stairwell to the lobby where he sat on a black leather couch to wait for his father. He pulled his phone from his bag and was surprised to find a message from Mackenzie. They had been working out in the mornings for several weeks now, but she rarely talked to him any other time.

>> *Weather looks bad tmrw. Probably no boot camp.*

Then, another message from ten minutes later:

>> *Since we don't have to get up early, want to go to Kemah 2nite?*

Alex stared at the message for a minute. Kemah was a small town with a boardwalk located on the channel between Clear Lake and the Gulf of Mexico. The boardwalk was a favorite local hangout with a few rides, tons of restaurants, and live music on a small stage several nights a week during the summer. Was she asking him on a date? Or was she going with a group of friends? He quickly tapped out a response:

>> *Sure, would love to. What time?*

He pressed "Send" and then wondered if his response sounded too eager. He stared at the phone, waiting for something to pop up, but he was interrupted by his dad marching briskly through the lobby in a blue and grey flight suit.

"How did the test go?" he asked.

"It was easy," Alex replied. His dad smiled and tousled Alex's hair as if he were still a child. They walked together to the parking lot. Alex took notice of how many more people stared at his father when he was wearing the flight suit. He really wanted to wear one himself. The training was supposed to be finished in one more week, followed by a physical fitness test. Then they would know for sure.

On the ride home, Alex kept checking his phone for a response from Mackenzie and wondering if she had changed her mind.

"What do you keep looking at your phone for?" his dad finally asked.

"Oh, I'm maybe going to meet some friends at Kemah tonight," he muttered.

"Hmmph," his dad grunted in the way that he did when he didn't think what you were doing was the best idea. "You know that you have school tomorrow and then a simulation in the evening."

"Yeah, I know Dad. I won't stay out late, I promise." Just then his phone dinged and a message popped up from Mackenzie:

>> *Sweet. Meet me at Eli's Ice Cream at 7:30.*

"Alex, I don't think you should be going out with friends right now."

"Dad, please, just for a little bit."

"Who are you going with? Tyler? You can see him on the weekend sometime."

"No, it's not with Tyler."

"Then who?"

"Just some new friends, Dad."

"What are the names of your new friends?" His dad just wouldn't let it go.

"Her name is Mackenzie."

"Oh." His father paused, and the silence hung thick in the air like the stifling heat of Houston, a palpable uncomfortableness. Finally, he said, "Well, I guess you can go for a little while. Just don't stay out too late."

Alex beamed. "Awesome. So can I take the car?"

His father groaned slightly. "Just be careful."

*****

Eli's Ice Cream Parlor sat across from the water between a seafood restaurant and a small pizzeria. Alex had rushed to change clothes when he got home but it had taken him longer than he expected and now he was running late. He power-walked through a crowd of people on the boardwalk, already feeling the sweat gathering on his forehead from the humid air.

When he arrived, Mackenzie was already seated at an outdoor table with a nice view of the murky brown water. There were two dishes of ice cream sitting on the table already.

"I ordered for you," she said with a smile as Alex sat down across from her. "It's called the Rocketman Sundae."

"Gee, thanks," Alex said, wishing he had arrived earlier so he could have at least paid for the ice cream. He looked around. "So are you expecting anybody else?"

Mackenzie laughed out loud. "No, silly. Just you and me tonight."

Alex smiled. "That's what I was hoping."

Mackenzie took a bite of her ice cream. "How's your training going? Or are we not supposed to talk about that?"

"We can talk about it, as long as you don't tell anyone."

"Cross my heart."

"I think it's going better. The test today was easy for me. But I don't think it was for Brock. I saw him looking at his phone during the test."

"No way! Did you tell anyone?"

"No, I thought about it but I'm sure he would have denied it."

"Alex, that could get him kicked out easy, even just the suspicion of it. You should tell someone." That was a good point Alex hadn't thought about.

"Maybe. It seems too late now. Anyway, I'm pretty sure I did better than him either way. And next week is the last week of training and testing and then it's all done. They'll have a decision."

"And you think it will be you?"

"I sure hope so. I mean, it's not just for me. It's for my mom and dad too."

"What do you mean?" Alex explained how he had found his mother's experiment notebooks and wanted to finish her research and how his father's ability to fly the first mission to NewStar One now depended on Alex passing all of his tests. Mackenzie listened silently and intently, her blue eyes probing Alex while he spoke.

"After what happened to your mom, aren't you scared to fly on a rocket?" she asked.

"A little," Alex admitted. They sat in a comfortable silence for several minutes.

"What's the most dangerous thing you've ever done?" Alex asked spontaneously.

"We went on a vacation to Mount Hood in Oregon and my parents let my brother and me go bungee jumping with them."

"No way! Are you serious?"

"Yeah, it was incredible. I was so scared jumping off that I thought I was going to have a heart attack."

"That's amazing. I'm going to think of that when the

rocket takes off. If you can do it, so can I."

They had reached the bottom of their ice cream cups. Alex took them to the trash and they walked along the boardwalk. A half moon reflected off the waves in the dark water below them. Mackenzie took Alex's hand.

"I really hope you get to fly in space," she said. They walked past the empty stage to a playground for children that was abandoned at this time of the evening. "I used to play on this all the time. Come to the top with me! There's a great view of the bay."

Alex climbed up the short ladder and Mackenzie followed him. The platform at the top of the playground from where the slide descended was small, but they squeezed in together. Alex looked out as a lone boat slowly glided into the marina. He felt Mackenzie's arm reach around his waist. He turned to face her and saw her blue eyes twinkle even in the dark. She moved closer to him. In seemingly slow motion, Alex brought his face down and their lips met. Hers were warm and soft and as she pulled his body closer to hers, Alex never wanted to leave.

CHAPTER 9

"ALL CREW MEMBERS, PREPARE FOR DOCKING," BOOMED ALEX'S father's voice over the speaker. Alex looked up from his seat on a rolling office chair inside a narrow corridor surrounded by blinking lights and displays.

This is so boring, he thought. This was the third and final simulation of their training program. Alex recalled how nervous and excited he had been for the first two, but he had quickly realized that most of the training involved routine maintenance tasks which he was not assigned to perform. This simulation was now entering its fifth hour, and so far the only thing Alex had done was to install and power up some computers in the simulated hotel rooms for the simulated arriving guests. Then he sat around playing games on his phone and thinking about Mackenzie. She had been texting him a lot lately, asking about his training and filling him in on gossip at school about people Alex either didn't know or usually didn't care about. He nevertheless replied enthusiastically and asked lots of questions. He found that he was learning a lot about social circles that he previously didn't even know existed.

Alex stood and walked the length of the corridor, stopping at an opening that looked out of the simulator and into the cavernous bay that made up the NewStar training center. Besides the space station simulator, the bay also held a capsule simulator of the Crew Transfer Vehicle – or CTV - that would carry them to and from the space station, an air-bearing floor for practicing two-dimensional zero-gravity tasks, a spacesuit training area with spacesuits and external tools and a robotics lab where NewStar was working on robotic inspection and repair techniques. Along the grey walls hung a gigantic United States flag and a flag with the NewStar Space Technologies company logo: a blue crescent Earth with rays of sun shooting out from the top in an orbital sunrise.

The space station simulator where Alex was stationed took up a full quarter of the enormous open floor. It consisted of a series of rectangular structures that looked like trailers connected together. Each rectangle was about 8 feet tall and about 30 feet long. They roughly approximated the modules of the space station which were cylindrical in real life but outfitted with racks and equipment that made them seem like rectangular rooms from the inside.

Since the simulator existed in earth's gravity field, the modules couldn't be placed the way they were in orbit. On the real station, the hotel rooms hung "down" from a long corridor and required one to reorient himself and think of the door to each room not as a hatch in the ground but instead as an upright door leading into a room with a large window at the end. None of this could not be accurately simulated in normal gravity. Therefore, the simulator modules that would be "up" or "down" on the real space station were simply placed side-by-side in the training center. This minor modification was not lost on Alex who imagined every time he moved across the training floor to the hotel room simulator that he was rotating his body in a gravity-free environment towards his home planet below.

There were three crew members involved in this simulation, the same as there would be when the first guests arrived at the space station: Alex, his father and a female chemist named Erica Reid. The simulation would be repeated tomorrow with Brock and Jim Abbott taking the place of Alex and his father. For this training exercise, Alex was the lone crew member assigned to the hotel section, while his father and Dr. Reid were practicing setting up equipment in the labs and monitoring the approach of the CTV. Alex always expected the simulation instructors to pepper them with scenarios of failed equipment or fires in space, but so far nothing out of the ordinary had happened as they prepared for the arrival of a ship full of passengers.

On the wall near Alex was a monitor showing a simulated camera view. The approaching ship appeared as a bright light against the dark backdrop of space, with the blue earth glowing beneath it. In the corner of the monitor, green numbers indicated that the ship was still 800 meters away and closing at 2 meters per second. Alex knew the ship would slow down once it reached 500 meters, and doing some math quickly in his head he realized there were at least 15 minutes before the ship would dock.

Alex returned to his chair and looked down at his phone to see if there were any new text messages. As he did, his eye caught a flashing red light on a panel at the top of the wall. For a moment, he froze, and then jumped up, knocking over the chair. He rushed to the wall and grabbed a black hand-held microphone.

"Depress, depress!" he shouted into the microphone, just as a blaring klaxon began to ring throughout the chamber. He knew from the classroom training that if the depressurization alarm went off, the crew needed to instantly inform everyone else and begin shutting the hatches to try to stop the leak. Alex ran into the nearby node module and slammed his hand against the "Close Hatch" button on the wall.

That probably wouldn't be so easy in space, he thought. He ran back to the other side of node towards lab module 1, his heart racing.

"Dad! There's a depress alarm!" he shouted, out of breath. His father was standing by a computer station, holding a laminated checklist and talking rapidly on the microphone to the control center in Houston.

"Copy, NewStar Control," he said, concluding his conversation with the mission control team on the ground. Alex had missed it all.

"Alright, guys and gals, you know the drill," his father announced. "Let's get to the CTV." While they were living onboard the station, the CTV remained docked and served as an emergency escape vessel for the astronauts and guests. With his father leading the way, the three walked briskly through the simulator towards their escape vehicle.

They quickly arrived in the node next to the hotel module where Alex had been stationed a few minutes ago. As they arrived, an instructor stood in the hatch at the end of the node that led to the docking compartment, his arms folded across his chest.

"Hatch is closed here," the instructor said as they approached the entrance.

"What?" Alex's father said. "Why would the hatch be closed?"

"Sorry, I'm just a hatch," said the instructor with a sly

smile.

"I closed it," Alex piped up. "When I heard the depress alarm." His dad did not look pleased.

"Why would you do that?" he practically shouted.

"I thought we were supposed to close the hatches to isolate the leak," Alex said sheepishly. He was sure that's what they had told him to do in class, but his father didn't seem pleased.

"Dammit, Alex!" His dad smacked the wall with his hand. "You don't close the hatches until all the crew is gathered at the CTV." As he talked, he moved to the wall and pushed the "Open" button for the hatch. It blinked twice, indicating the hatch failed to open.

"Sonova bitch," his father grumbled. He walked over to a display on the wall and jabbed at it with his fingers. He seemed to calm down a little as he looked at the data. "OK, it's just what I thought. The leak is on the other side of the hatch, in the corridor between us and the vehicles. Most of the air leaked out of the node and it's at low pressure. The pressure in here is stable but pushing against the hatch so hard we can't open it. Which means we can stay here and be safe but have no way to leave the station, or we open the valve to equalize pressure, leak a bunch of air out of here and hold our breath trying to make it to the CTV."

After his dad finished speaking, the room was silent except for the whirring hum of the computers. Alex suddenly felt alone, as if he were standing on a stage with a spotlight focused only on him. He should have remembered that the hatches had to be closed behind you as you made your way to the CTV. He had acted quickly without thinking or talking to anyone. In a real emergency, his actions would have wasted precious time and oxygen as they tried to equalize pressure and open the now vacuum-sealed hatch.

"Dad, isn't there anything else we can do?" Alex hated that his voice sounded tiny, like a small bird.

His father sighed. "I'm afraid in this case, we would have to feed the leak with more space station air and take our chances."

The instructor jumped in, "That's a correct assessment. You would repressurize the leaking module and then go back to the usual evacuation procedure. It just would take a little bit longer to get the pressures equalized, so you have a higher risk of the leak rupturing out and becoming catastrophic. Time is always of the essence when there is a cabin leak onboard."

Alex's father nodded agreement. The instructor decided to end the training session with that lesson. Alex watched him type notes into a tablet. He didn't want to know what was being written about his performance. Things had been looking up for him lately and now he had made a mistake during what was supposed to be an easy exercise. After the instructor dismissed them, Alex started to walk off the floor briskly. Hot tears began to streak down his cheeks. He broke into a run. Without even looking, he could feel his father chasing behind him.

Alex flew into the locker room and furiously unzipped his flight suit that they wore for the simulations. He pulled the padlock from his locker and threw it violently at the ground. Then he slammed the door open and shut four times, causing a cacophony of echoes in the small tiled room.

His father came around the corner. "Feel better? Because I'm sure the locker doesn't."

Alex fell back onto the bench and buried his face in his

hands.

His father sat next to him and put an arm around his back. "Son, we all make mistakes. Don't beat yourself up."

"I keep messing up. They're never going to let me fly. I'm never going to get to finish mom's experiment."

His dad took a deep breath. "This is not easy training for someone your age. I've heard that Brock has had some struggles of his own. Like Grandma used to always say, when the going gets tough, the tough get going. Don't let these things stop you from going on."

Alex shook his head. He couldn't understand how his father could be optimistic in the face of everything that had happened during the past five weeks. "I don't know how they would ever let me fly after this, and the vomit comet, and the hyperbaric chamber thing. Plus Brock is going to destroy me in the physical fitness test."

"It's not a competition, just a test. As long as you pass, you are qualified to fly. Alex, I can't predict what the company might do. But please don't give up." His father's voice cracked. "Ever since Mom died...well, I haven't been the best dad I could have been. It was hard for me. But now I see what I've been missing. You're an amazing boy, almost a man, and after all we've done together, I can't imagine doing this mission without you." His father pulled his arm back and covered his face, leaning forward to place his elbows on his calves. The two sat on the bench in nearly identical poses, looking like mirror images separated only by time.

Alex broke the mold first. He pulled his face from the depths of his hands and turned to face his father as if seeing him for the first time. It hadn't really occurred to him that his dad wanted Alex on the mission as much as Alex wanted to be there. After the initial reluctance, it seemed to Alex that his dad was doing this to honor his mom, not because he really wanted Alex to do it. But now he could see that the mission was more than that to his dad – or at least it was now, even if it hadn't been that way from the start.

"You're right," Alex muttered. His voice grew stronger as he spoke. "I won't give up. I'm not going to make any more mistakes. I'm going on that flight."

His dad pulled his head up and smiled weakly. He wrapped an arm over Alex's shoulder. "You may still make mistakes. Just never give up." Alex nodded. His father added, "I love you son."

Alex leaned into his dad's embrace. He still didn't think the company would let him fly, but it was good to know his dad was on his side. His voice was almost a whisper. "Love you too, Dad."

CHAPTER 10

THE PHYSICAL FITNESS TEST TOOK PLACE ON A CLOUDY AND muggy Saturday morning just six weeks before the launch. Stewart had promised them a quick decision and announcement following this final test. There had been no indication at all about how either boy's performance in the training so far might impact their chances to fly. All Alex knew was that he was still here, which meant he was still a candidate.

Unlike the simulations which were conducted separately, both Brock and Alex would be completing this test together, at the same time. It felt like a race, even though they had been assured that there was no winner, just a minimum set of standards that had to be met. The course consisted of a three-mile run, followed by a series of obstacles that would test balance, agility and body strength. The obstacles included monkey bars, a rope climb, a rope bridge, a series of balance beams and then wooden vaults. Finally, there was a 200-yard swim wearing clothes and then ten minutes of treading water.

Alex had continued his exercise program with Mackenzie and Emily, and he felt significantly stronger and more confident than he did several weeks ago. Still, this was a challenging course and Brock had a clear advantage having been an active athlete for most of his life.

Braddock Wilson, NewStar's physical fitness coach, jogged over to meet them. Braddock had been a Sergeant in the Army before joining NewStar, and he had a reputation for being tough. Everyone called him "Sarge" as if he were a drill sergeant even though he had worked in artillery and small arms repair in the Army. When Sarge reached the two of them, he explained the rules in a succinct lecture, even though both boys had already heard them several times. Both Brock and Alex's fathers were watching from the side, along with several other instructors and some of the company management. Stewart was not there.

"Alright boys, are you ready for the test?" Sarge asked. They nodded. "Good luck to you both. Now line up to start, the first section is the three mile run which must be completed in less than twenty-five minutes. After that, continue directly into the obstacles. Alright, get ready, set, and...GO!"

Alex took off at what felt like a blinding pace, but Brock managed to speed in front of him with apparent ease. A few times during training, Alex had pushed himself hard in an effort to impress Mackenzie, and he had always ended up sitting out at the end of the session. This time, he forced himself to keep a reasonable pace, even if it meant Brock was ahead of him. He knew that he could complete the three miles in the allotted time, and there was a lot more of the course to go once the run was finished.

Alex settled into a rhythm and pushed Brock and the spectators out of his mind. He focused on taking deep breaths of the damp air and pounding his legs steadily against the track. After a short while, he was trailing Brock by a hundred yards or more, but the gap seemed to have stabilized.

The three mile run required six laps around a large rectangular track which surrounded the obstacle course that would follow the run. Alex was still running as Brock completed his laps and started across the monkey bars. By the time Alex reached the finish line, he was sweating buckets and panting heavily, but he didn't feel completely spent yet. He paused with his hands on his knees to catch his breath and then jogged to the start of the obstacle course, leaped up to the bars, and began swinging from one hot metal bar to the next.

Once across the monkey bars, there was a tall rope climb to a platform nearly fifteen feet in the air. Brock was nearly at the top by the time Alex reached the base of his rope. He pulled himself up and snaked the rope under one foot and over the other so that he could push himself up the rope with his legs. Sarge had taught him this technique after several failed attempts to climb the rope by pinching it between his feet. Even with the new technique, though, it was slow work to inch up the rope, and Alex's hands were slimy with sweat. He was about eight feet up when his foot slipped off the rope. He squeezed his hands tightly to arrest his fall, but with his feet free, his hands began to slide and the rope burned against them fiercely. Alex let out a cry and tried to hold himself up but his grip wasn't strong enough. His right hand fell loose as he clawed desperately at the rope with his left, but before he could even register what was happening, his body came crashing down into the white sand.

The shock of the fall thundered through him, and, for a moment, bright spots danced in front of Alex's eyes. Pain shot up his back, centered on his tailbone. He groaned loudly. *It's not that bad,* he told himself. *I'm not going to fail this test.* He managed to roll over and push himself up onto his knees, as slowly diminishing waves of pain echoed throughout his body. A shadow blotted out the sun, and Alex looked up to find Brock standing above him. *Great, just the guy I need to add insult to injury.*

"Are you OK?" Brock asked. Determined to not be bested by this overachieving brown-noser, Alex nodded his head and rose to his feet. Sarge was running towards them. "Brock, keep going. I'll take care of Alex."

"Got it," said Brock, and he started to shimmy back up the rope.

The sharp pain in Alex's back was already beginning to dull as Sarge checked him over. With a quick examination, Alex was declared fit to continue and he pulled himself back onto the rope, determined more than ever to keep going. He moved quickly but carefully this time, trying not to spend any more upper body strength than necessary. By the time he reached the top and stood on the wooden platform, he could see that Brock was already working his way across the fourth obstacle, the balance beams.

Alex still needed to complete the third obstacle - a rope bridge that consisted of a single thick cable with two thinner rope handrails at arm level. Alex quickly donned his safety harness and attached the tether to one of the handhold ropes. Although he had walked this passage a few times in training, he was always afraid of falling, even with the safety harness. He took a deep breath and began to carefully make his way across, watching his feet closely as he placed them carefully one in front of the other on the teetering cable. In just a few minutes, he reached the other side without incident.

After quickly ditching the safety harness, Alex descended a wooden ladder and then walked carefully down a series of angled, descending balance beams with his arms extended. Finally, he rushed over seven wooden vaults to the end of this part of the course. With Sarge following him, he jogged to the nearby fitness center for the swimming portion of the test.

Alex was not a great swimmer, but he completed the laps quickly even if his form was less than ideal. He then doggie-paddled for ten minutes while Sarge counted down and shouted out supposedly inspirational tidbits like, "Just five minutes and you can get a hot shower and eat a tub of ice cream" or "This pool is for warriors, if you want gentle yoga try your neighborhood hippie gym."

Brock finished nearly three minutes before Alex, leaving Alex alone in the pool finishing off his doggie paddle while Brock stood at the side with a towel over his shoulders. When Alex finally finished, he pulled himself up the pool ladder, still wearing his dripping wet shirt. Sarge handed him a towel. "Nice work, young man. You completed everything in the allotted time, although that fall put you real close to the limit on the obstacle course."

Alex hadn't even been thinking about his times; he had been too focused on getting through the course and trying to stay at least within a reasonable distance of Brock. He smiled widely as he wrapped the towel around his body. He had done it.

*****

As promised, Stewart asked to see them that very afternoon. Alex and his father arrived at the office first and were escorted in by Stewart's young female assistant. She offered them drinks which they both declined.

Alex nervously tapped his foot while he waited, much in the same way he had during their first meeting in this office. After several minutes, Jim and Brock Abbott were ushered in, and they sat down on the couch. Stewart followed behind them. He casually dropped a folder on his desk and then strode over to the couches and stood in front of his enraptured audience.

"Well, boys," he began. "I'm quite pleased to say that you both passed your qualifications. From the company perspective, you are qualified to fly as crewmembers for NewStar Space Technologies." Alex felt his heart beating quickly. They were both qualified, which meant that there was no reason he should not be the one to fly. Despite all his struggles, he hadn't messed up so badly that they didn't think he could do this. His moment was finally here.

"Now is the difficult part," Stewart continued. "I won't mince words. Our original plan, of course, was to have Mike fly the first mission and bring Alex along as the third crewmember, thus satisfying our client that teenagers can safely and effectively live and work on our station. However, we need to have the crew that will be most efficient and effective as well." Alex didn't like the way Stewart was looking at him. He suddenly felt nauseous.

"After careful consideration of the results of our training program, we think the best choice for this mission is to send Brock to the station." Alex froze. He shook his head in disbelief; surely he had heard wrong. On the other couch, Brock was hugging his father.. Hadn't Stewart just said Alex was qualified to fly? He was ready to go; he had his experiments all planned out. They couldn't send Brock in his place!

Stewart had resumed talking and Alex realized what he was now saying. "...so after that reconsideration of my original position, Mike will continue to command this first mission. I trust, Brock, that you will be able to follow all..." Alex suddenly felt like he might throw up. His mother had died on her way to space and left him notebooks so that he could finish her work. Alex knew in the deepest part of his soul that he was meant to go on this mission. It didn't make sense that a patronizing jock who knew nothing about science would go in his place! His father would do something to stop this. He would know what to do. Alex felt an arm on his back. He looked over at his father whose eyes were set firmly upon him, his face warped in a sympathetic and concerned expression. Alex waited for him to do something, to force Stewart to let him on the mission. But his father just whispered, "I'm sorry."

Alex stood up, interrupting Stewart's ongoing monologue. He needed to leave this place. He turned towards the door, broke into a run, and disappeared down the hallway.

CHAPTER 11

MIKE STONE COULD CONFIDENTLY COMMAND A CREW THROUGH a reentry with half of the spacecraft's thrusters failed, but he was a frazzled bundle of nerves as he stood at the kitchen island and called Alex's phone for what felt like the fourteenth time. He told himself over and over that Alex was old enough to take care of himself and he just needed some time alone to deal with the news. It had been a shock to both of them, but Alex had taken it particularly hard, and before Mike could catch up with him, Alex had disappeared out the front entrance of the NewStar office building and was nowhere to be found. He was probably safe at some park or field somewhere working things out, but Mike had driven around for over an hour and couldn't find Alex anywhere. Now it seemed like nothing could loosen the knot of worry deep in his stomach.

The doorbell rang, and Mike sprinted to the front of the house. Through the adjacent window, he could see right away that it wasn't Alex. He opened the door to reveal a pretty blond girl with tanned skin.

She smiled at him and asked, "Is Alex home?"

"I'm sorry, but he's not here right now," Mike replied.

The girl looked disappointed. "Do you know where he

is? He wasn't answering my calls and I just wanted to see how his test went today."

Mike eyed her suspiciously. "How do you know about that?"

With a guilty look, she quickly said, "Oh, I just meant the math test today at school."

Mike cocked his head to the side. "Why don't you come in for a few minutes? Alex might be home soon."

The girl eyed him nervously. "That's OK. I've got to go." She turned to walk back to her car parked in the street.

"Wait," Mike called after her. She stopped and turned around to face him. Mike stared at her for a moment before he decided to take a chance. "He's missing. I don't know where he is." He felt ashamed telling a strange girl that he had lost his son, but he had a feeling she might be able to help. She stood in silence for a few moments watching him, as if trying to decide if he was trustworthy.

Finally, Mike broke the silence. "If you have any idea where he might be, please help me find him." After only a brief moment, the girl began walking back towards the house.

*****

It was dark when Alex finally returned home. A light drizzle had started falling an hour ago, and even though it was barely a mist, by now Alex's clothes and hair were sopping wet. He had walked for hours, at first sneaking through the back streets of Clear Lake until he had reached the University of Houston satellite campus. At the edge of a cluster of brick buildings sat a large bayou with trails snaking along its muddy edge, and Alex disappeared into the trees. Once he was alone deep in the woods, he began shouting furiously with an uncontrollable rage that he hadn't known he possessed. He snatched up a fallen branch and began hacking at the trees around him. He was surprised and satisfied at how easily some of the drier branches could be severed with a satisfying slice of the thick limb he held in his hands.

"Take that, Stewart, you asshole bitch!" He sliced a branch from a tree.

"Brock is a piece of shit primitive monkey!" Another tree lost a limb.

"My mom would have kicked your ass!" Tears streaked down his face as he lashed out at the vegetation.

Eventually, he grew tired and breathless and sat down by the water, trying to think of nothing but unable to avoid the reality that he would soon return to school as just a regular student. Even worse, it would become public news that Brock was flying to space with his father. Which meant everyone would ask the obvious question: why not Alex, the intelligent son of two astronauts who had been dreaming for years of flying to space? Why not the nerdy boy who kept working on science experiments in the biology lab in his free time? The one who everyone avoided because his mother was gone and nobody knew what to say to him. Why not him?

Alex tried to comprehend where he had gone wrong, what he could have done differently. The answer was too complicated for his exhausted mind to understand. Eventually, with the sky growing dark and the misty rain beginning to fall, Alex had stood up and slowly trudged along the trail towards an entrance to a neighborhood near his house.

He could see his dad's car in the driveway, so he

sneaked around to the back door that led to the kitchen, hoping to make it to his room without running into his father. But when he pulled open the door, he was surprised to see Mackenzie sitting across the kitchen table from his father and sipping something from a coffee mug. Alex wanted to disappear, but before he could realize what was happening they both surrounded him and he was lost in a maze of arms and sobs.

Alex had not expected his temporary disappearance to cause such a commotion, but he was touched that both his father and Mackenzie had worried about him so much. He was suddenly relieved to no longer be alone in his anger, shock and disappointment at losing his chance to fly to space. His dad rushed away to get Alex a towel, and Mackenzie stayed with her arms wrapped around him.

"I'm sorry," she whispered in his ear. "I know how much this meant to you."

Alex didn't know what to say. He managed to choke out a "thank you."

The three of them sat at the table, but there was not much that could be said and after a while Mackenzie left, telling Alex she would see him at school tomorrow and that NewStar was run by a bunch of idiots if they picked Brock over him. When she was gone, Alex returned to his room and his dad followed him. He stood in the doorway as Alex sat down on his bed.

"Alex, I..." he began but then paused, unsure of what to say next. "Well, I guess part of me wishes that I hadn't brought you into this, but if I hadn't, I'd never have been able to see you do all of these amazing things. I'm so proud of you. The company made the wrong choice; I'm sure of that. And there's nothing I can do about it, but having seen what you've accomplished in school and out of it, I know you can become an astronaut one day if that's still what you want to do."

"Maybe," Alex mumbled. He had wanted to fly in space since he was a little kid, and the fact that space travel had taken his mother from him never deterred him; instead, it had strengthened his resolve. But now that he had seen the kinds of things it took to really become an astronaut and he had been bested by a local boy, in a competition that was significantly smaller than the huge national talent pool making up astronaut candidates, he felt that he might not be cut out for spaceflight. Maybe he hadn't inherited the right stuff from his parents. And maybe his mother's experiments were never meant to be finished.

His father eventually left, and these thoughts followed him into sleep.

CHAPTER 12

THE NEWS BROKE THE FOLLOWING WEEK WITH A NEWSTAR PRESS conference. While the story did not get a lot of national attention, in the space-crazed culture of southeast Houston, everyone was talking about the new commercial space venture and the youngest person to fly to space. As soon as Tyler found out, he came to talk to Alex at his house, but Alex didn't have much to say and Tyler eventually left frustrated. Mackenzie also came to see him, but Alex was so lost in grief that he only managed half-hearted smiles at her attempts to cheer him up. At school, Alex did his best to keep his head down and avoid contact with anyone. As he suspected, rumors began to fly through the school. His mother's accident played heavily in many of these rumors. Some speculated that his father had refused to allow Alex to fly. Others wondered if Alex had even been asked. However, a few rumors came far too close to the truth and stung like fire-ant bites.

Alex stayed late at school a few times to work in the biology lab on his DNA correction virus, but his heart wasn't in it. He didn't pay close attention and would make solutions incorrectly or forget a critical mixing or centrifugation step. He got no positive results and made no progress creating the magic protein that he needed.

Alex's father was back to work to continue his training, which would only intensify in the coming weeks. Things were slowly returning to normal, and Alex could feel his father slipping away from him again. After all the time they had spent together these past few weeks, it was a painful separation.

Two weeks after the final test, Alex was invited to a pre-launch party at NewStar headquarters. He didn't want to go, but his father was insistent and spending another quiet night in an empty house was so unappealing that Alex finally acquiesced, stating that he would just stay for an hour.

The NewStar lobby was decorated heavily to the point of being almost unrecognizable. The main lights were off, replaced by the glow of blue and magenta LEDs from special lighting units hidden behind tables and planters. Tables loaded with food and drinks surrounded the center of the lobby while waiters in black tuxedos circulated among the guests. Speakers had been set up around the edges of the lobby and they pumped out a stream of mellow guitar tunes. Alex had never been to such an upscale event, and he had to admit that he was impressed.

Shortly after they entered the lobby, Alex's father was overrun by people wanting to talk with him. Alex wandered over to one of the tables and ordered a Sprite from a waitress. As he took his glass and turned away from the drink table, he spotted Brock walking towards him.

"Hey, man," Brock said with a wide smile. He was wearing a navy blue and grey flight suit. Alex wanted to punch him in the face. He barely managed to mutter, "hi" in return.

"Look, I hope there's no hard feelings," Brock said. "I actually never thought they were going to pick me over you. It seemed like you knew way more about the space station, and plus with your dad and all..." Brock trailed off, and an awkward silence hung in the air. Alex couldn't understand why Brock was even talking to him. Was he just feeling guilty about taking away Alex's chance to continue his mother's work? *He should feel guilty.*

Finally, Brock said, "Anyway, it was really great training with you." He reached out his hand to shake, but Alex just turned and walked away.

*****

At the end of the week, Mackenzie invited Alex to an arcade in Houston. It was the kind of place where you could play everything from Skeeball to laser tag to air hockey and win prizes if you earned some ridiculous amount of points playing the games. Alex was grateful for the chance to get out. They rode with Mackenzie's sister, who was meeting some friends at a restaurant near the arcade. Sitting in the back seat of the run-down Mazda, Mackenzie and Alex held hands and sang loudly and badly along to whatever was blasting on the local radio stations. For the first time in a while, Alex started to feel like maybe things were going to be alright.

Mackenzie's sister dropped them off near the entrance, and they ambled slowly towards the glass doors in the thick, humid air. Mackenzie wrapped her arms around Alex's waist as they walked. Before they reached the entrance, she stopped walking, her head tilted up to the clear sky. The moon hung brightly above them.

"It's beautiful, isn't it?" she asked. Then she planted a

kiss on Alex's cheek. He followed her gaze upward, but looking at the few visible stars felt like a harsh reminder of what he would soon be missing out on.

"Let's go inside," he said.

"Oh, come on, don't be a sourpuss," Mackenzie berated, slapping him gently on the chest. They walked the rest of the way to the arcade and felt a rush of cool conditioned air as they slid into the building. Inside, the lighting was so dim that it was difficult to see. The games blasted noise from all directions - bleeps and blares and the sounds of explosions filled the air.

Only a few minutes after they purchased their game cards, Mackenzie pulled on his arm and pointed excitedly. "Look, it's Heather!" Alex looked and was disappointed to see Heather Townsend and a group of other kids from school crowded around a motorcycle racing game that was being played by two boys who Alex recognized even though he couldn't quite remember their names. He badly wanted to spend time alone with Mackenzie, and he definitely didn't feel like facing anyone from school or any questions about the upcoming NewStar mission.

"Let's go say hi!" Mackenzie squealed, as she grabbed his arm and started towards the group. Alex begrudgingly followed. As they approached the group, Heather spotted them and broke free to run and give Mackenzie a hug. She beamed at Alex and said hi, and Alex said hi back with a forced smile. In no time at all, they were surrounded by energetically twitching bodies and recognizable but intimidating faces. Almost everyone hugged Mackenzie, but most didn't seem to know what to do with Alex. He wasn't popular like her - he didn't have any inside jokes to share or common friends to ask about. One or two of the boys offered a fist bump or a high-five. A girl he knew as Evelyn hugged him and said, "Good to see you, Alex." He was surprised she knew his name.

The group meandered through the dark and noisy arcade, and Alex found himself separated from Mackenzie, trailing along like a lost puppy. His thoughts drifted inward. So many games involved futuristic spaceships battling aliens or dodging meteors. Alex couldn't help but think again about where he had gone wrong. What could he have done differently to be where he would be the one maneuvering a spacecraft in for a docking in real life? He watched Mackenzie talk to Heather while one of the other boys sidled up to her and tried to join in the conversation. Alex began to feel totally alone in the crowd. He started to wonder if Mackenzie had known all along that the group from school would be here. Maybe she was trying to get him to hang out with others. Or maybe she just didn't want to be alone with him, especially lately when his mood had been sour.

Mackenzie suddenly was at his side, tugging at his sleeve. "Come on, let's do a race." She was pointing to a bank of race car seats with steering wheels. Two of the seats were already taken by Heather and a boy with spiked black hair and a tank top that exposed muscular arms. For some reason, Alex found himself shaking his head no.

"Why not?" Mackenzie probed. "Is everything ok?"

"I just thought we were going to be able to spend time alone together." Alex almost had to shout over the noise of the arcade. As soon as the words left his mouth, he hated himself for saying them, for the way he sounded so desperate and needy. Mackenzie frowned at him.

"Let's just do a few games with everyone," she

countered. "It would be rude to just ignore them." Alex felt himself tense. This was not at all his idea of fun. He wanted Mackenzie to himself, and he wanted to be able to forget about NewStar and Brock Abbot and his mother. It seemed incredibly unfair that Mackenzie's friends were here tonight, miles from home, yet coincidentally in the same place. After all he had been through in the past few weeks, he just wanted her to care about him and him alone.

"I don't want to play," Alex said simply.

Mackenzie put her hands on her hips. "Don't be a jerk," she said.

"Did you know they were going to be here tonight?"

"What? Of course not," Mackenzie said, but Alex thought he detected a hesitation in her voice.

"I just wanted time for the two of us to spend together."

"Yes, I know. But these are our friends."

"No, they're your friends. I hardly know any of them."

Mackenzie shook her head. "You know, I thought you were a better person than this. I thought you were one of the nicest boys in school." She opened her mouth as if to say more, but then seemed to change her mind and turned away from Alex to walk to the race car game. She sat down and said something to Heather, turning and pointing back towards Alex. He wanted to disappear off the face of earth.

Unsure of what to do, Alex walked towards the restrooms, but then he passed them by and continued on to the front entrance. He burst out of the doors and paced along the sidewalk underneath the searing glare of an overhead LED on a tall post. He mumbled under his breath about how unfair Mackenzie was being, but he didn't sound convincing even to himself. He had ruined his chance at flying to space and now he was ruining his first relationship. He felt like a complete loser. He kicked at the base of the lamppost, lightly at first but then harder.

"Damn it!" he shouted. "Piece of shit!" He wasn't sure if he was referring to the lamppost or himself. He reached into his pockets and grabbed a receipt which he wadded and flung furiously into a bush. The only other thing he had with him was his phone. He hoisted it up over his head. He wanted to smash it to the ground, but for a second he just held it aloft. Then it started to ring, shocking Alex into dropping the phone. Instinctively, he tried to grab it, and the glowing, vibrating device fumbled about his hands like a slippery fish, but he finally managed a firm grasp.

The screen read "Dad" which was not at all what Alex expected to see at 9 PM on a Friday night. Maybe something was wrong. He quickly tapped the screen and held the phone to his ear.

His father wasted no time saying, "Alex, I need you to come to Clear Lake Hospital immediately."

Alex's body tensed. "Dad, are you alright? Is everything OK?"

"I'm fine, Alex. I can't talk on the phone. Just come quickly."

The phone clicked off. Alex hesitated a moment and then rushed back inside. When he found Mackenzie and explained that his father needed him to meet at the hospital, she rushed to call her sister and get them a ride home. In almost no time at all, they were back in the car. Mackenzie's sister was annoyed at being pulled away from her friends early. Mackenzie also seemed annoyed at Alex and they rode in an awkward silence down I-45 with the tall buildings of Houston at their backs.

The music was turned low, in stark contrast to the happy dance-party atmosphere of their earlier drive into the city. Alex's mind raced through possibilities to explain why his father was in the hospital. He'd said he was fine, but maybe that's just what people say. He had been in a simulation earlier in the day, but there was no way he should have been hurt doing that. Had he had a heart attack?

Alex looked over at Mackenzie who was sitting silently with her arms folded across her chest. Even in that pose, she looked incredible, with her smooth skin highlighted by the glow of yellow street lamps and passing headlights. He didn't want to lose his chance with her.

"Mackenzie," he whispered, hoping to not let her sister in the front hear. She looked over at him. "I'm sorry I got upset. This week just sucked and I'm not really popular like you, so I don't really know a lot of those kids."

Her expression softened, and she uncrossed her arms, bringing one hand over to rest on his leg. "It's OK," she whispered back. "I just don't want to have to choose between you and my friends."

"You don't. I'll hang out with them next time. I was just in a bad mood tonight."

"Alright," she said, finally smiling. She scooted into the middle seat and laid her head on his shoulder. "I hope your dad is OK," she whispered.

"Me too."

*****

At the hospital, they entered the lobby and went to the information desk to ask for Alex's dad, but before they reached the desk, they spotted him walking briskly across the polished white floor.

"Dad," Alex said, surprised. "I thought something had happened."

"Actually, a few things have happened," said Alex's dad. His face was drawn tight and serious, but his eyes were puffy and tired. "It's been quite the day." He looked over at Mackenzie, as if just realizing that she was standing there. "Mackenzie, could you excuse us for a moment?"

"Uh, yeah, sure Mr. Stone," Mackenzie answered. She walked towards the front entrance to the lobby, looking lost, before she finally decided to settle into a chair halfway across the room.

"What's going on, Dad?" Alex inquired.

"Alex, I'll get right to the point. Brock was taken to the hospital this afternoon with abdominal pain. He has been diagnosed with kidney stones. He had been training hard and not drinking enough water. He will almost certainly be disqualified for flight."

"What?" Alex couldn't believe what he was hearing. Did this mean he was going to get his chance after all?

"As you can imagine, this is very hard for Brock and Jim. But there's something else. NewStar One had an anomaly this morning before any of this came up. The gyroscopes that are used to maintain attitude control are failing. The station is in danger of losing control and going into a free drift tumble. Because of this, the launch has been accelerated so I can conduct a repair."

His father took a deep breath. "Alex, the company is asking me if we can launch in two weeks. That is not a lot of time to refresh your training."

Refresh my training? That means they do want me to fly! But two weeks did not sound like a lot of time at all. "I can do it, Dad!" Alex said. "I swear, I can be ready to go. I swear on mom's..." He couldn't finish the thought. He saw the hesitation in his father's eyes. "Please."

His father stared at him for what seemed like an eternity, his stoic face unflinching. He was the perfect commander, in control of his emotions and himself. Finally, he nodded his head. Alex jumped and wrapped his arms around him.

"Son, we have a lot of work to do," his father said. "But first, you need to go see Brock." Alex cringed at the thought of another confrontation tonight, but he knew his dad was right.

*****

Inside the hospital room, the lights were dimmed and a series of monitors bleeped peacefully. Brock was sitting in the bed partially upright and looking like he might cry. Alex tiptoed to the bedside.

"Hey, Brock," Alex said softly. Brock looked over and frowned.

"I guess you're getting my ticket," he finally said hoarsely.

Alex looked at his shoes. "Yeah, seems like it." Bleeps echoed around the room.

Brock shook his head. "You know, I really meant it when I said at the party. I thought you deserved that slot in the first place. But you are one sore loser, bro. You wouldn't even shake my hand and then I heard you've been telling your Brookdale friends that I'm just a meathead jock. I didn't realize what an asshole you were."

Alex took a step back and felt as if he had been stung. Where had Brock heard those things?

Without even thinking, Alex found himself saying, "You're calling me an asshole? You were the one cheating on tests to take away my chance to do my mom's work!"

"What the hell are you talking about?" Brock's face was turning a flushed red and his eyes narrowed to daggers.

"I saw you looking at your phone during our written exam. I should have told Emily right then, but I didn't."

Brock was shaking with fury and he looked like he might jump out of bed and attack Alex, who took a step back.

"Bro, you better watch yourself," he said. "I was looking at my phone because my grandma had been taken to the hospital and my dad was texting me about it. So I'm sorry that I was distracting you from the exam while I dealt with some stuff!"

Alex froze and a knot twisted his stomach. He could see now that he had unfairly judged Brock. In fact, he had disliked him from the very first time they had met. Alex had wanted to fly to space so badly that it had never occurred to him that someone else's passion and talent might equal or surpass his own. Alex looked uncomfortably out the window at the end of the room for a minute before he said so quietly it was nearly inaudible, "Wow, I really am an asshole."

Brock's expression softened slightly. "Yeah, you are a bit. Look, I get that you lost your mom, but you can't use that as an excuse to walk over people either."

Alex was so ashamed he could barely look at Brock. "I'm sorry," he said. "It's just...when my mom died, she was trying to finish these experiments. And when this whole thing came up, I thought I would finally get a chance to try and finish her work." He took a deep breath. He didn't want to admit this, but it was true, so he said it. "But you were better than me and it was ruining my chances, and I got pissed off."

Alex finally looked up at Brock who was watching him intently. Alex felt like he should say something else, but he couldn't think of anything. Brock finally spoke. "I don't know what I'd do if my dad got in an accident."

After a pause, Alex realized there was not much more to say. He needed to repair his relationship with Brock, but it would take time. He said, "I really do hope you get better. I didn't want to win this way."

"Yeah, well, can't do anything about it now." Brock looked up at the ceiling. He looked tired. "Just make sure you get those experiments done for your mom. It's a once in a lifetime chance."

Alex suddenly wanted to hug Brock, a sentiment he never could have dreamed he would have. Instead, he walked over and grasped his hand with a bent elbow and gave him a light punch on the shoulder.

"Thanks, man," Alex said. "I'm sorry I was an asshole to you."

"Alright, get out of here. I'm tired and you probably have some work to do."

Alex nodded and turned away from the bed. He left the room feeling humbled but determined. He needed to be successful now - for his mother's legacy and so that Brock's fateful loss of this opportunity was not in vain. He strode quickly down the hallway towards his new future.

PART 2:
SPACE

CHAPTER 13

THE NIGHTMARE ALWAYS BEGAN WITH A SPACEWALK. ALEX WAS floating inside a spacesuit, with the earth spread out below him, entire continents passing slowly under his feet. In the dream, he was using handrails above him like monkey bars to move to the outermost module of the orbiting outpost. When he reached the end, he knew he should stop but for some reason, he kept swinging forward. There was no handrail past the end of the module and Alex suddenly found himself flying freely away from the space station. The earth glowed indifferently below him as he turned back to see NewStar One grow smaller and smaller.

Suddenly something caught in Alex's mouth. He tried to reach in and pull it out but his gloved hands could not enter the helmet of his suit. He banged his hands furiously against the glass of the helmet until a crack started to appear. He realized with terror that he was only making the situation worse. The crack spread and grew wider. Alex's eyes bulged out of his head, but there was nothing he could do. The helmet shattered all around him.

Alex jolted awake and sat straight up. He was panting heavily in the darkness of a strange room. He gingerly touched his cheek and was relieved to feel his intact face with his fingers.

On the wall opposite his bed was a digital clock which read out two times in dim blue numbers. The top row of the clock showed that it was 3:37 AM local time. The bottom clock read L-09:43. It was slowly counting backwards to launch, less than ten hours away.

Alex's room at the NewStar One "astronaut prelaunch hotel" was small but well-appointed. The bed was huge, and Alex felt like he might get lost in its massive layers of blankets. The bathroom featured a Japanese-style toilet with controls and features which Alex was afraid to explore. The walls were heavily decorated with photographs of planets, stars and the space station he would soon call home.

The hotel was designed primarily as a place for the tourists to stay in the days leading up to their spaceflight, but since there were no tourists awaiting flights just yet, NewStar had allowed the crew to stay in the guest rooms. Alex had heard that normally the crew would be housed in much sparser rooms on the bottom floor of the building.

Alex lay his head back on the pillow and stared at the ceiling. *Ten more hours to go.*

They would be flying on Venturer, one of NewStar's newest Crew Transfer Vehicle capsules, which the company designed and produced in Houston and then shipped to Florida for launch. The CTVs were all very similar and there was a growing fleet of them to transport the guests to and from the station on a regular basis. The capsules splashed down in the ocean, were retrieved by boat and were reused after a two-week maintenance and test period.

Alex picked up his phone from the nightstand. Not caring that it was almost 4 in the morning, he tapped out a quick text to Mackenzie:

>> *Getting nervous, less than 10 hrs! Wish you could come too. Miss ya already.*

Deciding that sleep was futile at this point, he turned on the lights and sat down at a shiny metal desk. The computer provided in the room included access to all the astronaut training materials from NewStar and a crude simulator. Alex opened the docking simulation and grasped the joystick-like controls provided with the computer.

While he was not officially trained to pilot the spacecraft, recent events had compelled him to spend time trying to learn as much as he could about how the space station and the Venturer spacecraft flew. Learning how to fly the CTV had been interesting and the simulator felt like a really slow-paced video game. Once he had taken some time to understand the controls and the counter-intuitive orbital mechanics that pulled the spacecraft in strange directions, he found it to be pretty easy. By now he was able to perform a docking successfully nine times out of ten in the simulator, even when he allowed the computer to introduce failures during his approach.

Recently, he had found the settings that allowed him to adjust the space station's simulated attitude control parameters. Alex thought for a few moments and decided to try a docking approach with the space station tumble rate at the maximum the engineers had predicted it might be due to the failing reaction control wheels. *I guess we'll see if this is really as easy as dad says it will be.*

Alex started the simulation. On his screen, an image of the round docking port appeared along with a cross-hair target. The goal was to center the target in the camera, which meant that the docking ports of the ship and the space station would also be aligned.

The cross-hair target began to skew to one side. Alex used the two hand controllers to chase it. As he moved the ship, he had to also rotate to align with the docking port. He rotated too fast though and found himself pointing the incoming craft at a solar array. The computer flashed a warning that his approach speed was too fast. He pulled back on the translational hand controller and the ship slowed. Then he realized the cross-hairs were getting smaller. He had fired the thrusters so hard that he was now reversing away from the space station.

Alex pressed forward and tried to catch the cross-hairs that were now dancing off to the side of the screen. His silent mutterings were interrupted by a high-pitched ding from his phone. He looked over to see that a message had come in from Mackenzie. When he looked back at the screen, the cross-hairs were completely askew. The computer flashed red warnings, and the simulation ended abruptly. A replay showed him hitting the docking port at an upward angle that would have probably dented the hatch and sent the ship bouncing off into space.

"Damn," Alex said. He picked up his phone and looked at the message from Mackenzie.

>> *don't b nervous. wish i could come 2. will be watching and thinking of you!*

Alex smiled and turned off his phone. Then he sat down at the computer and restarted the simulation.

*****

By 6:00 AM, Alex had made eight simulated docking attempts and only succeeded once. He finally decided this was not the morale boost he had hoped for on launch day. He showered and left the room to look for breakfast.

His dad was already seated in the dining room when Alex arrived. He was sitting across from Erica Reid, the chemist/astronaut who would be flying with them on this mission. The two were chatting animatedly and sipping steaming coffee from white mugs. Alex sat down in a plush and comfortable blue chair next to his father.

"Are you ready for the big day?" his dad asked, smiling widely.

"I think so," Alex muttered, still thinking about the simulator. "I didn't sleep that well though."

Alex's father put a hand on his shoulder. "Alex, when I was getting ready for my first flight, I had a great commander, Tom Harding. And I remember him saying on the morning of my first launch, 'Mike, you might never get another flight again. You've worked your life for this. There are about twenty thousand people on the ground working out the details of this flight. It's your time to sit back and enjoy it.' That's the best advice I've ever been given. You can't control much of what will happen today. But you can control how you feel about it. Space flight has some risks in it, just like everything worthwhile in life. But today is not the day to worry about that. Today is the day to enjoy the ride of a lifetime."

Not sure how to respond, Alex just nodded and sipped some water. His dad was right, he knew, but he couldn't completely let go of the nervousness that gnawed at his guts. He looked at the spread of food before him on the table. There was buttery French toast, crispy bacon, eggs, muffins and juice. But as good as it all looked, Alex decided to only sample small bits of everything. If his zero-gravity training flight experience was any indication, there was a better than decent chance he'd be seeing whatever he ate this morning again later in the day.

*****

After breakfast, the three crew members were escorted to a brightly lit room filled with reporters. Alex was asked several questions, including whether or not he had a girl-friend. His father jumped in and sternly told the reporter that personal information wasn't relevant to the mission. Perched on an uncomfortable chair with lights and eyes all fixed on him made Alex uncomfortable and nervously sweaty, but he did his best to smile and answer politely.

Following the press conference, the crew was taken by van to a small gray building where they were given a quick medical exam. After that, they started suiting up in their bulky launch suits that were designed to keep them alive even in the event of a catastrophe. Alex tried to shut out the images from his nightmare as the technicians secured his gloves and boots in place with locking metal rings.

The crew was then taken to the launch pad in a spacious van. Each of them took up what would have been two ordinary seats. Alex's father and Dr. Reid were talking with each other and laughing about something. Alex sat quietly and stared out the window as the gleaming white rocket grew larger and larger in front of him.

Steam drifted lazily away from the base of the rocket. Alex now understood that this was caused by the liquid oxygen in the rocket's tank boiling off slowly in the Florida heat. He looked proudly at the American flag painted on the rocket below the NewStar logo. His mother must have felt the same excitement and pride before her fateful launch. Today will be different, Alex told himself. Today her experiments will get a second chance. Inside his personal luggage, he had several biological samples hidden in tightly sealed sample containers that were stuffed into the pockets of his clothing. They should be loaded into the capsule already by now, he realized.

Before long, the van arrived at the base of the rocket. The driver opened the door and one by one the three crew members stepped out into bright sunlight and vast emptiness. There was nobody at the launch tower except for the crew, their driver and three technicians. Everyone else was far away from the dangers of a rocket filled with enough explosives to take out a small town.

Alex felt a fluttering in his stomach and cold sweat on his body. It was the same way he felt when standing in line for a big roller coaster at the amusement park, especially one that had a massive drop at the start. As he approached the tower elevator with his father and Dr. Reid, he felt like he was next in line for the big ride.

"Here we go," Alex's dad said with a smile when the elevator doors closed. Alex's stomach felt like it stayed below as the elevator rose. He took a deep breath and held it.

When the elevator stopped at the top of the 140 foot tower, Alex could see for what seemed like miles along the coast and out into the ocean. But his eyes quickly fixated on the hatch to Venturer, just across a metal bridge, as he walked slowly towards the capsule. Alex had been in mockups of the spacecraft before, but his breath was still taken away by the sight of the real thing, glistening in white paint with cool green lighting inside, the screens powered up and lights blinking. It looked like a scene from a science fiction movie, but it wasn't. This spaceship, this rocket and this mission were all real! Alex smiled as he ducked his head and entered the capsule.

He crawled into his seat below the control panel and lay on his back with his feet raised above him. The capsule could hold up to six passengers and a pilot, but today it would carry only three. The remaining space was filled with dozens of bags of supplies - food, clothing, spare parts, spacesuits, computers, scientific equipment and hotel amenities. The bags were neatly arranged and held to the sides and bottom of the capsule with black straps that would prevent them from floating freely when they arrived in orbit and lost the sensation of gravity.

Venturer was designed to take tourists to space, so several round windows dotted the capsule's hull. Alex checked the display above him and saw that they were a little more than two hours from launch. He remembered watching his mother before her flight. It was the last time he had seen her and she had been smiling with nervous excitement. She hadn't had any idea what was about to happen to her. Alex wanted to feel the same blissful excitement she had experienced, but he couldn't shake the image of exploding light from his mind. His father reached over and patted Alex on the knee as the technician closed the hatch to the capsule, sealing them inside. Alex tried to look over and see his dad's face, but the bulky helmet made it impossible.

"Ready for the ride of your life?" Alex's dad asked over the private channel of the radio.

"Yeah, I think so," Alex replied nervously. "I just wish we could hurry up and get this over with. I'm so scared I feel like I'm going to pee my pants."

"Venturer, this is NewStar Control," came a voice on the radio. "Check your mics please."

Alex's father started laughing, his chuckles booming into Alex's ear. Then Alex realized that he'd pressed the wrong button on the wrist of his suit before speaking into the radio. He'd been speaking on the public channel that was sent to mission control. Wait, didn't they say that they were going to air that channel on TV live? *That means everybody heard that. Oh God, even Mackenzie probably heard that!*

"Don't worry, Alex," his father finally said when he finished laughing. "We've all made that mistake before."

Alex refused to speak after that. The control center began rattling off steps in their procedure, checking oxygen levels and pressures and fuel quantities. Alex was asked to do a voice check and he meekly responded that he could hear the control center fine. Before long, the display in front of him showed only 5 minutes left until launch.

"Alex, is your suit configured to launch mode?" his dad asked.

"Yes," Alex responded.

"You're on the private channel now, you don't have to answer in just one word," his dad said with a chuckle.

The clock continued to count backwards and was joined by voices from the control center.

"One minute to launch."

"30 seconds."

"Auto ignition is ready."

"10"

"9"

"8"

"7"

"6"

"5"

"4"

"3"

"2"

"1"

Alex felt the world shaking. His seat bounced so hard that for a moment he thought it would break loose. He reached up and grabbed a support bar with both hands, squeezing tightly. The rumble of the capsule was far more violent than Alex expected. He felt sure something was wrong.

"Liftoff!"

Alex squeezed his eyes shut, waiting for the capsule to come apart around him. Instead, he felt a sudden force push him down into his seat. He opened his eyes and looked out the window to see the clouds above them rushing closer. He let out a breath. They were flying!

Alex tried to look over at his father, but he could not make out his face. His dad was all business, calmly checking the displays and rattling off numbers to the NewStar mission control. His father's ability to remain calm in the middle of a literal fireball was impressive.

As the shaking and rumbling subsided, Alex felt himself being pushed harder and harder into his seat. They were accelerating faster now and were past the most dangerous aerodynamic loading on the rocket. A smile swept across Alex's face as he began to feel that everything was going to be fine, and he started to relish the thrill of being shot skyward on a pillar of flame. He was surrounded by the sensation of the rocket's vibration, the rumbling of the powerful engine and the force of the rocket pushing him back into his seat. He closed his eyes again and let the excitement wash over him.

That's when the alarm sounded.

CHAPTER 14

ALEX'S EYES DARTED AROUND THE DISPLAY, TRYING TO FOCUS ON what was happening. He heard his father say calmly, "NewStar Control, this is Venturer. We see the DP alarm. Five minutes until we hit the abort decision threshold."

Alex knew that DP stood for "De-Pressurization." It meant that air was leaking out of the capsule. Alex started breathing heavily.

Don't panic, don't panic. The suit will still hold air in. You can still breathe.

"Copy Venturer. We see the same," said the voice on the radio. "The leak rate is 2 pounds per hour. We recommend abort."

Alex looked at the window above his head. The blue sky was beginning to darken. The rumbling had calmed significantly, but there was still a swirl of what appeared to be dust dancing around the window.

That's strange. I don't remember it being so dusty when we first took off.

"Alex, pay attention!" his Dad shouted into the radio. Alex pressed the button for private radio.

"Sorry, dad."

"You need to set your suit to launch abort mode. The

valve on your chest." Alex remembered and turned the valve. He looked up and again saw a white plume swirling by his window. He tried to turn his head to look at another window. His head felt heavy and turning it made him dizzy. But he could see enough of the other window to realize that it didn't have the same dusty swirl.

"Dad! I think I know where the leak is!"

"Where?"

"Out my window. I can see some dust or something being sucked up."

"You're right! I see it too."

"Can we use the leak repair kit on it?" Alex asked.

"That's designed for on-orbit use only. It's safer to abort."

Alex remembered the abort training. They would separate from the rocket, hoping not to hit anything. The capsule would fall freely for miles, until parachutes would open and put them in the ocean. If the capsule filled with water, they would have to swim. This was an unplanned abort so it would take hours or more for rescue ships to reach them, depending on where they landed.

"We have five minutes before we have to abort," Alex said quickly. "Just give me two minutes to try!" Before his dad could respond, he had unbuckled his safety harness. He could hear his father yelling at him to stop, but he continued to roll out of his seat. He struggled to get to his knees as the rocket's acceleration pulled him down with nearly two and a half times the force of gravity.

The leak repair kit was located in an orange emergency box mounted to the wall. Using all the strength he could muster, Alex raised a shaky arm to the box's latch and opened it. The kit contained a spray that should form an airtight seal that would dry within seconds. He reached inside and grabbed the spray bottle. A package of first aid supplies was knocked loose and came crashing down, but Alex had the can in his gloved hand.

Alex tried to turn to the window, but his suited body in the cramped space couldn't bend the way he needed. He rolled over onto his back and reached his arm up. He was still a few feet from the leak. He needed to sit up, but it felt as if there was another person sitting on his chest. Alex strained and pushed his stomach muscles, willing them to do more.

"Alex, we have three minutes and then we have to abort! Get your seat belt back on!" His Dad's voice was loud and clear in his ear. Alex screamed and pushed with all his might. Shaking madly, he managed to bend his upper body upwards until the bottle was just a few inches away from the bottom of the circular window where most of the dust particles seemed to be dancing.

Close enough.

Alex squeezed his finger down on the bottle's trigger. A white liquid goo splattered onto the edge of the window. As best he could, Alex tried to trace the lower part of the window until his stomach muscles gave out and he collapsed back down onto the floor of the capsule.

He lay there, panting heavily, and heard nothing but the rumble of the rocket in his helmet. After what seemed like an eternity, he heard the voice from NewStar mission control say, "We see the pressure stabilizing at 8.6. We consider it safe to press to orbit if you concur."

"Concur," said Alex's father. "But stay ready for an early re-entry in case this patch doesn't hold. We have enough air in the suit reserves to last at least a couple orbits in the worst case."

"Good plan. And expect main engine cutoff in two minutes."

Even though his entire body felt weak and rubbery, Alex managed to slide back into his seat. Dr. Reid helped him buckle his harness back around his bulky suit.

"Hey, Alex," his father's voice came into his headset. "Don't ever disobey an order from me again. That was a stupid move to unbuckle your harness while in powered flight when we could have aborted."

Alex didn't say anything.

"Having said that, you did a nice job thinking quickly and getting the repair done. But next time, you let me make the decisions."

"Yes, sir." Alex clicked off his radio. Despite the reprimand from his father, a smile stretched across his face. He knew that he had just saved this launch, and nothing his dad might say could take that away from him.

Two minutes later, the main engines stopped and the vehicle was suddenly silent and still. Then Alex felt the familiar feeling from his flight in the vomit comet. His guts seemed to disappear, as if he never recognized the weight of them before now. The bulky suit no longer pressed down on him, but instead he floated loosely inside it. Ordinary objects inside the capsule came alive. The loose ends of straps began to dance in a rhythm of their own. The can of sealant which Alex had dropped after spraying the window now flew up towards the top of the capsule and bounced off the curved wall.

Alex tilted his head back towards the window and suddenly had to catch his breath. Outside the window, he could see the darkest black imaginable give way to the bright glowing blue of the planet. From this height, he could see clouds below float near the African coastline. The sandy deserts bordered lush green forests. The beauty of the colors overwhelmed him. Alex felt his throat swell and his eyes begin to water. He made a noise somewhere between a laugh and a cry that nobody but him could hear inside his helmet. A tear caught in the corner of his eye, and when he shook his head, it floated away freely in the helmet.

Alex smiled and sobbed quietly. He couldn't be sure if he was crying from the beauty of the Earth or the relief of making it through the launch alive. He poured his emotion out inside his helmet for what felt like minutes and then took a deep breath and tried to remember what he was supposed to do next.

He looked over and saw his father tapping buttons on the control panel. Eventually, his father said, "Alright, guys and gals. We made it. I've been watching the pressure and we seem stable, but let's not take off the suits until we're sure."

"Do you think it could blow out?" Dr. Reid asked.

"The sealant is supposed to be an effectively permanent fix, but you never know. I'm going to get some pictures and send them down to Houston to have a look at."

"You stay here and keep an eye on things. We should have the orbit circularization burn in another 30 minutes. I'll get the photos," Erica responded. She unbuckled herself and pulled her body upright. Pushing off the seat with her feet, she shot up towards the window.

Alex watched her pull a camera from a bag and begin to take photos. He was starting to feel nauseous, the way he had in the training aircraft.

"Dad," he said into the radio. "I think I'm going to be sick."

"Damn," his dad said. "Can you wait a few more minutes? Let's just see what Houston thinks about the leak repair. I don't want you to take off the helmet until we're sure it's safe."

"I'll try."

Think of something else. Think about Mackenzie. She's probably watching the mission news. What would she say if she saw you puking? Not cool, not cool. Just keep it in.

Alex began to sweat and he nervously tapped his fingers against the panel, trying to contain his growing nausea. He watched Dr. Reid working with the camera and then connecting it to a computer to send the pictures to the ground via satellite. He took deep breaths to calm his stomach. Finally, they received a call from mission control.

"Venturer, the engineers have taken a look at the leak seal. There are two silicone seals to hold air into the window. The engineering team suspects that somehow some debris got into those seals and left a small gap. That would explain the low leak rate..."

Yeah, yeah, hurry up and tell us what we need to do! I'm going to hurl!

"...based on those results, and the test data from the leak sealer, we are confident the vehicle will be flight-worthy for the remainder of this mission. So we're comfortable with you taking off suits and continuing on with the planned NewStar One docking tomorrow."

Alex couldn't wait any longer. He released the latches and ripped the helmet from his head. He reached for one of the white plastic bags in his leg pocket. Before he could even get it to his mouth, his stomach let loose and he sprayed vomit out of his mouth. Only about half made it into the bag.

*****

After several hours, all three crew members had removed their bulky launch suits in favor of comfortable cloth jumpsuits, folded the seats out of the way and unpacked the personal gear they would need for the night. Their launch timing did not allow them to arrive at the space station until tomorrow, so they would be spending their first night in space in the cramped capsule, which felt to Alex like sleeping in a car.

Luckily, Alex's nausea was diminishing and he was even able to eat a small snack of crackers and cheese spread around dinnertime. Every experience in space seemed new and different. When he opened a package of mixed nuts, he found the nuts inside dancing around the bag instead of resting at the bottom like he expected. The sun set shortly after they had arrived in orbit, but then rose again only forty-five minutes later.

Alex's father was serious about getting work done, as always, but he went about his business in a playful way, doing back flips as he bounced from one place to another, or letting droplets of water hang in the air before scooping them up with his mouth. Alex felt like he was seeing the fun-loving childish side of his dad for the first time in years, or maybe ever.

Whenever he had a moment free, Alex found that he could hardly take his eyes off the window. Watching the planet was an amazing experience that he couldn't get enough of. He stared down as they soared over cities at night and shining lakes in the daytime. He saw glaciers and snow-capped mountains and huge sandy deserts that would take days to traverse on foot whiz by in just minutes.

"I guess it's time to bed down for the night," his dad finally said when all of the items on their post-launch checklist had been done and they had made a final call to the mission control center for the evening.

"Where are the sleeping bags?" asked Alex.

"Good question," his dad said. He began to rummage through the large bags of equipment strapped to the walls and floor of the spacecraft. Alex and his Dr. Reid joined him, but after twenty minutes of searching they couldn't find the sleeping bags.

"Well, I guess we better ask the ground where they hid them," his dad said. He reached for a small hand-held microphone that was velcroed to the wall. Pressing the button on the square blue box that held the microphone, his Dad said, "NewStar Control, Venturer on channel 1."

"Go ahead, Venturer."

"We are having a little trouble locating the sleeping bags. Could you let us know where in the capsule they are stowed?"

"Sure thing, give us a minute to check with the logistics team."

It took ten minutes before the mission control voice returned with a sheepish answer. "Venturer, um, we talked to the logistics team. It seems that because of the late launch date change, they never packed the bags on Venturer. NewStar One has a full supply set, but with the old launch date you would have arrived the same day as launch and not had to sleep on Venturer. Sorry about that. If you'd like, our engineers have some suggestions on how to improvise a sleeping bag."

Alex's dad frowned. "Those friggin' idiots," he said. Then he pushed the button on the microphone and said, "Copy, Control. We can make do up here. Talk to you in the morning."

"Sorry again, Venturer. We'll see you tomorrow."

"What are we going to do?" Alex asked. His father shook his head and let out a sigh, but Dr. Reid smiled broadly.

"We're going to tie you to the wall," she said. Laughing, she grabbed Alex, pushed him up against the wall, and pulled a cargo strap around his torso. Alex was annoyed at first that this strange lady just felt like she could grab him and tie him to a wall, but the whole thing was so comical that he couldn't help but laugh, and his father quickly joined in the fun. Using spare black cargo straps, Dr. Reid and Alex's father were able to fasten him like a piece of cargo to the bulkhead.

Once he was trapped like a bug in a spiderweb, his father took a photo and then proceeded to help strap Dr. Reid to another bulkhead. Alex eyed the pair suspiciously. His father seemed to be getting awfully close to the younger, blond scientist. The last thing he needed right now was his dad to have a live-in girlfriend on their first trip to space. Their faces were nearly touching as his father pulled straps around Erica's shoulders.

"This feels weird," Alex said loudly to interrupt them. "I like having a sheet when I sleep."

"I know," his dad said, turning briefly to look at him. Alex thought he sensed a tinge of annoyance in his voice. "I turned up the temperature so it should warm up a bit. Just relax and close your eyes. You'll get used to it."

Alex waited until his father had separated from Dr. Reid and loosely strapped himself to another side of the ship before he closed his eyes. He wanted to press his head against something, but there was no pillow. At least the sleeping bags they would get on the space station would have a built-in pillow and strap to attach it to your head. But with your head floating freely, it probably would feel weird anyway, since there was no real feeling of laying down against something.

Every few minutes, Alex found his head bumping against the wall or his arms getting caught in the straps. It was hard to get used to this strange way of sleeping. Still, Alex was tired and after about twenty minutes, his mind drifted. He thought about the docking tomorrow and his failed attempts with the simulator to catch the moving space station. After a while, he gave that up and started thinking instead of the beautiful views he had seen of the planet below. Soon he was fast asleep.

CHAPTER 15

WHEN ALEX'S EYES OPENED, HIS FATHER WAS ALREADY BUSTLING about the spacecraft cabin, preparing breakfast and getting the seats ready for docking later that day. Alex tried to free himself from the webbing that made up his bed, but his straps were too tight. His father looked over and saw him struggling.

"Well, I wish we'd had this option when you were a little boy and didn't want to go to bed," his dad said.

"Very funny," said Alex. "You wouldn't have needed it. I was an angel as a child. Now could you let me out of this?"

"For a Stone boy, you've got a terrible memory," his father retorted as he began releasing the tangled web of straps. Alex was free in short order, and he floated to the bottom of the capsule. He retrieved a small plastic pouch filled with water from a storage locker built into the floor. A straw protruding from the pouch was capped by a small valve that opened when it was squeezed. Alex bit down on the valve and slurped a slug of water into his dry throat.

Erica Reid woke up next and after using the "bathroom," which was little more than a vacuum hose and seat behind a curtain, the three of them gathered near the control panel to talk about the plan for the day.

His dad started, "Houston called us and said the control wheels are jittery, which they think is a sign they are close to failing. If that happens, the station will be in free drift and will start tumbling faster. We really need to make that docking today and probably spacewalk tomorrow to make the repair."

"What happens if the wheels fail before we get there?" Alex asked.

"Well, we might still be able to dock but it would be really difficult. From the data the engineers sent, we'd probably have three or four hours after a failure to dock before the rotation rates would make it impossible."

"And if that happens?"

"If that happens, we head home and I start looking for a new job. But let's not focus on that. Dr. Reid and I have trained a lot for this docking. When we did the training, Brock would use the laser range finder to get a secondary range measurement and he would call out our alignment based on the guidemarks above the hatch. Do you remember how to do all of that, Alex?" Alex replied that he remembered.

"Alright," his dad said. "We've got two hours until we'll be close enough to see the station. Get breakfast and get yourselves ready. It should be a fun day."

Alex heated up a package of oatmeal and another of freeze-dried scrambled eggs. Since he had barely eaten the night before, even this bland food tasted wonderful and he scarfed it down. Then he took a few minutes to open up a laptop computer and check his e-mail. NewStar wanted to make sure that the guests going to the hotel would have all the amenities of home, so a slow but effective satellite internet link was provided on all spacecraft.

Alex had 184 messages waiting for him. *Wow, this astronaut gig really makes you popular. Too bad you have to leave the planet and can't actually enjoy being popular.*

Scrolling quickly through the messages, Alex found one from Mackenzie from the night before.

Hi Alex, I watched the launch today, it was amazing! Hope you enjoyed the ride. I found out on the news later there was some kind of problem with the capsule?? Hope you're OK and everything will be fine the rest of the trip. My family's heading to the water park tomorrow. Should be a blast - wish you could come with us ;)

Miss you already! M

"What are you smiling at?" his father asked, floating nearby.

"Nothing," Alex said quickly, closing the screen. "Just reading my e-mails."

His dad smiled at him but said nothing else.

"Guys, come take a look," Dr. Ried called from across the capsule.

"What is it?" Alex's father asked. He pushed off the side of the wall and propelled himself like Superman towards the hatch where Erica was hovering and looking through a window. Their bodies were touching and it almost looked as though Alex's father was going to put his arm around Dr. Reid. Alex quickly flew over to join them and jostled his way between the pair.

"What are you looking at?" Alex asked as he squirmed towards the window.

"See for yourself," his dad said, moving aside. Alex looked through the window at the round curvature of the earth. The sun was setting behind them and the earth below was quickly fading to black as they flew eastward towards the shadowy night side of the planet. Then Alex saw it. It looked like a bright star rising out of the darkness until Alex realized it was getting bigger the longer he watched it. Then he saw the object brighten considerably and he realized the brightness was the glint of light reflecting off a solar array. NewStar One was directly in front of them.

"Wow, it's beautiful," Alex whispered, mostly to himself.

"She sure is," his father replied. "I'm glad we have a chance to save her. This station will bring great experiences to a lot of people and hopefully some great scientific discoveries as well."

The trio floated motionlessly, staring at the bright dot hovering above the horizon until the sun set behind them and blackness swallowed up the distant space station.

"Time to get ready," Alex's dad said. He floated over to a nearby bag labeled DOCKING AIDS. He opened it up and pulled out several items. He handed a pair of binoculars and a small laser range finder to Alex. Alex's father explained again how to use the laser ranger to take measurements of the space station's distance.

"This is much more accurate than the GPS sensors we will be watching on our screens, so call out the range at least every 30 seconds once we are within 200 meters."

"Don't worry, Dad. I've got it."

"Alright. And if you see anything you don't like, let me know. This is going to be tricky with the station rotating."

"Yeah, I know."

Dr. Reid had already strapped herself into a seat in the lower part of the capsule where the controls were located. His father joined her and began tapping buttons to set up the screens and cameras the way he liked them.

Alex stared nervously out the window. He tried to make out the space station in the distance, but he couldn't find it.

"Looks like we are coming to 10 kilometers range," his dad announced.

"I can't see anything yet," said Alex.

"We should be coming into sunrise in about 20 minutes," his dad responded. "By then, we will be close enough to get range marks." Alex couldn't believe the sun would be rising again so soon. At the speed they were traveling in orbit, they circled the planet every 90 minutes, which meant the sun would rise or set about every 45 minutes as they moved between the day and night sides of the earth. It was very difficult to get used to after spending your whole life with a half a day between sunrise and sunset.

Alex slipped his feet under a metal handrail to keep from floating away and hovered in front of the window. Nearly three hundred miles below him, the lights of dozens of cities drifted by. Relaxing his muscles, his arms floated up and swayed like kelp. He folded them across his chest to keep them from drifting loose.

Before long, the sun rose above the horizon. The sunrise did not come slowly like on earth. It happened with stunning speed due to the high velocity of their spaceship hurtling around the planet. An orange glow hit the walls of the cabin as the sun's light refracted through the atmosphere, but in just a few minutes it had turned into a bright white.

Alex spotted the space station right away, but he had to squint through the sunlight. It was hard to tell if it was aligned the way it was supposed to be, with the solar arrays rising high above the structure and the hotel "rooms" hanging down towards the earth with their glass-bottom views of the planet.

"Distance is five kilometers," Alex's dad announced. "Alex, can you get a range mark yet?"

Alex lifted the laser ranger to the window. He looked through the scope and tried to center the cross-hairs on the space station, but with the glare of the sun he wasn't sure if he had it. He kept pressing the trigger to get range measurements, but each time the display read "ERR" for error.

"Sorry, Dad, I can't seem to get it."

"OK, let's wait until we get a little bit closer."

"Are you OK?" Alex heard Dr. Reid say in a low voice. "You seem tense."

"I'm fine," his dad replied. "Just hoping this docking is...not impossible."

Alex waited a little longer, until the sun was a bit higher in the sky and then looked through the binoculars.

The station's solar arrays spread out like wings from the central mass of cylindrical modules. Alex tried to spot the round circle that outlined the docking module. In the simulator, it was always easy to find, but with the real space station in front of him, he couldn't seem to locate it. He pushed the binoculars aside and tried a measurement with the laser ranger. Finally, he was able to get a reading as the laser bounced off the station's structure and back to the sensor in his hand-held device. *2650 meters.*

"I got 2650 for the range, Dad," Alex said.

"Great," his father replied. "Can you tell how the alignment is?"

"It's hard to tell," said Alex. "I can't see the docking port yet."

"OK, keep looking," his dad said. "The docking port should be clearly visible when we get within 1 km, which will be in about 10 minutes." Alex put the binoculars back up to his eyes. The details of the space station were becoming more clear every minute, and Alex searched for the bright red docking port alignment indicator he remembered from the simulator. The shadows made it more difficult to find than it was on the computer screen, but eventually Alex's eyes settled on the spot.

"I see the docking port, Dad!"

"Great, how is the alignment?"

"Um, looks good." Alex wasn't entirely sure if it was good with the harsh light and shadows, but he didn't see anything obviously wrong.

"NewStar Control, Venturer, we're ready to approach," his father announced. Alex put the laser range finder back up to the window and began taking range measurements as the spacecraft crept forward, its jets pulsing periodically as his dad gently pushed and pulled on the joysticks.

"600 meters," Alex announced, trying to use the bold and confident voice he heard his father use when he was doing something serious. Inside, his stomach was tumbling and jittery. They continued to creep slowly towards NewStar One.

The station was large enough now to make out some details. The red lights marking the docking port flashed. The solar array wings that stretched out from the sides of the station were rotating slowly. If he watched long enough, Alex was pretty sure he could tell that the station was wobbling slightly, as if it were adrift on an ocean with gentle waves swaying it from side to side. They continued moving forward, slowly and smoothly now, as momentum carried them through empty space with no resistance. There was only an occasional thruster jet pulse as Alex's father used the controls to make small corrections to their course.

Alex pointed the laser ranger at the space station again. The digital readout showed 284 meters. They were almost there. Almost at the strange new place they would call home for the next six months.

"OK, crew," his father said, all business. "We're going to do a hold at 100 meters. Alex, call out the last 20 meters so I can slow us down appropriately."

"Yes, sir." Alex started taking measurements every few seconds and dutifully called out all the readings from 120 down to 100. Then he looked back at his father who let out a deep sigh, unbuckled, and floated up to the window where Alex was posted. His dad looked out the window for a while and then looked back at Erica who was seated in the co-pilot's chair watching the displays.

"It sure is wobbling a lot," he said.

"Yeah, more than I thought," Dr. Reid replied, her eyes still fixed on the displays. "What if we try to match it's rotation?"

"I'm not sure how well I can do that."

"What if I handle the forward motion and you just try to work the rotation?"

His dad paused. "That might work." Returning to the controls, his father began playing with the joystick. Pretty soon he said, "Hey, I think I've got it." Alex looked out the window and saw that the station had stopped wobbling. But then he looked up at the earth and saw it tilting from side to side. The station wobble hadn't stopped - they were just wobbling with it. The sight of the earth shifting made him feel like he was on a boat. His stomach began to tremble, and he clamped his mouth shut in case anything decided to come up.

"Here we go," Dr. Reid was saying as she pushed the controller to thrust them towards NewStar One. Alex reached for a white barf bag. He squeezed his eyes shut and spit into the bag, but nothing else came out.

Alex kept checking out the window, but tried not to look up at the earth. When he looked back, his father and Dr. Reid were intensely focused on their screens, giving each other small commands and suggestions as they approached the docking port.

"Try a little more roll to the right."

"Move up towards the cross-hairs."

"Slow the approach, slow it!"

Soon, they were within a few meters of the docking port. Alex felt like he could reach out and touch it. The sun was moving towards the horizon. They needed to dock while it was still daylight.

"OK, let's go for it," his dad said.

Venturer slid forward. As it did, the round docking port ring seemed to twist away from them. Alex's eyes opened wide with terror.

"Hold on!" his father yelled. The ship twisted violently. Alex looked back and saw his dad jerking the control joystick to the side. Then a loud bang pierced the air and the ship shuddered violently.

CHAPTER 16

ALEX LOOKED AROUND THE CAPSULE HELPLESSLY. WARNING alarms were sounding, but everything else was still. A nearby monitor listed what seemed like a dozen messages, none of which made sense to Alex. Below his feet, Alex's father wore his usual mask of calm despite the crisis.

"Control, this is Venturer. Looks like we've got a partial capture," he said flatly.

"We see the same, Venturer. You should release the latches and back away."

"We're not releasing. If we let go, we might never make it back."

"Venturer, we would *strongly* suggest you release latches. With the latches not fully engaged, any small disturbance could break or damage the docking mechanism."

As if on cue, a large groan came from the hatch area above Alex's head. Alex looked over at a monitor and saw an image of the round ring, and one portion was flashing red. Unfortunately, he had no idea what that meant. Alex had never studied the docking port in any great detail. The company had let him skip a lot of training with the understanding that his work would be centered around cleaning, preparing meals, keeping the guest rooms in order and doing light maintenance. At the time, he had been happy to have fewer classes, so he could spend more time with Tyler and Mackenzie and miss less school. But now he was wishing he had asked for more training. He was amazed at how many things there were to learn and how every little detail seemed so critical.

At the bottom of the capsule, Alex could see his dad and Dr. Reid conversing intently in their seats, but he couldn't hear what they were saying. After a few seconds, they both unbuckled and joined Alex at the front near the docking mechanism.

"The engineers on the ground want to play it safe," his father started saying to Alex as he unscrewed the cover of a panel next to the closed hatch. "But they don't realize that playing it safe from a mechanical perspective is not always safest overall. If we back away, then we have to risk another approach to the station and we might not make it."

By now the panel was removed and his father had put on a headlamp and taken a large wrench from the tool kit.

"I would much rather take a risk of damaging the mechanism, which can later be fixed, than have to sleep in this capsule again tonight, not knowing what will happen tomorrow. That way, we can get to fixing the reaction wheels and get this station stable."

His father was grunting now as he turned the wrench hard.

"What exactly are you doing, Dad?" Alex asked.

"I'm attaching us to the station manually," his father replied with a smile. "You want to see?"

"Sure," said Alex. He struggled to fit his head into the hold behind the panel. Inside, it was cramped and dark. His father was applying a wrench to some kind of metal rod.

With each twist, the rod retracted further into a metal cylinder at the very front of Venturer.

"This is the latching mechanism," his father explained. "It does the final attachment to the space station. Normally motors turn these rods to move the latches, but they clearly aren't working the way they should." Alex looked around the tiny compartment. There were wires going everywhere. He noticed a number of round connectors on the hull that had nothing attached to them.

"What are all those connectors and why is nothing attached to them?" he asked.

"Oh, those connectors are a legacy item," his dad replied. "They provided power to some of the mechanisms on the docking port that were used when the space station was first being assembled. The docking port was installed by a ship like Venturer which came back to earth after it delivered the module. That ship was flown robotically with no crew onboard, and these ports were connected to this ship's batteries and used to power the mechanisms. All the ships have the same design, so we have those connectors even though they aren't needed anymore."

Alex looked around the tiny and dark compartment. He was amazed at how much complexity was hiding behind just one single panel of their spaceship. Finally, he tired of the cramped area and pulled his head back out into the relatively spacious main cabin of the ship.

About twenty minutes later, his father announced that they were fully attached to the space station. The mission controller on the radio did not sound happy, and grumbled something about the mechanism probably being damaged by manually forcing the latches closed.

"Well, I guess it's time to move into our new home,"

Alex's dad said. He turned to Alex. "Do you want to do the honors?"

"Sure!" Alex exclaimed excitedly. "Select hatch controls from the panel, right?"

"Well, don't forget that there's no air in the vestibule between our hatch and the NewStar One hatch. All the air pressure from our cabin..."

"...will push on the hatch and we won't be able to open it," Alex interrupted impatiently. "Yeah, I remember. So I have to open the pressure equalization valve on the hatch to let the vestibule fill up with air."

"You got it," his father said proudly. Alex moved quickly to the touch screen panel on the wall. Moving rapidly so it seemed like he knew what he was doing, Alex found the hatch controls display screen and selected "equalization." Air hissed through the valve that opened. Alex's ears popped as the pressure changed. The hissing stopped and without waiting, Alex pressed the buttons to begin the hatch opening sequence. Motors whined as they pulled the hatch up into a recessed panel overhead, revealing a small and dark space called the vestibule.

At the end of the vestibule was another gray metal hatch, emblazoned with the NewStar One logo. Just a few minutes ago, this hatch had been exposed to the vacuum of space. Alex put his hand up and felt the smooth metal. It was surprisingly cold. Unlike the motorized hatches in Venturer, the hatches onboard NewStar One were all manually operated. In the middle of the square-ish hatch was a hole where a wrench needed to be inserted to open it. Alex thought about the fact that there were no locks or keys needed to gain access to this multi-billion dollar space station. Anyone with a basic hex-head wrench could do it.

Well, as long as they had a rocket, a spaceship and a docking port to get here in the first place.

Alex's father silently handed him a hex wrench with a long crank handle. Alex accepted it and looked back at his dad. He realized he was waiting for permission, but his father wasn't giving instructions or reminders this time. He was giving Alex this moment all to himself.

With a nod of his head, Alex inserted the wrench into the hatch. He tried to turn it, but his body twisted and flailed like a fish at the end of a line. He put his feet up against the narrow wall of the vestibule and twisted as hard as he could. The wrench wouldn't budge.

Frustrated, he turned back. "Dad, I think it's stuck."

"Here, let me try." Alex's dad grabbed the wrench handle and braced his feet. He grunted loudly as his arms strained against the wrench. It didn't move.

Alex's father looked sheepishly at Dr. Reid. "Wow, it's really tight."

She smiled back at him, and barged her way forward to take the wrench handle. She twisted her body so that both feet were against the "wall" and put both of her hands on the side of the handle. She looked like she was trying to do some kind of strange push-up. Holding her arms against the handle, she pushed up forcefully with her legs. She let out a loud cry as she pushed. "Arrgggghhhhh."

The wrench handle jumped forward and Dr. Reid spun around, bumping against the wall and then the hatch and finally bowling into Alex and his father. The three of them tumbled in a mess of limbs into the Venturer, finally coming to rest against a stack of bags filled with clothes.

Alex's father separated himself first. "Are you OK?" he asked.

"Aside from my pride, I'm fine." the scientist said, smiling at Alex's father in a way that made Alex very uncomfortable.

"Well, I guess we know who's opening all the pickle jars on this mission," his dad said. He floated back to the hatch area and tried the handle. Dr. Reid had managed to break the stuck bolt loose and the handle moved easily now. Alex's father twisted the handle and the gears grumbled until they reached the end of their travel with a satisfying click.

"Alex, would you like to do the honors? I think you'll have better luck this time."

Alex slid past his father. He put his feet against the side of the vestibule, grabbed the handle on the hatch and pushed. The hatch yawned open with a slight metallic whine and revealed an empty black corridor. The stale and cool air from the space station washed over him. It smelled a bit like paint mixed with the plastics of a new car.

Alex moved forward, feeling a bit apprehensive in the darkness of a seemingly abandoned station in space. His hand groped around until he felt the cold metal of a handrail, which he used to pull himself into the space station docking hub. For his entire journey, he had thought of the hatch on Venturer as either "up" or at least the "front" of the capsule. But now he had to shift himself to an entirely new orientation, where what would have been the ceiling was in fact the length of a hallway and what would have been a wall was now a floor. A bit dizzy from this disorienting change, Alex pulled himself in front of a panel with dimly lit buttons. He purposefully pressed the glowing blue ON button under the label LIGHTS. At first, nothing happened, but then something clicked deep behind the walls and lights began to blink on down the corridor. Alex looked down the passageway that seemed vaguely familiar - from the simulators - and yet new and exciting.

Alex moved ahead into the depths of the space station. He followed the corridor out of the docking hub to the first node and switched on the lights there. Moving forward from the node, he entered one of the two laboratories. His eyes grew wide as he looked around. There were two gloveboxes, racks of plasticware, glassware and chemicals each held to the shelf with individual clamps, a PCR machine for sequencing DNA, a 3D printer, several cold storage freezers and refrigerators and a large table in the middle of the room that ran the length of the module. There were no chairs, just straps on the floor to slip your feet into while working at the standing-height table.

His mother would have worked in a laboratory like this. Alex felt sure she would have discovered something incredible. He felt a tingle run up and down his body and he shivered for a second uncontrollably.

"Pretty neat, huh?" Alex turned to find his father hovering in the middle of the node.

"It's unbelievable."

"I know we've talked about this, but your main job here has to be taking care of our hotel guests."

"I know, Dad."

"But I'm sure Dr. Reid wouldn't mind you helping her out in your free time," his father said with a wink. Alex nodded, sharing the silent understanding that the best way to honor his mother's sacrifice would be to complete her work. He couldn't wait to get started.

CHAPTER 17

THE BEEPING ALARM INCREASED IN VOLUME UNTIL IT FILLED Alex's head. He grunted and slammed his hand blindly against the wall until his palm caught the "Off" button. He moved his hand and flicked the light switch. Nothing happened.

"Not again," he grumbled as he pulled himself out of the straps holding him to the foam mattress on the wall. He grabbed a flashlight that he kept velcroed to the wall and switched it on. The beam of light hit the top of his phone booth-sized sleeping quarters and provided a dim and un-even light to the rest of the compartment.

They had lived on NewStar One for a full week now. His father had performed a spacewalk the day after they arrived and replaced several pieces of equipment outside the space station. In addition, the mission control team had uploaded new software to the space station to correct some of the control algorithms that they believed had over-worked the reaction wheels and caused the failure in the first place. After these fixes, they were all optimistic that NewStar One was ready for business.

However, it was quickly becoming apparent that the space station was not designed to the same high-quality standards his dad was used to from NASA programs. Although the fixes to the reaction wheels and software gave them stable attitude control, they had found numerous other problems. Lights didn't work right, computers rebooted spontaneously and often at the worst possible time, and improperly installed sensors frequently provided inaccurate information.

Alex was inexperienced in the diagnosis of space station problems and the use of tools, but he found that he enjoyed working with his hands and taking apart things to see how they really worked. He had never realized how much the job of an astronaut involved being a plumber, electrician and mechanic to a highly sophisticated piece of machinery that needed to function flawlessly to keep you alive in the harsh conditions of space.

Alex took a wet wipe from a small bag and wiped his face in front of the tiny mirror attached to his sleeping compartment's cloth door. His face looked puffy and more full than it had on earth. The trainers had told him to expect fluid shifts in microgravity to change his appearance slightly, but it was still hard to get used to.

Unzipping the cloth door to his "room," Alex entered the central corridor of the crew quarters module. The entire module was 35 feet long and 12 feet wide, but much of that space was taken up by the soft-sided sleeping compartments like the one Alex had just emerged from. Those compartments lined both sides of the module, while the center of the corridor was occupied by a long table which was used alternately as a dining table and office space. Eventually, there would be as many as ten crewmembers in the module, but with only three onboard the station right now, the room felt fairly spacious.

Alex headed towards the common toilet at the end of the module, but when he noticed the red "Occupied" sign illuminated over the door, he floated instead to the table and pulled out a laptop from a storage shelf underneath it. He placed the computer on a Velcro pad on the top of the table, opened the lid and browsed through his e-mail. There were two messages from Mackenzie, including one with a picture of her in a blue and black bikini at the beach. Alex enlarged the image and stared lustfully at her gorgeous body, now nicely tanned from her summer adventures. Her blond hair swept around her shoulders and one hand rested on her hip near her exposed belly button. Looking at that picture, Alex wondered if their short-lived relationship would survive the summer. With a beach body like hers, Mackenzie surely had lots of guys going after her. Alex had never had a girlfriend before her, and the thought of losing her was almost enough to make him wish he was back on earth.

Alex wrote a quick response to her e-mails, exaggerating his mechanical prowess as they repaired the station and telling her how much he missed her. He hoped that letters and phone calls would be enough to keep their long-distance romance alive. By the time he pressed send, his father was leaving the toilet, so Alex closed the laptop and took his turn.

Inside the tiny stall, Alex unhooked a hose from the wall. He selected his personal "cup" from the cabinet, which he attached to the end of the hose. He flipped a switch to start the vacuum. This part always felt strange. He placed the cup between his legs and tried to let go. Even after a week, he still had some performance anxiety with the cup and vacuum system. He tried to think about other things - the repairs he had to do today, what he would have for breakfast, anything. Finally, a stream began to flow into the vacuum hose. After relieving himself, Alex shut down the vacuum, wiped everything down with alcohol wipes, rubbed some hand sanitizer into his palms and left the tiny room.

Back in the main module, Alex's dad was preparing oatmeal with dried fruit and yogurt for breakfast. Alex drifted by him, went back to his sleeping quarters and changed clothes into a fresh blue jumpsuit. When he came out, he found his father floating at a corner of the table near Dr. Reid, who was laughing at something he had said. The two of them seemed to be getting very close, and Alex wasn't very happy about it. He understood at some level that his Dad would probably not remain single the rest of his life, and for all Alex knew he could have been dating women back on earth when Alex thought he was staying late at the office. Still, the thought of his dad with another woman felt like a violation of his mother's memory. Alex floated over to join them at the table, hoping to interrupt their camaraderie.

"NewStar says they are on track to send the second crew complement and our first guests in two weeks," Alex's father said as Alex approached.

"You mean the Fritzers?" Alex asked.

"That's right. They'll be coming up on Destiny with Jim, Doug and Megan."

"Are we really going to be ready for guests in just two weeks?"

"Well, we're going to have to be ready. I've told Stewart again and again about all the issues we're having. He says we can't afford any delays. Honestly, I think the company is running out of cash. If we don't start getting guests into the hotel and science grant objectives completed, I'm not sure NewStar One will be around much longer."

"Well, the lab is in pretty good shape," offered Dr. Reid. "Once Doug and Megan get up here, we should be able to get a lot of work done."

"Great. Now we just need to get the hotel ready to go. Alex, why don't you go check out guest rooms 4 and 5 today? Make sure everything is working - all the lights, the computers, intercom, toilets, everything. Then afterward you can help me clean the spacesuits. We need to get them ready for Jim and I to do another spacewalk once he gets here."

"Yes, sir."

"Oh and let's get our blood draws done for the day after you finish breakfast." Alex scowled. He hated the blood draws, but the doctors had insisted that they be done every two days for the first few weeks so the medical data could be sent to the Fritzers to prove that there were no adverse effects on his teenage body from the exposure to zero-gravity and radiation. His arm was starting to look like a dart board. Plus he always felt a little dizzy watching his own blood get sucked out of his arm into the little test tube where it danced around in zero gravity as if it were trying to escape.

After he finished his breakfast, Alex put everything in the trash. His dad performed the blood draw, taking two times to find a vein this morning which made it even worse than normal. Thankful to be done with that, he headed away quickly to the hotel module.

He used the handrails to pull himself into the corridor of the guest area. This corridor had green walls with gentle

LED lighting. Along the side of the corridor were five rectangular doors labeled with the numbers one through five. These were not airtight hatches like the ones that connected all the other modules together, but rectangular sliding doors that looked a lot like normal doors on earth.

Alex positioned himself in front of the door labeled "Four" and slid his feet into straps that rested on the floor. With his body secured, he grabbed the large door handle and slid it open. As the door opened, lights immediately came on and illuminated the room in a gentle blue glow. Opposite the door was a curved wall made mostly of clear glass that offered an incredible view of the planet below.

On the left side of the room, a mattress was attached to the wall. There were two pillows secured to the memory foam, each with a strap to hold the occupant's head against the pillow. The bed was dressed with a navy blue blanket made of soft fuzzy material that was ribbed with five straps designed to comfortably keep a guest pressed against the mattress. Alex heard that the designers were worried that guests waking up to find themselves laying against what seemed to be a wall would be disorienting, but nobody knew this for sure and eventually management decided this orientation enhanced the uniqueness of the experience of sleeping in space.

On the wall opposite the bed was a built-in touchscreen monitor that served both as a control panel and entertainment system. Next to this was a small closet-sized area which housed the zero-gravity toilet. Once the guests arrived, he would have to clean and maintain these machines, in addition to trying to keep the toilets in the crew quarters clean and functional. He grimaced at the thought of what hotel guests in space might do to their toilets.

Alex circled the room and checked out everything and was pleasantly surprised to find everything working as expected. It seemed that the engineers had spent more time on the luxury guest rooms than the rest of the space station, including the functionally necessary parts.

With his work completed a little sooner than he'd anticipated, Alex decided to switch on the television. They received television by satellite, since most satellites orbited higher than the space station. They also had an online database of movies and other videos that was regularly updated and allowed guests to watch shows on demand.

Flipping through the channels, Alex stopped on a sitcom called "Baby Fever." It was a show produced by John Fritzer and he also played a minor character. On the television, John was coming out of a bathroom at a party when he spotted a girl in the corner of the room. He made an awkward attempt to hit up a conversation with her, but she left when he started talking about his last girlfriend leaving him. His character began bumbling and starting to cry. The performance was hilarious and wonderfully played.

Alex watched, hardly able to believe that the man he was watching on TV would be staying right here in this room in just a few weeks. He looked around and then went and closed the door. With the TV still on, Alex slid himself under the elastic straps of the covers on the bed. He imagined that John Fritzer slept on the right side of the bed, so he wiggled over there, pushed his head against the comfortable memory foam pillow, and watched the rest of the Baby Fever episode before deciding to get back to work.

Down the corridor from the hotel rooms, there was a general-purpose module for guests called the Commons that would be used for meals and recreation. Guests had the option to dine in their rooms or in the Commons with the other guests. In addition, the Commons would be used to host various activities, including games, movies and classes taught by the crew members.

Alex entered the Commons headfirst and floated to a compartment built into the wall from which he extracted a computer tablet. He pushed the power button, but the tablet did not respond. He tried plugging it into the wall with a cord he found in the compartment, but it still wouldn't turn on. Finally, he gave up and pulled another tablet which booted instantly.

Alex used the tablet to open up the procedures for setting up the room for different activities. He began working his way through each of them, turning on the movie projector, pulling the fold-away table from it's stowed location in the floor, checking the equipment lockers for balls and hoops and nets that would be used for zero-gravity variations of various sports.

There were more problems than Alex had expected. Two equipment lockers had broken hinges and the doors fell off when opened. The projector would not show any video, and the wires leading out of it didn't seem to be connected to anything. Also, the room control panel sometimes displayed mysterious "System Error" messages and would stop working until it was rebooted.

With some help from his father, Alex fixed the locker hinges and projector. He also replaced the room control panel with a spare. Tired from all of this work, Alex left to get lunch and then clean the spacesuits with his father. By the end of the afternoon, he was exhausted, but he still stopped by the lab. Dr. Ried was working sorting out some equipment and looked up at Alex hovering in the hatchway.

"Your dad said you were interested in some of the science work," she commented.

"My mom was a scientist."

"I know. A really good one from what I understand." Alex just nodded, but Dr. Reid continued, "Do you want to help me start up a few growth plates? I need to try to replicate a few viral samples in different host cells."

"Sure!" Alex said. He grabbed a pipette and some gloves and soon found himself listening to Erica Reid's rock-heavy playlist and carefully injecting drops of blue liquid onto petri dishes inside a glovebox. He was in heaven.

CHAPTER 18

JOHN FRITZER WOKE UP EARLY BUT DIDN'T GET OUT OF BED. Instead, he shifted his body closer to the woman lying next to him and felt her warmth on his back. After a few minutes, she woke also, wrapped her arm around his chest and kissed him gently on the back of the neck.

"Morning, astronaut man," she said sleepily, her breath tickling his shoulder.

"Morning, gorgeous," he said as he rolled over to face his second wife. The dim blue light of Newstar's prelaunch hotel room made her skin glow. He kissed her deeply on the lips. Then the doorbell rang, with a pleasant tone that sounded like something from a sci-fi movie.

"What is it?" Jennifer shouted, her voice no longer sweet or sleepy. Her shrill response shattered the morning peacefulness.

"Let me in, it's launch day!" came the excited reply from John's daughter. John smiled, but his wife did not. He rolled out of bed and started to pull on a shirt and pants.

"I don't see why we can't have some time to ourselves, John. This is our vacation too. Tell her to come back in an hour."

John looked over at his wife. She was beautiful, her

brown puppy-dog eyes pleading for him to come back to bed. He wasn't sure if that look was because of how much she loved him or how much she disliked Elodie, who was born from one of John's previous relationships. The tension between the two had never let up in John and Jennifer's seven years of marriage - a lifetime by Hollywood standards. Now that Elodie was fifteen, a full-blown teenager, things had only become worse.

John loved Elodie more than anything. It had been a mistake to have her with Tanya, the wild partying girlfriend he'd had for a couple years in his early twenties. Tanya never wanted a child and she was on birth control, but she tended to forget to take her pills when she stayed out until 4 AM drinking on John's tab, partying with the D-list celebrities who had been John's early career companions. Tanya had disappeared from John's life shortly after Elodie was born, but he didn't care. He didn't really think she was right for raising a child anyway.

When John married Jennifer, she had promised to be a good mother to Elodie. From the start though, the tension in Jennifer and Elodie's relationship was evident. Elodie resented Jennifer for taking away her father's time. Jennifer thought Elodie was spoiled and ungrateful. Jennifer had tried in those first few years, John had to admit. But both women were stubborn and their sour relationship never sweetened. John was disappointed about that, but he loved both of his girls too much to let their animosity get in the way of his happiness.

John opened the door to the hotel room, and Elodie bounded in. She had been very excited when John had brought up the idea of taking a trip to low earth orbit. Then Jennifer had found research showing that teenagers were vulnerable to radiation in space. John was sure it was just an attempt to keep Elodie out of the vacation, but the doctors had agreed that it was not a great idea to bring her. However, NewStar One was adamant that the risks were negligible, and they had even sent the teenage son of one of the astronauts to the space station as a hotel assistant. After John had met Mike Stone and looked at the medical reports in detail, he'd decided the risks were indeed small. Besides, Elodie had never seemed so excited as she had been for this trip.

"Dad, did you see the TV trucks out in the parking lot?" Elodie asked. She practically bounced over to the window to look out. "There are so many more here than even at home!"

"Well, I guess we're a novelty out here, sweetie. Back in LA, people are a little more used to seeing us around."

"It was such a good idea to have a red carpet on the way to the launch pad. This is going to be such an exciting day!"

"I'm glad you're so excited," John said with a smile.

"Do you want to get breakfast with me?"

"Sure, let's all go. Jennifer, breakfast?"

"I need to get dressed," his wife replied. "I'll catch up with you in a bit. Unless you want to get dressed with me." She raised her eyebrows.

"Eww, gross," Elodie said. John laughed and said he was ready to go now. He and Elodie left the room. Jennifer scowled and slumped her head against the pillow before finally getting out of bed to hunt for some clothes.

When John and Elodie arrived in the hotel restaurant, John recognized their pilot, Jim, who had introduced himself to them yesterday. He was sitting at a table with a cup of coffee and a newspaper. There was no food in front of him.

"Mind if we join you?" John asked.

"Please," Jim said, gesturing to the other chairs around their table. A young twenty-something man with tousled brown hair and a starched white shirt came to take their orders. John noticed him staring at Elodie, and to his dismay she returned the attention with a conspiratorial smile. His daughter had become more flirtatious than he would like in the past year.

Elodie ordered fruit, yogurt and juice in a voice dripping with sweetness. John asked for eggs, bacon and toast.

"I wouldn't eat too much today," Jim cautioned.

Jennifer joined them after a few minutes, and the four nibbled at their food. Elodie asked questions of Jim nearly continuously, wanting to know about his previous missions as an astronaut and what to expect during their vacation in space.

Finally, Jim looked at his watch and said, "Alright, guys and gals. Time to suit up." John grabbed Jennifer's hand and smiled. She beamed back. This trip was a good idea, John thought. The excitement of an adventure like this was bound to bring all three of them closer together, and hopefully improve Jennifer and Elodie's relationship.

They went back to the hotel rooms, changed into the jumpsuits provided by NewStar One and then left to meet the cameras. On the way, they were joined by Jim and two scientists who would be traveling to the station on today's flight. Doug Williams was a gregarious, balding biologist with dark skin. Megan Sanford was a chemist with dark hair and pale skin who would be conducting experiments with Erica Reid. She was shy and said little to John after he

introduced himself. They six of them left the building together to head towards their rocket.

The red carpet John had arranged to have placed on the
way to the launch pad was a media circus. John, Elodie and
Jennifer strutted forward into the familiar chaos of shouting
reporters and flashing bulbs. John was able to steal a glance
back at the pilot and scientists behind him, looking be-
wildered and uncomfortable in the eye of this media hurricane. He chuckled at their deer-in-the-headlights looks. It
didn't really matter since none of them would get any actu-
al coverage unless they did something stupid or embarrass-
ing.

John stopped along the way and spoke briefly with reporters he recognized and even one or two new faces if
they had a network logo on their name tag or microphone.
The media was eating this story up - the first private family
to take a vacation in space, the first famous family to visit a
privately owned space station.

They finally made it to the launch preparations building across the street from the hotel. All three were in a fab-
ulous mood after the attention they had received. Nothing
boosted one's spirit like being loved by strangers.

John joked casually with the suit technicians who fitted
him into the bulky pressure suits that would protect them
in case of an emergency.

"So if my baggage ends up in Chicago, do I get a free
night's stay?" They all laughed at his jokes and told him
how much they loved his shows and how he seemed like
such a nice guy in person. It was the same story and stale
jokes everywhere he went, but John loved it.

Before long, the family was sitting in the van with the
other three crew members and driving towards the launch

pad. Elodie was talking to Jim about how the suit worked.

"Remember, if you do need to talk for any reason, use the PRIV button for a private channel just to all of us in the capsule. The PUB button will make a public call back to the launch control center. You shouldn't have to use that except in an emergency or if the control center has a question for you."

"Is that why that kid a few weeks back talked about how he felt like he was going to piss his pants during the launch?" Elodie asked.

"Exactly," Jim replied. "Alex thought he was using the private channel and just talking to his dad and crew."

"He seems like a dork, but I still feel bad for him for that. It was all over the Internet. I must have gotten it from like a hundred friends since they all knew I was going to take this trip."

"Well, he's a good kid. You'll meet him when we get up there. He's going to be taking care of you folks."

"Good, at least there will be somebody my age to hang out with."

"Don't get your hopes up too much. Alex is a crew member so I don't think he'll be able to hang out much."

"Then I guess I'll have to hang out with you. My disgusting parents are just going to want to stay in their room and have sex the whole time."

Jim blushed and was speechless for nearly half a minute. "I'm sure they'll do other things, too," he managed to finally say. They rode in silence the rest of the way.

*****

When the van arrived at the launch pad, the towering rocket stopped all conversation. Even the normally gregarious John was awestruck and speechless. They rode the elevator in silence. It took two trips. Jim and the science crew went first and the Fritzers followed on the second trip.

At the top of the tower, John grabbed hold of his wife and daughter's hands through the thick gloves of his launch suit.

"Whatever happens," he said in a whisper, "we are going to be part of humanity's great explorations today. And like we always do, we're going to have a damn good adventure doing it."

"Dad, stop making it sound like we're going to die," Elodie said with a hint of annoyance in her voice. "This company knows better than to blow up people as famous as us."

"Geez, Elodie, you sure know how to ruin a moment," John responded, moderately annoyed.

The three of them marched together across the bridge from the elevator to the small anteroom surrounding the capsule hatch. Several technicians were waiting and helped the family into the capsule. John looked in amazement at the pristine interior of the spaceship. There were three seats in a row at the bottom with a set of control panels in front of them. Jim, Doug and Megan were already in those seats. Jim was pushing buttons on the controls while Doug and Megan appeared to be just laying there as if they were lounging.

Off to the side of the crew seats and raised slightly above them was another row of three seats mounted to a track. The seats were centered right underneath a series of windows built into the side of the capsule.

Elodie was seated first, followed by John in the center seat and his wife was finally strapped in on his left side.

Helmets were placed over each of their heads and the technician talked to each of them to make sure their radios were working properly.

After checking a few more things and wishing the six of them a safe flight, the three technicians left the capsule and closed the hatch. Everything was silent.

"OK, folks," came Jim's voice in the helmet radios. "We are just finishing up our capsule checks and topping off the fuel. Once the technicians close out and clear the pad, we should be ready for launch. The launch window opens in one hour. Right now, weather is looking good and everything is on track for an on-time launch. So just relax and if you have any questions, hit the private channel button and I'll be happy to answer anything."

"Can we use our phones in here while we're waiting?" Elodie asked immediately.

"Well, I've never had that question before," Jim answered. "I don't think you'll get any signal in here and anyway, you need to stay in your suit. I don't think you can use it with the gloves on."

"OK, so what are we supposed to do?"

"Elodie, just sit tight and have a little patience," Jennifer chimed in. "Your dad has paid a lot of money for this and wants to enjoy it."

"Whatever. I just think they should have some entertainment options if they're going to have us sit in here for an hour with nothing to do but stare at the clouds."

"You don't need to be on your phone *all the time*. This is a once in a lifetime experience. You don't want to miss out on it because you're texting with friends. You can do that any other time."

"OK, OK," said John. "Let's not fight. We'll be launching before you know it. Just relax, girls. This is going to be the ride of your lives. Get stoked!"

The capsule was quiet then. John tapped his foot against the wall nervously. He looked over at Elodie who was sitting with her arms folded across her chest. He couldn't see her face to tell if she was upset. She probably was. *That girl can be so stubborn sometimes. But once we lift off, her attitude will change.*

After sitting in a reclined position for a while, John began to feel himself getting sleepy. He had been full of ad-renaline going into the rocket, but the long period of wait-ing with nothing to do had relaxed him to the point of nearly dozing off. His eyes drifted open and shut until the launch control center finally announced it was time for the final poll before launch. John became much more awake now.

The monitor in front of the Fritzers showed 2 minutes to liftoff. John looked over and noticed Elodie fidgeting in her seat.

"You getting excited, girlie girl?" he asked on the ra-dio's private channel.

"Dad, we're going to be OK, right? I mean, it's just like a roller coaster ride, isn't it?"

John smiled. *I knew reality would break through that shell eventually.* "Sweetie, it's just like a roller coaster, only better."

"Your dad is right," Jim added from behind them. "This roller coaster ends with a view like you've never seen. Hang on tight!"

The clock ticked down through the last minute of launch. As the control center verbally counted the final ten seconds, John felt the powerful rocket begin to rumble until everything was shaking and he was pressed back into his seat. He could feel his pulse pounding in his ears as he looked out the window at a clear blue sky streaked by an occasional wisp of smoke whizzing past the window.

"Wooooohhhh, this is awesome!" John shouted into helmet radio.

His wife and daughter responded with screams of their own, as if they were tumbling down a log flume at the amusement park. The rocket continued its ascent for nine minutes until the sky faded to black and the curved edge of the earth became visible in the windows.

As the rocket engine cut off and the rocket separated to fall back and land in Florida, John Fritzer felt his body lift off the seat.

"Welcome to low earth orbit," said Jim.

CHAPTER 19

ALEX RACED DOWN THE CORRIDOR OF THE SPACE STATION towards the docking port. He was late setting up the camera equipment for the Fritzer's arrival. For the past two days, his dad had been hounding him constantly to clean something, repair something else, upload the latest movies from the ground...the list went on and on. He had barely had any time to work on his experiments, and he was getting angry at his dad for not letting him have some time. Didn't he care about mom's scientific work that she had died for?

The docking hub was dark, but motion sensors activated the lights as soon as Alex flew headfirst into the module. John Fritzer wanted as much of his vacation filmed as possible; he was planning on making a television special about the journey. NewStar was footing part of the bill, and that meant that Alex needed to hurry and get the equipment set up.

With the successful launch on time earlier that morning, the orbital mechanics lined up for a same-day arrival at NewStar One. John and his family, along with three other crew members would be arriving at around 1600, or 4 PM, which would put them onboard just in time for the first ever tourist dinner service aboard the station.

The space station in theory could use any time zone to operate. The orbiting complex did not belong to any particular part of the earth and made a complete lap of the planet every ninety minutes. Still, it was necessary to pick a time zone to use as a reference for day and night. So NewStar had decided to keep the station on Eastern Standard time in the United States, breaking with a long-standing tradition of using the international standard Universal Coordinated Time, which is based on the time in Greenwich, England. Using Eastern Standard Time made it easier for those launching out of Florida to adapt to their new environment without having to worry about shifting their body clocks to a foreign time zone.

Alex grabbed a bag of camera equipment and unstowed the video cameras, lights and lots of long cables, which danced around him like kelp in the ocean. He followed the instructions on the tablet computer for mounting the camera to its stand. The cables had become totally entangled and he struggled to pull apart the various power and video cables and connect them to the right places. When he finally finished, the extra lengths of cable continued to dance all over the docking port, so Alex carefully coiled up the loose segments and secured them with Velcro straps to the walls or the camera stand.

With everything finally set up, Alex had a chance to peek out the window in the center of the hatch. Outside, he could see the Destiny spacecraft coming towards them, looking like a bright star as it reflected the sun's light from a few kilometers away.

"You got a tally ho?" came a voice from behind him. Alex turned to see his father pulling himself into the module.

"What's that?"

"Oh, it's just an expression we used to use when we could spot an incoming spacecraft. Tally ho!"

"That's weird, dad, but yeah, I can see them out there."

"Looks like they're about 1.1 kilometers away," his dad said as he looked at some data on a wall-mounted screen. "Should be docked in about 40 minutes. Everything ready in their rooms and for dinner?"

"I've cleaned their room about twenty times, since you've been bugging me every hour about it this past week. And the dinner packages are all out and in the rehydrator, I just need to turn it on and it'll be ready in ten minutes. So relax."

"Good, good. And the table is all set up in the Commons in case they want to eat there?"

"Yes, dad. Jeez, give me a little credit. Everything is set up."

"Don't get smart with me. I'm the commander and it's my responsibility to check that everything is taken care of." Alex fumed silently - his father was becoming more and more confrontational lately.

The speaker on the wall crackled, and they heard the voice of Jim come through professionally but excitedly. "NewStar One, Destiny. We are approaching 1 km range and slowing for final. Please confirm you are in attitude hold."

Alex's dad checked the wall panel. He then pushed a button and spoke at the microphone embedded next to the panel. "Destiny, NewStar One. I can confirm the station is in attitude hold mode and we have a visual on your approach. We're following you in and ready to welcome you aboard."

"Copy, NewStar One. Be there soon."

The approaching ship glided in slowly over the next fifteen minutes, gradually becoming larger and more visible. Alex could see the flashing lights on the capsule and the solar arrays spread out like wings on both of its sides. Eventually, the sun set, leaving only the lights of the capsule visible against the black sky.

When Destiny was about 100 meters away, it slowed even more. Alex's dad talked on the radio nearly constantly with Jim at this point, giving him updates from his point of view of Destiny's alignment and speed and reminders about the checklist items that needed to be done to get ready for docking.

Alex stared out the hatch window as the craft approached. By now, he could just barely make out faces staring back at him from Destiny's windows. He was jealous of Jim piloting the spacecraft. He wanted a chance to try it himself, especially after all the times he had done it in the simulator. But he knew that his father would never let him have a chance at something like that. He barely trusted Alex to get beds made properly.

Then he noticed the girl's face in the window. Elodie Fritzer. He recognized her from a couple of photos he'd seen. She was never really in the media spotlight like her father, but on occasion, her name or picture would come up in some magazine or website. She had flawless tanned skin and dark brown hair. Alex could see it was currently pulled up in a bun, probably to avoid it flying around in zero gravity. *She looked a little tired, or maybe nervous. I wonder if she's scared to be flying up in space.*

The ship continued to approach and eventually Alex's

dad asked him to move back away from the hatch. He watched the camera views on the video monitor attached to the wall. Floodlights illuminated the docking mechanism. Destiny's docking ring approached the space station with its probe extended in front. Alex watched as the probe slid into the capture cone of NewStar One's docking port. The metal screeched slightly as the two made contact.

Gears whirred as the mechanical hooks joined the two vehicles together with an airtight seal. Unlike the docking with Venturer, Destiny was connected to the station with no problems. Alex bounced around the module, double-checking the cameras and making sure everything looked clean and nice. He had never met anyone famous like John Fritzer before. He knew his dad had met John before launch, but he didn't say much about the encounter aside from the fact that John was a nice guy and they'd all like him. That could describe anyone!

Finally, the leak checks were finished. Alex watched as the hatch slid open a few inches, and then all the way along the track until it was fully inside NewStar One and Jim's smiling face could be seen on the other side.

"Permission to come aboard?" he said with a chuckle.

"Granted," Alex's dad said, giving Jim a hearty hand-shake before pulling him into an embrace. The scientists followed him. Then came John Fritzer, who shook Alex's dad's hand and then came over to Alex.

"You must be Alex. I've heard a lot about you from your dad. John Frizter."

"Hi," said Alex, taking the hand offered to him. John shook firmly, and Alex tried desperately to think of something interesting to say. "It's, uh, nice to have you in space."

"Good to be here," John said without missing a beat. "And this is Jennifer, my wife, and Elodie, my daughter." Alex hadn't even noticed them coming through the hatch. He shook Jennifer's hand and then Elodie's. She met his eye with a mischievous smile on her face.

"You look like you could be fun," she said simply before moving away to greet Alex's father. *What on earth does she mean by that?*

After all the introductions were made, Alex's dad offered to take the guests on a tour of the space station.

"And while we're doing that, Alex will take your bags to your rooms," he said.

"But, dad, I can help out with the tour too," Alex said. He hated being left out.

"I think I can handle it," his dad said with a smile. "Now get Destiny unpacked." His voice made it clear that there was no room for disagreement. Alex scowled and moved towards the hatch.

"Don't worry, I'll take a private tour with you later," Elodie said as Alex was leaving. Alex turned back and Elodie winked at him. John shot his daughter a look, but nothing more was said. Alex slid into Destiny as everyone else left for the tour.

The Fritzers each had a bag full of clothes and personal items. Elodie's was the largest by far. Alex grabbed all three bags and dragged them behind him as he headed towards the hotel module. He left Elodie's massive bag in room four, attached to the wall with a few bungee cords. Then he took John and Jennifer's bags to room five and attached them similarly to the wall.

Alex returned to the ship and took another load of bags to the crew area for the scientists. Everyone else was just coming into the crew habitat as part of their tour.

Alex worked quickly to put away the crew's bags, hoping to have a chance to join the rest of the tour. He wanted to make friends with the Fritzer family. Secretly, he dreamed that he would impress them with his knowledge of the space station and they would invite him on some exotic vacation when they got back to earth. Maybe he would join them on their yacht for a wild celebrity party and meet other actors and musicians and athletes. All his friends would be so jealous. He would bring Mackenzie with him. Maybe they'd offer her an acting job and they could move to Los Angeles and live a life of fame and fortune.

"Alex, once you're done with those bags, please go prepare dinner for our guests and the crew," his father said, interrupting his daydreams. "The Fritzers have invited the entire crew to join them tonight in the guest dining area, so set up the table for all nine of us to eat together. We should be ready in about thirty minutes."

Disappointed that he would miss the rest of the tour, Alex said, "Yes, sir," and left the module. At least he'd get a chance to talk to the Fritzers at dinner. He should try to think of something interesting to talk about. Maybe he should tell them about how he had sealed the leaking capsule during launch. Or would that scare them too much? Come to think of it, Alex wasn't sure if they had been told about that incident, or if it had been made public at all. Alex certainly didn't want to cause trouble for the company, so he decided to keep his mouth shut. Maybe it would be better to ask John about what it was like to be in movies. Surely nobody ever asked him that, he thought, chuckling at his own self-criticism.

Alex hurried into the Commons. He had set up everything to make a shrimp cocktail appetizer followed by beef roast with vegetables and chocolate pudding. Now he had to get six more servings ready and prepare the trays that held the food and silverware. He quickly grabbed more food packets from the storage closet at the far end of the module. The beef roast was sealed in a silvery package that could be heated in a small oven. After he added the six new packets of beef and vegetables and started the heater, he moved on to the shrimp cocktail.

The shrimp was dehydrated in vacuum-sealed clear packages mixed with a dried spicy tomato sauce. It was based on a recipe that was a favorite of NASA astronauts. Astronauts for years have noted that tastes change in space, and most people find spicy foods appealing in zero-gravity even if they dislike them on earth. Alex found this to be true, and he loved the shrimp cocktail even though he never ate shrimp back home. He'd eaten the dish three times already in the past week.

All of the food was rehydrated with an injection of hot water. The rehydration machine had room for ten food packages at once, so it was nearly full with the nine Alex inserted into the slots. He closed the door and pushed a few buttons which started the automated process which inserted needles into the packages and injected them with hot water.

While the food was being prepared, Alex retrieved six more trays from the storage below the food warmer. He took the trays to the table where they were secured with Velcro to the surface. Then he laid silverware onto magnetic strips at the side of each tray.

Alex had just finished laying out the silverware when

he heard a mixture of voices and laughter growing as the rest of the space station occupants came through the hotel corridor towards the Commons.

He quickly checked the food in the warmer and began moving packages over to the trays on the table.

"...and so I told her she was going to have to dye her hair blue for the part. And she wouldn't do it! That's why Katheryn Goodwin was cast as Claudia in the movie," John Fritzer was saying. Alex's dad laughed. Elodie was talking to Jim, and the scientists were engaged in a conversation with Jennifer Fritzer. *This sure is an interesting crowd,* thought Alex.

Elodie floated over to him as he was taking the shrimp cocktail packages out of the rehydrator. She came to an awkward stop, holding onto the edge of the shelf that held the equipment, her legs and feet flying up above her head.

"Still getting used to zero-g, huh?" Alex asked.

"Yeah, it's totally wild. I love it! You seem pretty used to it."

"It took me a while, though. I was bumping into things all the time the first few days. I still wake up confused once in a while."

"Sleeping is going to be crazy. But I'm so tired I don't think it's going to be a problem. What's for dinner?"

"Shrimp cocktail, beef with vegetables, and chocolate pudding."

"I don't really eat crustaceans. Can I have something in place of the shrimp?"

"Um, I can try to find something else. But I've heard a lot of people like the shrimp cocktail even if they don't usually eat it on earth. I've had it a few times. It's pretty good."

"No. I can't eat those nasty looking creatures. They're

so slimy and gross."

"Let me see what else we have."

Alex pushed off and landed in front of the food pantry. He searched for something that might appeal to Elodie as an appetizer. She followed behind him and looked over his shoulder.

"Oooh, I'll try the macaroni and cheese!" Elodie exclaimed. Alex laughed.

"Seriously?" he said. "All these choices and you want mac and cheese?"

"Yup," Elodie said with a smile. "It's my favorite. My daddy used to make it for me all the time as a kid and I still love it. Especially if you mix it with a little salsa."

"Well, we don't exactly have salsa, but there is hot sauce I can inject into it."

"That would work. What do you mean 'inject in'?"

"You can't just pour sauces onto food in zero gravity," Alex explained. "So the rehydrator machine has some different sauces you can inject into the food with a needle and then mix them around. In fact, that's how you add salt to your food if you want it. It comes in a solution. No salt shakers in space."

"I never would have thought about that. You guys have everything figured out up here."

"Yeah, we kind of do," Alex said with a smile.

Everyone was settling into their spots around the table now. Alex quickly heated up the macaroni and cheese for Elodie, selecting to inject a burst of hot sauce with the rehydration from the menu on the control panel. Then he grabbed drink bags of water for everyone before joining the crowd around the table.

"Hey, Alex, what do you say we bring out a drink bag

of wine for everyone also?" his Dad said.

"Just for the adults, right?" Alex asked.

His father smiled. "You know technically, we're outside of US legal jurisdiction. There's no drinking age up here." Turning to John, he asked, "Is it OK for Elodie to have a little wine?"

"Absolutely! Wine for everyone!" John replied enthusiastically. Alex retrieved a pouch of chilled white wine for all of the guests in addition to the water and brought them back to the table.

"This is just amazing - our first meal together in space," John said. "Can I get a picture of this?"

"Definitely," Alex's dad said. "Here, I can take one for you." He grabbed the camera and took a photo of John and Jennifer in front of their rehydrated shrimp cocktail.

"Here, Dad," said Elodie. "Get one of my mac and cheese. And the amazing chef." Elodie held up her food and put her arm around Alex while her dad took a picture.

After a few more pictures, John put away his camera and offered a toast. "I just want to say thank you to the crew of NewStar One for your hospitality. This really is an unbelievable place you've got here, and Jennifer, Elodie and I are just thrilled to share it with you all. And really for us, it's an escape like no other. Honestly, this is the first time in a very long time we've found a way to get away from the damn paparazzi!"

Everyone laughed.

John continued, "I also want to give a special thanks to Mike and Alex for arriving here early and getting everything set up. I understand you guys hit a few bumps on the way and that without your bravery and hard work, this vacation wouldn't be possible for us. And also thanks to Jim for flying us up here with skill and of course to Erica, Doug and Megan for coming up to do important research that will help us all on planet Earth. I hope this station is just the start of large parts of humanity reaching beyond our planet. Cheers."

Everyone tapped their drink bags together, which lacked the satisfying clink of glass. All of the space travelers brought their straws to their lips, pinched the valve that held the liquid in with their teeth and took satisfying slugs of wine into their throats. Alex had tried beer once on a dare, but never wine. The burn in the back of his throat as he drank came as a surprise. He decided he didn't like the sharp sour taste of the drink.

Alex turned to Elodie. She seemed to have no problem with her wine and in fact was taking what appeared to be a big gulp from the bag. Then she picked up her fork and took a bite of macaroni and cheese.

"Thanks for making this special for me," she said with a smile. "It's nice and spicy, really good."

"Sure, no problem," Alex said. He took a few bites of shrimp cocktail, slurping up some sauce that escaped from his fork. "So do you want to be a movie star like your dad?"

"Actually, I want to be a model," Elodie replied. "I might do a few movies, but I don't like having to memorize lines and stuff."

"Have you ever done any modeling before?"

"Not yet, but I might get a chance soon. I was invited to do a photo shoot to show off a new line of clothing in Glamour magazine. My dad said he'd think about it. He thinks I'm not old enough yet. I'm like, come on dad, I'm almost sixteen, and lots of models start as little kids."

"Well, if it makes you feel better," Alex said, his voice

lowering to a whisper, "Sometimes I'm pretty sure my dad thinks I'm not old enough to be here."

Elodie smiled in a conspiratorial kind-of way. "Parents don't know what we're capable of," she said in a low voice. "They just want to hold onto that quaint notion that we're still their little helpless babies so they can feel important."

"I know exactly what you mean."

"It's even worse with step-parents," Elodie said. "They have something to prove."

Alex instinctively looked over at Dr. Reid talking to his father. Elodie noticed and caught Alex's eye when he turned back. "A little drama going on in our little space team?"

"No," said Alex. "Well, actually, I don't know. I hope not."

"She's cute and your dad seems like quite a catch."

Alex frowned. He still wasn't ready to imagine his dad with anyone besides his mother, even after seven years. "Let's talk about something else," Alex suggested.

"Alright," said Elodie, taking a bite of macaroni and cheese. "What is there fun to do up here?"

"We have lots of games, movies, exercise equipment, or you can just watch the planet. It's pretty amazing - I feel like I could stare at it for hours."

"What kind of games are there?"

"There are some magnetic board games and we have the space versions of basketball, laser tag, and dodgeball."

"Which one is your favorite?"

"Honestly, I haven't played any of them," Alex admitted. "So far I've just been working."

"Will you play basketball with me after dinner?"

"Sure!" *The customer is always right, isn't that what they say?*

They continued eating and talking for another hour. John Fritzer dominated much of the conversation, and when he wasn't talking to Elodie, Alex loved hearing stories about John's adventurous travels around the world making movies and doing charity work. Alex served dessert, and slowly the adult guests dribbled out of the room, leaving Elodie who waited around for her promised game of space basketball, a game that Alex was pretty sure the company had made up.

It took Alex about twenty minutes to clean up from dinner. He was a little annoyed that Elodie didn't even make an effort to help, but then he realized he was being foolish - after all, he was the hired help and she was on vacation. Elodie floated nearby while talking constantly about her modeling friends and how they were so stuck-up and not even that pretty, which meant that she should have a *fantastic* chance at making it big.

When all the trash from dinner was thrown away and the trays cleaned and stowed, Alex recessed the table back into the floor of the module. With the spacious room now effectively empty, he mounted up two circular hoops with nets to the opposite walls of the module. Then he clipped the ends of the nets to hooks on the walls so they wouldn't float around like seaweed in the ocean. Finally, he grabbed a small handball from the recreation stowage closet.

Elodie finished up her last phone conversation and flew over to Alex. "So how do we play basketball in space?"

Alex smiled. "Actually, I have no idea. They provided some instructions, but I think someone on earth made them up who has never been in space. Supposedly, instead of dribbling we are supposed to toss the ball between our hands while we move, which seems ridiculous to me."

"Alright," said Elodie. "Well, let's try it." She took the ball from Alex and tossed it back and forth between her two hands. After about three passes, she missed and the ball flew out of her hand. She threw her head back and laughed. Alex laughed with her.

"Not as easy as it looks, huh?" Alex asked.

"No, I guess not. But I'm up for the challenge! Game on?"

"I haven't finished reading all the rules yet," Alex said.

"Who cares? It can't be that hard - just try to get it into the basket. Let's go!"

Boy, she's pretty impatient, Alex thought. *Impatient but fun.*

He let Elodie start with the ball first. She tossed it quickly back and forth between her hands and pushed off the floor gently with her feet. Her push was too gentle though, and her body slowed to a stop in the middle of the module. Her hands were busy with the ball, her eyes focused on the orange blur passing between them. There was little she could do to advance any further.

Maybe we need to rethink the rules on this game, thought Alex. But this thought didn't stop him from pushing off with his feet and snatching the ball from between Elodie's hands. He curled into a somersault position as he soared towards the overhead panel and let himself rotate until his feet were touching a handrail. Then he extended his body quickly, pushing off the handrail towards his net. He tossed the ball into the net just before his body crashed into the bulkhead at the end of the module. As he looked back he saw that Elodie had come after him and was now on a collision course. Her mouth was opened and her eyes wide as she realized she was about to smash into Alex. He put out his arms and grabbed her, slowing her a little before they both hit the wall and tumbled in an awkward embrace.

Both of them were laughing by now, their bodies entangled. Elodie held on longer than necessary. Her face was just inches from Alex's, her arms still wrapped around his torso when she whispered, "You're a good space basketball player."

"Thanks," said Alex and he freed himself from her arms. He went to retrieve the ball from the net. Elodie followed him and as soon as he had the ball, she put her arms around him again and said, "Can we try dancing in space next?"

Elodie pulled him close and inched her face towards his. Alex's mind went blank as their lips briefly touched. Then he pulled back.

"I'm sorry," he said. "I can't do this. I have a girlfriend back home."

Elodie smiled sweetly. "Well, it's not like she'll ever know. We're far away from everything on earth up here." Alex hesitated. Elodie had a point. She was gorgeous up close, with smooth skin and a small trace of freckles across her nose. As a nerdy loner at school with only one close friend, Alex had never known any girls to be interested in him, and now he suddenly found himself torn between two, including a famous movie star's daughter!

Elodie mistook Alex's hesitation for consent, and she pulled him in for another kiss. Alex relented for a moment, tasting her tongue and feeling her warmth against his body, but then he pulled back again.

"No, Elodie. Even if nobody else would know, I'd know," he said. "I can't."

She smiled and released Alex from her embrace. "Oh, don't worry, you'll change your mind before the end of the week," she said with an unnerving certainty. "I need to get to bed. Stop by anytime you want though."

With that Elodie Fritzer, the incredibly beautiful and famous girl who Alex had just rejected, left the room.

CHAPTER 20

ALEX HIT THE SNOOZE BUTTON ON THE ALARM AND THEN banged his head back against his pillow. It was 0600 and he was supposed to get up, but he didn't want to move. Last night, he had barely slept thinking about Elodie and Mackenzie.

How many guys would have a chance to be with a girl like Elodie Fritzer? How often in his life would he meet someone so famous and gorgeous...and RICH! He might never have a chance like this again. Actually, he almost certainly would not.

And I've only been dating Mackenzie for a few months and most of that time I was in training and barely saw her. Who knows...she might even be seeing another guy right now.

Alex banged his head against the pillow a few more times. Did he really even have a chance with ditzy Elodie? The reality was he had nothing in common with her. She lived in a world of money and modeling and fame. He was a nerdy high school nobody. What did Elodie even see in him?

"Alex, are you in there?" It was his dad outside his quarters. Alex groaned in response. "The Fritzers will probably be up and wanting breakfast soon. You need to get dressed."

"OK, OK. I'll be out in a minute." Alex said, and he pulled himself out of his sleeping bag.

"Five minutes and then you better be on your way to the hotel." Alex scowled but started pulling on his jump-suit. After quickly using the bathroom, he grabbed a cereal bar and banana for breakfast, and then headed to the hotel module. Orange lights above doors 4 and 5 indicated that the Fritzers were still in their rooms, probably sleeping. It was ridiculous to ask him to be at the hotel by 0630. No hotel guests in their right mind would wake up that early. With no famous guests to attend to, Alex decided to use the time to call Mackenzie. He needed a reminder of why he had pushed Elodie away last night. As he had done several times before when he wanted privacy to talk to his girl-friend, he slid into the vacant hotel room 1. Once inside with the door closed, he tapped the touchscreen on the wall to dial Mackenzie. It was still early, but Mackenzie was an early riser and even when she wasn't awake, she would get up to take his calls.

Mackenzie answered right away and turned on the video camera on her phone. She was wearing pajamas and her hair was a mess, but she still looked amazing with her smooth, tanned skin and blue eyes.

"Hi, Alex," she said groggily.

"Hey, you," Alex said, smiling. "How are you?"

"Sleepy. I was out late last night."

"Oh yeah, what were you doing?"

"A bunch of us went to the boardwalk to see Glass Crutches play." Alex had heard of the band, but had never actually listened to any of their music.

"That sounds like fun. Wish I could've been there."

"Me too," Mackenzie replied. "I saw on the news the Fritzers arrived yesterday."

"Yeah, they got in last night and we had a nice dinner," Alex said casually.

"I bet. How is Elodie Fritzer?"

Alex felt his stomach churn as if he had been spun around in the vomit comet. Surely Mackenzie couldn't know anything, right? "I mean, she seems pretty nice," he said, but his voice felt squeaky. It seemed like Mackenzie was eyeing him suspiciously.

On the screen, Mackenzie's door opened behind her, and she turned away as her mother came in to tell her breakfast was ready. "Hey, Alex, I have to go," Mackenzie said, turning back towards the screen. "Call me tomorrow. I miss you."

"Yeah, miss you too," he replied.

"Alright, bye." She blew him a kiss and then the screen blinked and showed the message CALL ENDED. Alex took a deep breath and looked out the window at the blue Earth passing below him. A map in the corner of the monitor showed they were over the Indian ocean. He wished he could just sit here all day and stare out the window and try to make sense of his conflicting thoughts. It was odd that Mackenzie had mentioned Elodie, and Alex didn't know how to feel about the fact that she was out having fun with a group of friends that he knew included several guys who would likely not hesitate to make a move on a girl as popular and good-looking as his girlfriend.

Alex decided to check his e-mail quickly before heading to the hotel. He scanned the list and his eye quickly settled on one from Tyler with the subject line "nice, Alex." He opened it with a smile expecting to find something funny to brighten up his morning. His smile quickly disappeared when he clicked the link Tyler had sent.

Alex stared at a picture Elodie Fritzer had posted online the previous night with Elodie holding her meal in one hand with her other arm wrapped around Alex's shoulder. The caption read, "This cutie made me my absolute fav - mac&cheese!" Had Mackenzie seen this? Is that why she was asking about Elodie? Alex suddenly felt the urge to call Mackenzie back and explain himself, but there was nothing he could explain. The truth was, Elodie clearly liked him and she was taking that flirtation to a public level. And the other truth was that they had kissed - sort of - and he didn't want to start a conversation that might lead down that path at all.

Disconcerted, Alex logged off the computer and left the room to get ready for breakfast service. It was 0830 by the time John and Jennifer emerged from their room. Alex offered them coffee and then rehydrated scrambled eggs with cheese. They accepted and ate in silence while Alex bustled around the module gathering food packets for lunch later in the day, setting up games he thought the Fritzers might like to try, and replacing empty coffee pouches.

It was after 0900 when Elodie finally arrived. She came directly over to Alex, who was cleaning empty food pouches off the breakfast trays and slipped her arm around his chest from behind him. Alex's muscles instantly tensed. She whispered in his ear, "Good morning, my space chef."

"Hi, Elodie," Alex said. He kept his eyes on his work and in his mind willed her to let go of him. He was angry at her for posting the picture of the two of them online. He also couldn't believe she was doing this right in front of her parents, who were looking out the window and probably pretending they didn't notice their daughter throwing herself at the help. Alex focused his thoughts on Mackenzie, her beautiful figure and blue eyes, what it had felt like to kiss her and feel her hands on his face and neck. Elodie hung on for a few minutes longer before finally releasing her grasp and letting out a sigh that made it clear she was displeased at the lack of response to her affection.

Alex asked Elodie if she wanted some scrambled eggs and coffee. She said she would and gave him a sweet smile that Alex couldn't help but return. *Knock it off,* he admonished himself.

While Alex made breakfast, John inquired about doing a workout that morning. Alex said that he could set up the exercise equipment in the Commons as soon as breakfast was finished.

"Great, I'll go get changed while Elodie eats. Do you want to work out with me, honey?" John asked his wife.

"I think that's an excellent idea," Jennifer replied, and the two left the Commons to change into gym clothes.

Alex brought Elodie her breakfast tray. "Can I get you anything else?" he asked.

"Will you join me?"

"I've already eaten," said Alex.

"Then just get some coffee and sit with me."

"I don't drink coffee."

"Well, then have some water. I'd just like some company. Is this how you treat guests?"

Alex was annoyed at Elodie using his position and "customer service" requirements against him, but he relented, pulling a pouch of orange juice from the refrigerated storage and returning to the table across from Elodie. She took a few bites of egg and drank some coffee and then looked up at Alex with an inviting pair of eyes.

"So now that the adults are gone, are you going to tell me if your dad is hooking up with that scientist?"

Alex was taken aback by her question. "I hope not! As far as I know, he hasn't seen anybody since my mom died." Alex paused for a moment as uncomfortable thoughts swirled in his head. He mumbled, mostly to himself, "But I guess maybe he could have and just never told me."

Elodie stopped eating and looked up at him. "You know, your dad will probably start dating other people at some point. He's a great guy, so he deserves it. It's not anything against your mom."

"Yeah, you're right," said Alex, studying his orange juice packet. He turned it around in his hands a few times and finally looked up. "I know the accident was a long time ago. I guess...well, I still haven't totally gotten over it."

"Has your dad?"

"I don't really know," Alex said. "My dad never really talks about it."

"That must be so hard. I couldn't imagine something like that happening." Elodie took a few more bites as a heavy silence hung in the air until Elodie broke it with another question. "So your dad raised you all by himself after your mom died?"

"Well, actually, he was never around very much. Always busy with work and all. Mostly my grandma raised me."

Elodie took another bite of eggs, and then said, "Well at least you have your grandma. Mine barely shows up. I think she hates kids."

The conversation fizzled out again for a few moments

and Alex decided to change the subject. "What was it like growing up with John Fritzer as a dad? I mean you must have gone everywhere."

"Not as much as you'd think. My dad used to take me on travel with him when I was really little. But when I got into second grade, he stopped doing that because he was worried I wouldn't learn anything from the random mix of tutors on the road. And he had just divorced my first step-mom, so he got a nanny for me. Her name was Margaret, and she took care of me almost all of the time."

"Wow, that must have been tough."

"Not really, she was awesome. She was from England and had this cool accent. We'd go shopping and out to eat and she drove me to school and horseback riding. We did everything together."

"Where is she now?"

"She moved back to England when I turned fourteen. I still keep in touch with her though. She's actually getting married this fall."

"That's pretty cool."

"Yeah," Elodie said. She stared absentmindedly at the earth out the window. Alex wondered what she was thinking about. Her face betrayed a tinge of sadness. Finally, she added, "Margaret was my best friend."

"Really? You must have tons of friends having John Fritzer as a dad. Your best friend was your nanny?"

"Yeah, my best friend was my nanny, OK?" Elodie sounded annoyed. "Sure, I have tons of friends in LA, but they are all my friends exactly because my dad is John Fritzer. They're all so fake sometimes."

Alex didn't know what to say. It had never occurred to him that Elodie's life was anything less than spectacular.

But maybe there was a price to pay for all the fame and fortune the Fritzer family enjoyed.

They sat in silence for a few more moments. Finally, Alex couldn't stand the awkwardness and he said, "Hey, I need to go down to the lab to do a quick check on some experiments."

"Really, what kind of experiments?" Elodie asked.

"It's genetics stuff. The kind of stuff my mom used to work on. Do you want to see?"

"Yeah, sure!" Elodie replied excitedly. "I don't really know much about genetics."

"Well, if you want to learn, you've come to the right place." That sounded really nerdy, but surprisingly Elodie smiled at him. After Alex quickly threw away the remnants of breakfast, the two headed towards the lab, flying through the corridors with arms extended like carefree superheroes.

CHAPTER 21

THE LAB WAS BATHED IN A DIM RED LIGHT WHEN ALEX AND Elodie entered through the hatch. Dr. Williams had been conducting experiments that were sensitive to blue and green wavelengths, and the red light had to be maintained to avoid invalidating the experiment. Equipment hummed gently, but there was nobody in the module.

Alex led Elodie over to a small bench at the end of the starboard equipment racks that the science team was allowing Alex to use for his experiments. Officially, he was not a part of the science team and his research did not generate any grant money for the company. But having his dad as the commander helped, and the ever-curious scientists were interested in his experiments, so they allowed him to do his work as long as he didn't use too many of the lab supplies. NewStar corporate management on earth would hopefully never know.

Alex pulled out a tissue culture flask from the incubator below the lab desk. He held the rectangular glass in his hands. It looked eerie in the glowing red of the module.

"What is that?" Elodie asked.

"It's a test to see if I got the right protein structure. I've been working on building a virus that can be used as a carrier of DNA corrections for patients with cystic fibrosis."

"You're kidding me." Elodie took the flask from Alex's hand and looked it over in awe. "You can make a virus? That's some serious evil scientist shit."

"Well, it's a good type of virus. Basically instead of taking over a host cell to create malicious RNA, it would insert DNA corrections needed to cure the genetic defect."

"That's insane. I've heard of cystic fibrosis but I don't really know what it is."

"It's a genetic disease that causes really thick sticky secretions from cells that produce sweat, mucus and digestive fluids. It used to kill kids at a really early age. Today, lots of people survive it into adulthood, but they have lots of problems."

Elodie turned her gaze from the flask with its floating mass of sticky goo to Alex's face. "How did you learn how to do this?"

"Mostly from reading my mom's notes." Alex took the flask back from Elodie. "The problem is that for the virus to be able to enter the infected cells, it needs a special protein called a receptor that will let it get past the cell wall. It's like finding a key to a lock. My mom could never create the right receptor and thought it might work better in zero gravity where proteins form differently. But so far I haven't had any luck with my first two attempts. This guy is my third try."

"How will you know if it works? Unless you're hiding some cystic fibrosis patients around here somewhere."

Alex smiled. "No, I have a marker inserted into the host cells I'm trying to grow the virus in. If the protein is correct, they will glow green under a microscope."

"Oooh, can we check to see if it worked?"

"This one needs another ten hours before we will likely be able to see anything."

"I want to see anyway." Elodie touched his arm and batted her eyes. "Plleeeaassseee."

Alex chuckled. He couldn't believe the girl who wouldn't stop talking about her modeling friends earlier now wanted to look at viral growth under a microscope. Maybe there was more to Elodie Fritzer than he had let himself believe. "Alright," he said. "Come over here."

Elodie followed Alex as he drifted slowly to the center of the lab and placed the flask inside the large microscope sample restrainer. After locking it in place, he flicked on a nearby monitor and began to adjust the position and magnification with a series of dials until finally an image sharpened on the screen. Grey and blue blobs danced slowly around the screen.

"What are those dots?" Elodie asked, pointing her finger at the image.

"Those are the nuclei of the host cells."

"There is something very sexy about a boy who knows how to do these things." Elodie's lips turned up into a sly grin. Alex froze as she drifted closer and reached her hand up towards his neck, trailing her fingers along his skin and causing the hairs on his back and arms to tingle. Her hand finally came to rest at the hairline on the back of his head. Alex felt his own hand reach for her waist almost involuntarily. She started to pull his face towards hers when Alex pulled away.

Elodie's face went sour as she moaned, "Oh, Alex, I really thought we had a connection, but if you're going to be such a prude..." She stopped talking when she realized that Alex wasn't even looking at her. His eyes were fixed on the computer monitor.

"Oh my God," he whispered. "It's turning green." Elodie looked over to see several dots on the edge of the screen whose blue color had changed to a brighter blue-ish green. As she watched, the color began to slowly brighten in front of her eyes.

"What does that mean?" Elodie asked.

"I think...I think it means it's working." Alex grabbed the controls and fiddled with the image until the amorphous blobs were centered and more focused. There were distinct blue borders but inside those borders, specks of green were beginning to appear like perpetual fireflies. "This means that the virus was able to enter the cells and combine with the probe RNA inside! Do you know what that means!?"

"Not in the slightest," Elodie laughed.

"It means the protein cap folded the correct way. We made the key to getting into the mucosal cells affected by the CFTR gene mutation! It's the right...my mom was right!" Alex grabbed Elodie in a bear hug and she smiled and laughed with him as he rambled on. "I can't believe it! 70,000 people in the world have cystic fibrosis and now we have something that might be able to cure them!"

Alex released Elodie who grabbed onto the table to stabilize herself as Alex began to type frantically on the keyboard. "What are you doing?" she asked.

"I'm taking some snapshots of this image and putting the finding into the lab notebook."

"Wow, that sounds...um...exciting." Alex rolled his eyes. He didn't care if she found writing lab notes boring - the finding had to be properly documented in case there was ever any question about what he had found.

After a few minutes, Elodie asked, "So, is this going to take a while? Because I might go back to my room."

"I'm almost done," Alex replied. He saved the photos and was about to press save on his notes when a loud buzzing sound filled the module. The noise seemed to come from everywhere at once.

"What on earth is that?" Elodie shouted, her hands covering her ears. The buzzing crescendoed and was followed by a pop. Then the module went dark.

CHAPTER 22

"WHAT THE HELL?" ALEX WONDERED ALOUD. WHEN HE finished saying those words, an eerie silence enveloped them, and Elodie clung to Alex's waist. All of the hum from the countless machines that kept them alive and surrounded their ears night and day was gone. In the near total darkness, Alex thought he could make out small specks of phosphorescence coming from the flask under the microscope. He wondered if his notes and photos had been saved. He had clicked the button right before the power had gone out - without that evidence, he doubted anyone would believe his discovery.

"What's going on?" Elodie asked, her shaky voice snapping Alex's attention back to the reality of their situation.

"I'm sure everything's fine," said Alex, trying to sound comforting. He didn't remember any training on what to do if electrical power was lost. The station had huge solar arrays and two backup sets of batteries. This shouldn't even be possible.

"There's a flashlight in the emergency kit by the hatch entrance," Alex said. "Let's try to get it and then head to the ships." His trainers always said in an emergency, all crew should gather at the ships in case there was a need to make an escape.

"Don't leave me here." Elodie's voice was a whimper.

"Just hang on to me. We'll go together." Alex slid along the table edge using his hands. Elodie was wrapped tightly around his side like a barnacle, so his movement towards the hatch was slow. When he finally reached the edge of the table, he stretched his arm out into the darkness in the direction of the hatch, but couldn't feel anything. It was too far away. "We'll have to make a jump for the hatch."

Without waiting for a response, Alex pushed himself and Elodie off the table and reached out in front of him. His hands felt nothing but then his head smacked hard against a cold solid surface. He winced in pain and specks of light flew around his field of vision, while his hands flailed around searching for something to hold onto. They finally grasped the thick metal bottom of the hatch.

"What happened?" Elodie asked fearfully.

"We almost went through the hatch but don't worry; I stopped us with my head."

"That bang was your head? Ouch!"

"Yeah, no kidding. I'll be fine though."

Suddenly, a glint of light reflected towards them from a distance. "Alex! John! Can you hear me?" His dad's voice was calm and confident. The light grew and Alex stuck his head into the corridor. A bluish-white beam hit him right in the eyes and he quickly shut them against it. "There you are!"

"Dad, what happened?" Alex shielded his eyes with his hands as he looked towards the headlamp and shadowy figure floating towards him.

"We've had a little electrical glitch, but Jim is working

on fixing it, and we should be back online any second. Elodie, where are your parents?"

"They were in their room getting ready to work out, I think," Elodie responded.

"OK, let's go get them." Alex's dad grabbed Alex by the hand and started down the corridor. They hadn't even made it to the Node hatch when the lights turned on. The fans began to spin back to life and they were quickly surrounded by the familiar hum of the space station. Alex's father continued into the hotel and found John emerging from his room wearing a concerned expression. Jennifer trailed behind him, looking visibly shaken.

"Guys, I'm terribly sorry about that," Alex's dad said to the Fritzers. "We had a minor glitch with the power, but everything is back to normal now."

"That seemed like a pretty serious minor glitch," John said wryly. "What happened?"

"Our power system just had what you might call a hiccup," his dad explained, sounding like this was a routine occurrence. "The power system tried to switch to the backup source, but unfortunately, we think a small software bug stopped it from switching automatically. We'll get it fixed and I promise there won't be any more power interruptions."

"Why were you switching to the backup power source?"

"It was an automatic switch. It appears that the electrical load was a little too high for a short period of time and it caused what was essentially a brownout. We are still looking into the primary power system, but that is why we have backups."

"Has this ever happened before?"

"No," his father admitted. "But we are still only in our first month of operations. There are always things you learn as you operate a new facility."

John seemed satisfied with that answer, but Jennifer was shaking her head. "This is insane, just insane," she said. "I will not have us staying on some experimental facility where you can't even keep the power on! John, we should have these people take us home right away."

"Doll, I'm sure Mike can take care of this. Mike, should we be worried about this problem?"

"Not at all," Alex's father replied. "We have more than enough backup capability onboard. The fact that it didn't kick in right away was just a minor glitch that can be easily fixed by our mission control team. Everything here is safe."

John turned to Jennifer and gave her a long look. "What do you think, sweetie? If you think we should go, then we'll go, but I think Mike and his team have it under control now."

Jennifer folded her arms across her chest. She hadn't had time to tie her hair up when they left their room after the power went out, and now her long blond mane was spread out wildly in all directions. She gave John a very clear you-better-be-right-or-else look and snorted, "Fine, but if anything else goes wrong with this place, I want out of here. I don't need to be frozen to death or suffocated in some outer space hotel experiment."

"Understood, loud and clear," Alex's dad said, his face deadly serious. "Why don't you all head back down to the commons and get comfortable and Alex will find you something fun to do."

"Alright, we were about to exercise, let's finish getting ready and try out the gym," John said enthusiastically, trying to cheer up his wife. She seemed to warm up to him a little and they returned to their room to finish getting dressed.

"I think I could go for a little exercise too after all that," Elodie said. "Thanks for being with me. It would have been pretty scary without you there." She gave Alex a hug while Alex's father watched with raised eyebrows. Then she disappeared into her room.

Alex was about to leave to set up the exercise equipment in the commons, but his father grabbed him by the arm and pulled him close. "Alex, I need you to keep the Fritzers occupied in the hotel for the next few hours. Don't let them out past the node."

"Why?"

"I don't want to scare them, but based on the alarms we got before the power went out, Jim and I are worried that the brownout was caused by a short circuit between the primary and first backup battery banks. If that is the case, two of our three batteries may be nonfunctional. They are offline at the moment. We want to do a spacewalk to visually see the condition of the batteries and try to see if we can find any source of a short circuit before we attempt to bring them back online."

"I thought we had three sets of batteries. Why did we lose power if the third set is still working?"

"The software was designed to go from primary to backup 1 and then backup 2, but in this case, it had to skip from primary straight to backup 2 which wasn't defined. Luckily Jim is a good electrician and he was able to manually jumper the backup battery onto the main bus, bypassing the other two battery banks."

Alex didn't know a lot about the space station's power

system, but he definitely understood the seriousness of a short circuit taking down two of their three battery packs. If the last one were to fail, they'd be a dead ship in space. The solar arrays would only be able to provide them power on the day side of earth, but on the night side, everything would shut down for much longer than just the few minutes they had experienced this time.

"OK, dad. I can keep them busy." Alex paused for a second before asking, "Dad, do you really think it's safe to stay here?"

His dad frowned. "Truthfully, I'm not sure, but panic won't help anything. Once I get outside and can take a better look, I'll know how bad it is. Maybe it's an easy fix."

"There seem to be a lot of problems with this space station. The reaction wheels, the computers, the batteries..."

"It definitely wasn't built to NASA standards," his dad admitted. "But we'll make her work." He gave Alex a smile, but it seemed forced. "Now get down there and keep our guests occupied."

*****

Stewart Sanders banged his fist against the table. His chief engineer looked like he was about to wet himself as Stewart began to lay into him.

"What kind of incompetent shit are you?! How could YOUR design created by the team that YOU hired have so many damn problems? Your ass is on the line! You will get this fixed. You will get this fixed NOW! No more excuses. Get your sorry ass out of here and FIX IT!!"

"Yes, sir," said the man. He adjusted his glasses and hurried out of Stewart's office as quickly as he could.

Stewart pounded his desk again with his fist after the

man had left. He had not cut corners, he told himself. Despite his rantings to the chief engineer, the design didn't seem to be the problem. The design is solid, Stewart told himself, but something had gone wrong with the manufacturing. Parts had been installed incorrectly or were badly made. That must be the issue. They should investigate the suppliers.

In the meantime, he had a crisis to deal with. He picked up the phone and told his secretary to fetch Melanie Howell on the double. Then he sat back and tried to clear his head.

Melanie appeared a few minutes later with a frown and a creased brow.

"You've heard about the battery failure?"

"Yes, the mission director just called me. It sounds bad."

"It's worse than bad. They are on their last backup. The crew is going to do a spacewalk and try to fix it, but I'm not sure the engineers even understand what the problem is."

"How are the Fritzers taking it?"

"I'm not sure. Which is why I want you here for the call I'm about to make. Nothing we discuss leaves this room, understood?"

Melanie nodded silently. Stewart picked up the phone and asked to be connected to NewStar One immediately. Then he pressed the speakerphone button and placed the receiver in its cradle.

A moment later, Mike's voice came on the line. "This is NewStar One."

"Mike, it's Stewart. What the hell is going on up there?"

"It's not good, sir. We've had two of three battery banks go offline. It's possible there was a common short between them. I'm getting ready to go inspect them and see if I can find the root cause. But even if I do, they may be toast."

"What a nightmare. I've got Melanie Howell with me. We need to be careful about how we handle this. What do the Fritzers know?"

"There's no hiding that we had a problem. The power was out for about five minutes, and Jennifer is not happy. She wanted to leave, but I convinced John that things were OK and he was able to calm her down."

"Shit. We need to keep her silent. Disconnect the Internet service, say it was related to the power problems. I don't want any of them sending out messages publicly until we can put together a story."

"Sir, are you sure that's a good idea? I don't think we can cover this up and delaying the publicity will just make it look like we're hiding the issue."

"Just do it for a few hours so we can get a story together."

"OK, you're the boss."

"Where are the Fritzers now?"

"Alex is entertaining them in the hotel. They had been getting ready to exercise when the power went out, so we're trying to keep them busy with that. Sir, they don't know that I'm doing a spacewalk. I didn't want to alarm them anymore because I was pretty sure they'd insist on leaving. I told Alex to keep them away from the airlock for a while. It's a pretty delicate situation right now."

"You're doing the right things, Mike. Just keep it up. I've got all the engineers down here looking at everything. No matter what, keep them happy and keep them from talking to anyone on the ground. We are not going to bring them home early."

There was a silence on the line before Mike spoke next. "Stewart, you know I'm loyal to this company and want to see it succeed. But the moment I start to think this station can't safely support its occupants, I'm going to order an evacuation."

Stewart's face turned red and Melanie watched him suck in air through his teeth. He spoke deliberately, his voice straining to maintain composure. "That's the wrong answer. We will talk together before we make that kind of decision."

Nobody spoke for what felt like several minutes.

Finally, Mike broke the silence. "Look, I need to get the suits prepped and get out to inspect the batteries. I'll let mission control know what I find."

The line clicked off and Stewart banged his fist against the desk yet again. Melanie flinched at the sound. Stewart finally waved her away, and she scurried out of the office.

CHAPTER 23

ALEX FLEW DOWN THE CORRIDOR AND QUICKLY SET UP THE exercise equipment in the Commons. The NewStar One fitness complement included a rowing machine, exercise bike, a resistance weight trainer and a treadmill. The rowing machine and bike worked generally the same as they would on earth, except that they were mounted in frames with springs, which allowed the exercise machine to move around but kept them from shaking the hull of the space station too much. These "isolation devices" were important to preserving the integrity of zero-gravity science, including Alex's own experiments.

The treadmill was also mounted on an isolator, and it required the runner to wear a special body harness that fit over the shoulders and around the torso. This harness was then connected to the sides of the treadmill with bungee cords, holding the runner "down" on the treadmill track. This gave some semblance of running in gravity, but it wasn't perfect.

The final machine, the resistance weight trainer, consisted of a standing platform with foot restraints and two large canisters that contained elastic twisted around a central core. The resistance of the elastic could be changed with a knob and then various implements attached to the canisters allowed for bench presses, arm curls, squats, tricep extensions and a variety of other exercises.

John and Jennifer arrived in the commons just as Alex finished setting up the equipment. Elodie showed up a few minutes later, and Alex gave them a brief tour of the available options. Jennifer decided to go for a run on the treadmill while John asked to try out the weight trainer. John got the hang of the resistance machine quickly, and Alex could tell from the high resistance he chose that he was no stranger to weightlifting. Meanwhile, Elodie had started pedaling on the exercise bike.

With all three of the guests happily occupied, Alex grabbed a tablet computer and drifted over to the huge earth-facing windows. He stared out at the rounded edge of the planet while he tried to process everything that had happened that morning. Had his experiment really worked? The green was a sure indication that the virus was entering the target cells in his sample. It was a small step, but one with huge potential. Then he remembered the lab notes he had been working on. Had they been lost? He quickly tapped through several screens on the tablet and to his relief found that his photos had been saved. The brief notes he had written were lost, but he could recreate those later. The photos were the most important evidence. He realized that in all the commotion, he hadn't even been able to tell his dad about the discovery. But by now, his dad was probably already outside doing his spacewalk.

Looking out the window, Alex suddenly had a panicky thought. What if the Fritzers could see the two spacewalkers as they did their inspections? But as he thought it through, he realized they were probably out of view. The airlock was two modules forward and up above the level of the hotel, and the batteries were located out on the solar array masts, nearly opposite of the window he was now looking out. At best, they might be visible from an angle at the edge of the window. Trying to appear nonchalant, Alex drifted closer to the windows and looked out edgewise, cocking his head to get the best view he could of the station structure. As he had suspected, he could barely see the edge of the airlock module and only at a sharp angle.

"What are you looking at?" Elodie asked. Alex turned to see her eyes fixed on him as she leaned over the handlebars of the bike and pedaled nonchalantly.

"Oh, nothing," he said quickly and hurried back towards the guests. "Just checking out the view. How is the exercise bike working?"

"It's a little weird but I'm getting a workout. I can definitely tell I haven't been using my legs much in the last few days. I've only been going about ten minutes and I can already feel the burn."

"I can lower the resistance if you want."

"No, thanks. I like a challenge." She winked at Alex as she said this. Alex pretended he didn't see it. The Fritzers continued their exercise, and the module was mostly silent for the next forty-five minutes while Alex retyped his lab notes and the Fritzer family sweated and panted in their first off-planet workout. Eventually, they tired of exercise and one by one the machines came to rest.

"I think I'm going to wash up and change clothes," said John. "Alex, do you think after that we could go see the labs? Erica offered yesterday to show me some of the work she's doing. It sounded fascinating."

"Well, um, I think I could definitely ask her that," Alex

said. "Why don't you all change clothes and meet me back here and I'll let you know?"

"That sounds good," said John. All three went into their rooms. Alex watched the doors close and then rushed to the crew quarters. Dr. Reid was not there, and Doug Williams informed Alex that she was in the airlock. Alex rushed back into the node and up to the airlock. Erica was talking on the radio, and Alex heard Jim's reply on a speaker.

"Dr. Reid," Alex said, slightly out of breath from rushing through the modules. "The Fritzers want to come see your lab. What should I tell them?"

"Your dad made it pretty clear that he doesn't want them to know about this spacewalk. Why don't you tell them that I'm doing a very delicate experiment right now and I won't be done for another two hours."

"How much longer do you think the guys will be out there?"

"They just got the cover off the battery bank." Dr. Ried tapped some commands into a laptop as she spoke. "If they find something obvious, it won't be long. But I have a feeling they may be tinkering around out there for a while. This isn't something we trained for."

"It's going to be really hard to keep the Fritzers distracted. If they come through the Node, they will probably see you up here."

"It won't matter as long as they don't come through when your dad and Jim come back through the hatch. I can just say I'm doing some maintenance up here. But if they see spacesuits, they'll probably be clued in. So just try to keep them in the hotel."

Alex's dad was calling on the radio now, impatient for

Erica to send some commands to test closing battery relays, and Alex was worried that the guests might be done changing and come look for him, so he rushed out of the airlock and back to the hotel.

John was emerging from his room just as Alex returned.

"That really felt great to exercise," he said. "I was pretty stressed out after that power outage this morning. But everything has been good since then, so I probably over-reacted to the whole thing."

Alex faked a smile and inwardly cringed. He hated hiding things from the Fritzers. Jennifer and Elodie emerged from their rooms.

"So I spoke with Dr. Reid," Alex said, "and unfortunately, she's right in the middle of a very delicate experiment that is going to take another two hours, so this isn't a great time to tour the lab. But luckily, I have a lot of other great things we could try. We have magnetic board games and a full selection of movies." The blank expressions facing him told Alex he hadn't caught their interest yet. "Or we could try some other activities. Maybe some zero-g basketball...or a lesson about cooking in space."

"Well, I didn't come all the way up here to watch a movie. I can do that on the ground. This cooking in space thing sounds interesting. What's that about?"

Shoot! thought Alex. He had made that last part up, not expecting a famous family that was used to having food prepared for them to want to cook. Cooking in space involved little more than reheating food that had been already prepared on the ground. Luckily, Alex had paid attention to his dad's stories about how he and his buddies would combine different foods to make new creations when they got bored with selections onboard the International Space Station. He decided he could invent an activity to hold everyone's attention.

"Great choice," Alex said with a smile and led the Fritzers into the Commons. After about twenty minutes of going through the food selections available onboard and suggesting a few tactics like wrapping food in a tortilla or combining the contents of different packages, Alex let the Fritzers go to work. He showed them how to use the rehydrator and small oven to heat foods. After about an hour of work, Alex was actually impressed with the creations that emerged. John used the beef wellington with some vegetables, rice and hot sauce wrapped in a tortilla to make a very tasty, albeit fairly messy, burrito. Elodie decided to spice up her usual mac and cheese with tomatoes, onion and chicken. Jennifer opted to create a dessert out of tortilla pieces smothered with chocolate hazelnut spread and topped with M&Ms.

While the three guests were tasting the foods, Alex sneaked over to one of the wall panels and checked the airlock pressure. It read zero, which meant his Dad and Jim were still working outside. He was starting to wonder if the situation was even more serious than his father had let on.

"Hey, Alex!" John was gesturing with his arm for Alex to come towards him. Alex moved back to the table where the Fritzers were standing in the foot restraints. "What do you think about us making our new creations for the crew for lunch? I think it would be a fun way to treat them for all they've done for us."

"Oh, that's probably not a good idea," Alex did not want to have to explain why several of the crew, including his father, were missing.

"Why not? It's really not any trouble for us, and I'm sure everyone needs to get some lunch pretty soon," replied John.

"Well, I just was thinking the crew is really busy and maybe they've already had lunch in crew quarters."

"It's only 11:30. Would you mind asking them for us?"

"Um, sure." Alex let out a sigh as he exited the Commons for what felt like the twentieth time that day. This ruse was becoming exhausting. As he left the Commons, John called after him, "We'll start getting some of the food ready and heated up." Well, at least they were staying busy, Alex thought.

He rushed to the airlock and found Erica in nearly the same position he had left her, standing in front of a computer terminal with her feet in restraints and a microphone in her hand. He quickly explained how the Fritzers wanted to surprise everyone with lunch.

"They aren't done working outside. Can you just make some excuses for a little longer? It sounds like they're about to give up."

"This is really getting annoying," Alex said, exasperated. "I've already tried telling them the crew was busy and had probably eaten lunch. I don't know what else I can do. They're going to get suspicious if I try to keep them there any longer."

Dr. Reid sighed loudly. "OK, let me talk to the man in charge." She squeezed a button and spoke into her hand-held microphone. "Mike, it looks like we've got a situation with the Fritzers. Alex had them making some kind of space food and now they want all of the crew to come for a lunch they made."

"Just have Alex keep them busy a little longer," came

his dad's reply. Alex threw up his arms.

Jim's voice came across the radio next. "I really think there's a short between the two channels, but I don't think we're going to find it by inspection. It's probably in the wiring harness underneath the batteries and we won't get to that unless we remove the batteries and the mounts, which would take hours."

Alex heard his dad sigh into his microphone. "Alright, let's replace the covers and head in. I guess we can go to lunch with John and the family."

Just then the alarm tone rang softly from the panel on the wall.

"What's that?" Alex asked.

"Oh, it's nothing," Erica said, looking at the display and then hitting a button to silence the alarm. "Your dad's suit oxygen flow has been a little high. Nothing to worry about, just another piece of quality NewStar space gear. Now go distract the Fritzers until your dad and Jim can get inside. It should only take them five or ten minutes to get in and then another ten or so to get out of the suits."

Alex nodded, grabbed a handrail and dove headfirst through the node hatch to head towards the Commons. As soon as he rounded the corner of the node, he almost bumped into John who was coming his way.

"Hey, there you are," John said. "Look, I'm sorry, but I think we might have broken the rehydrator. I was trying to rehydrate some of the rice and it started making a funny noise and steam started coming out, so I turned it off."

"Oh, don't worry," Alex replied. "That sometimes happens when the needle is only partially into the food package. Come on, I'll show you how to fix it."

Alex started back towards the Commons with John

when a dull thud sounded from the hull above them.

"What was that?" asked John.

"I'm not sure," said Alex, even though he strongly suspected that one of the spacewalkers had hit a piece of equipment, or maybe a boot, against the outer shell of the node.

"That didn't sound good." Jim was inching forward into the node and looking around. Alex wondered how close the crew was to repressurizing the airlock and coming inside.

"I'm sure it's nothing," said Alex quickly. "Why don't we head back to the Commons and I'll take a look at that rehydrator?"

Just then, two more thuds echoed in the node, and John pulled himself all the way into the module and looked up in the direction of the airlock where Dr. Reid was stationed. Alex looked up too, afraid that any second the airlock door would open and his dad would enter the station furious to find John right in front of him.

"Oh, hi, Erica," said John. "Did you hear that noise?"

Dr. Reid looked down from her post and glared at Alex for a split second before smiling and responding to John. "Yes, sorry, I'm doing a little maintenance up here on the life support system. I heard there will be lunch in a few minutes. As soon as I'm done I'll join you."

"Oh, OK. Sorry to bother you. We'll see you in a few minutes for lunch."

John was satisfied and let Alex lead him back to the Commons. As they prepared food, Alex thought he could hear the sounds of hissing air coming from the airlock, but the Fritzers didn't seem to notice anything at all.

About thirty minutes later, the entire crew came into

the Commons, including his father and Jim. Alex breathed a sigh of relief. As the crew and guests mingled, Alex's father pulled him aside.

"Nice work," he told Alex in a low voice. "You did an excellent job keeping our guests occupied."

"Did you find anything?" Alex asked.

"Unfortunately, we didn't. I would like to try to restart the batteries, but the mission control team wants to think about it a little more. The data they looked at strongly suggests there is a short circuit somewhere even though we couldn't find it. If we restart the batteries and the short circuit is present, we could damage the system further. Besides, everything seems to be working fine on the current backup set."

"Yeah, I guess that's good." Alex was proud that his dad was confiding such technical details to him. He felt almost like he was part of the adult crew, and he swelled with pride.

His father smiled at him and patted him on the shoulder. "Thanks again for handling this, Alex. Unfortunately, I had to rush through the post-spacewalk checklist. so I'll need your help to clean the suits after this is done. No good deed goes unpunished."

Alex made a sour face, but he was proud to be trusted enough to work on something as complicated as a spacesuit. Only a month ago, he had been sure that he would never be allowed to travel to space. A few months before that, he doubted his dad would have trusted him with a power drill. And not only had he earned his father's trust, but he had completed the first step of his mother's experiments! He opened his mouth to tell his dad about the finding when John called them over to the table. His father turned away before Alex had a chance to tell him about the breakthrough.

Alex trailed his father to the table and listened as John Fritzer explained the foods his family had prepared. None of them suspected that by rushing through the post-space-walk checklist, Mike and Jim had missed a critical issue. And so as they began to eat their lunch, a spacesuit hanging neatly on the airlock wall hissed quietly, as a stuck-open valve inside it slowly leaked out highly flammable pure oxygen.

CHAPTER 24

ALEX FINISHED CLEANING THE TRAYS AND STACKED THEM NEATLY in the cabinet, their magnetic bottoms holding them to each other and to the metal shelf they were stored on. Elodie was hovering near the window of the Commons and chatting on the phone, bragging to some friends back in California about a vacation none of them could ever afford. Jennifer was feeling tired and had left to take a nap. The rest of the crew had filtered out of the Commons to return to their duties, except for Alex's dad who still hovered at the table, talking and laughing with John Fritzer. The two seemed to delight in sharing stories from their adventurous lives, and over the past few days Alex had enjoyed lingering nearby and listening to both of them. But right now, he just wanted them to stop talking so he could tell his father about his virus protein success.

Alex hovered and waited. He didn't have any pressing work to do at the moment, but his dad seemed to be enjoying the conversation too much to want to stop. After a few minutes, Alex's dad and John left the table and headed towards the hatch.

"Where are you going, Dad?" Alex called after them.

His dad stopped and turned to face Alex. "I was going

to show John the onboard trainer for the CTV. He was asking about how we fly them. You want to come?"

Alex had used the trainer many times. He would normally delight in showing it off to someone like John Fritzer, but his mind was too focused on other things at the moment.

"Maybe next time," Alex said, "But when you're done, can I show you something in the lab?"

"Sure thing, bud," his dad said with a smile.

Alex watched the duo leave the Commons, and with a little time to spare, he decided to get some exercise. Even after just a few weeks in space, he could feel his body growing weaker in an environment where most movements required very little muscle exertion. He rarely had to break a sweat or do anything that put him out of breath. He actually missed playing basketball, feeling his heart pound as he raced across the court, dripping sweat. Running on the treadmill with the bungees holding him down didn't give quite the same effect, but it was the best he could do.

Alex set up the treadmill and grabbed his phone which had a huge collection of music on it. He popped in his earbuds, selected a high-energy playlist and began jogging. The treadmill faced the window and he imagined he was actually running across the African desert, which was spread out below him.

Elodie was also in front of him, upside down with her back to him and her feet tucked into straps at the top of the window. She was on her third phone call of the afternoon. With the music pounding his ears, Alex couldn't hear what she was saying. His eyes drifted across her body. She was beautiful even in a utilitarian jumpsuit. She had selected a suit that was slightly small on her and accented her body's curves. Alex had to remind himself again that he had a girl-friend back home and that Elodie could vaccilate between sweet companionship and stuck-up flirtation with almost no warning.

He increased the treadmill speed until he was at a seven-minute mile pace. With each step, the treadmill bounced and Alex caught it on the next step as his bungee harness pulled him back to the oscillating platform.

After about five minutes, Alex began to sweat. The motion felt good and he took deep heavy breaths. It felt like he was moving more than normal, shaking the entire space station as his legs pumped up and down. He pushed harder. Fall Out Boy was screaming loudly into his ears, which seemed to pop a little bit. Maybe he should turn the music down. The vibrations were getting harder, so he tapped the control panel to reduce his speed.

Then he looked up and saw that Elodie was no longer talking on the phone. She had released it and it was tumbling around in front of the window. Her mouth was wide open.

Alex reached up and removed an earbud, and as soon as he did he could hear her screaming. His ears were still popping, even with the earpiece removed. He reacted instinctively, and before he could even fully comprehend what was happening, his hand had slammed down on the STOP button of the treadmill. Alarms screamed wildly and the air stirred around him, pulling quickly together into a steady breeze. He had not heard the thunderous explosion behind his loud music, but he knew right away that there was a leak, and he tore off the treadmill harness, threw his phone and headset away and pushed himself forcefully towards the hatch.

He shot headfirst through the hotel corridor just as Jennifer pulled open the door to her room and looked out. He soared past her with his arms at his side and his jaw clenched. He had fixed the leak in Venturer during launch, and he could fix this one. But as he approached the node, his eyes widened as they took in an unfamiliar scene.

The walls of the node were blackened and thick smoke swirled and rushed up towards the airlock. Alex could smell burnt rubber and sulfur. Then a burst of light and heat hit him directly in the face and knocked him back against the hotel corridor bulkhead. His head slammed the metal panel with a force he could hear and his ears, already popping from pressure changes, began to ring.

Alex blinked several times but he could barely see. Pain ripped through his head. He tried to shake it out, but it just made him feel worse. Despite the fog in his head, the pain through his body and the sounds coming all around him, one signal kept coming to the front of his consciousness. His ears popping meant that the pressure was going down fast, air leaving the module. Memories rushed to him from training at NewStar...the altitude chamber when he removed his oxygen mask...first nothing, then headaches, flush face and euphoria...he was silly...hungry for more air.

Now he had the same feeling. He was losing control of himself but there was no mask to put on. Panic rose in his belly.

He tried to move his limbs. They resisted, but he pushed them harder. In a daze, he moved towards the hatch and grabbed it.

His hands touched metal, found the handle, and tried to pull the hatch closed. It wasn't moving. He looked at his hands. They were covered with red blisters and some blood.

He kept pulling but it seemed hopeless. His muscles strained , but even with his feet braced against the ceiling, the hatch did not want to budge.

Then suddenly another pair of hands was there with him, trying to help. He pushed. The other hands pulled. The hatch started to move. It slid along the track and then was all the way closed. He twisted the crank to latch it. Then he collapsed, but he didn't fall to the ground. He just drifted, unable to think about moving a muscle again.

As he was drifting, another jolt hit the station. Alex flew uncontrollably towards a bulkhead. He tried to stop himself, but his hands couldn't come up quickly enough to stop his head from rocketing into the structure. Suddenly everything went black.

*****

Alex awoke with a groan. He was in a guest bed in the hotel. The room was dark. As his mind began to stir, he wondered if he'd had a bad dream. He leaned forward and the slight motion made his head throb. He pulled his hands up and saw redness that stretched across the back of them from his fingertips to his wrist. It hadn't been a dream. There had been a fire.

The windows were darkened. Alex reached up and flicked a switch on the wall and they instantly became transparent. The bright light stung his eyes. They were on the daylight side of the earth at the moment. Alex wiggled out of the elastics holding him to the mattress with great difficulty. Every muscle ached and complained as he moved, but he was soon free of the bed and floating towards the door.

Alex opened the door and saw the closed hatch leading to the node. He suddenly felt a surge of panic.

Where is my dad? What happened to the rest of the crew? And where are the Fritzers?

"He's awake!" Elodie's voice came from the Commons. Alex turned and saw her and Jennifer looking at him through the hatch. Her face looked puffy and her voice sounded raspy, devoid of its usual pep.

Alex moved quickly towards them. Elodie grabbed him in a tight embrace, and Alex thought she might never let go. She buried her head in his shoulder.

"We didn't know what to do," she said.

"How long has it...I mean how long was I out?" Alex asked. The shakiness in his voice surprised even him.

"I think it's been two hours."

"I don't remember falling asleep."

"After you got the hatch closed, there was some kind of explosion and we were all pushed against the wall. You hit your head hard and were knocked out. We tried to wake you, but you wouldn't respond, and we didn't even know if..." Elodie's voice trailed off.

Alex felt his face with his hand. His whole head hurt, and he could feel the blisters on his skin and a large painful bump on the back of his head.

"Have you heard from the rest of the crew?"

"No."

Alex noticed Jennifer floating at the table. She was just staring at them, saying nothing. Her hair was loose and floating wildly around her head in every direction. She looked angry and shocked. She didn't even make a move to approach Alex.

Alex freed himself from Elodie's arms. "We have to try

to contact the others," he said. He went to a panel on the wall and pushed a few buttons. Then he noticed the red icon in the corner. They were not connected to the station's central computer. The main computer was housed in the node and probably destroyed. There was a backup in the lab, but that one might have been damaged also, or the data lines connecting the modules might have been severed. It was actually a miracle they still had power.

Alex checked the pressure. It was around 8 psi, pretty low but still manageable. He knew that oxygen was piped into the air from big tanks on the outside of the space station, but he didn't know if the ducts went through the Node to reach the hotel. He also knew that there were carbon dioxide scrubbers in several modules, but he couldn't remember which ones or how they were powered. He was going to have to check that.

"Is it working?" Elodie asked.

"No, we can't seem to connect to the servers and all the communication runs through them."

"What are we going to do?"

"I don't know."

Suddenly, Jennifer turned to Alex with dagger eyes. "You don't know! You don't KNOW! NewStar sends us to space with a teenager on the crew. One who doesn't know anything! Just to prove how safe it is in space. Look how safe it is!" Alex was stunned into silence.

"Jennifer, stop it!" Elodie practically shouted at her stepmother. "He's just trying to help!"

"We are going to die up here!" Jennifer shouted hysterically as she threw her hands up in the air. "My husband might already be dead!"

Alex didn't know what to say. He wanted to disappear,

but he coudln't escape the domestic squabble of these two stubborn and persistent women.

"Are you crazy?" Elodie screamed. "It's not Alex's fault that we're in here. We're lucky he happened to be here and we're not alone!"

Jennifer glared at them for a few seconds and then turned away. She hid her face from them but her sobbing was easy to hear. Alex was still in a stunned silence. Elodie came over and hovered above him. Alex couldn't help but feel that maybe Jennifer was right. He was the crew member, the one who was supposed to know what to do. The rest of the crew might not even be alive. The thought made him shudder.

Alex looked around. If he was the only trained crewmember available, he would have to figure this out. He tried to assess their situation. They had power and breathable air, at least for a while. They also had plenty of food and water in the galley supplies. But they couldn't live in the hotel forever, they needed some way to get home. And to do that, they needed to go back into the node and then out to the docking compartments where the ships were located. He remembered his father's lesson about always going to the ship before closing hatches.

So much for that rule. There's no way we could have made it to the ships alive with a fire and an air leak. I didn't think there was supposed to be anything flammable up here. How did this happen?

Alex tried to think through what he'd seen. The node had been burned by a fire. An explosion or fire would have released a lot of gas into the atmosphere. Since they were in a giant closed can, those gasses would have increased the air pressure to a point where it might have damaged the station's structure. Alex vaguely remembered something about pressure relief valves. Maybe one of those had opened to let out the extra pressure.

If a valve had opened to let out the pressure, maybe it had closed again, which would mean that some air might be left in the node. They could try to open the hatch and see if they could make it to the ships. It would help if there was a way to check the pressure in the node before opening the hatch. But with the computers down, he wasn't sure how to do it.

"What are you thinking about?" Elodie asked.

"I'm wondering if we should try to open the hatch to the node," Alex said.

"We talked about that while you were out," Elodie said. "We weren't sure if the fire might still be going on."

"It's more than the fire I'm worried about," Alex said. "The air was leaking out of the station, and there might be no pressure left in the node."

"That sounds bad. Can we just hold our breath and go fast?"

"No, it's not just that you won't have air to breathe. If you take away the air pressure around your body, the air inside your lungs and blood vessels would explode your body like a balloon."

Elodie cringed.

"Let's go have a look," suggested Alex. "There might be a way we can measure the air pressure before we try to open it."

"OK," said Elodie. She looked over at her stepmother, who was crouched near the window with her head buried in her hands.

Alex decided to try and make peace with her. "Jennifer,

I'm going to go check out the hatch and see if there is something we can do. Just wait here. I promise I'll figure out a plan for us."

Jennifer turned her head to look at him but didn't say anything. Her blue eyes were moist and she rolled them slightly to show Alex that she did not trust him at all to better their situation.

Alex decided to ignore her and he turned away and headed into the hotel corridor with Elodie by his side. They approached the hatch and floated silently in front of it for several minutes.

Elodie finally asked, "Do you think we could open it a little and see what it looks like?"

"I'm not sure," said Alex. He tried to think about his training, but there wasn't anything to cover this type of case. He supposed if there was air on the other side of the hatch, it should be safe to open. And if there was no air, then the pressure inside the hotel would push against the hatch and make it difficult or impossible to open. "I guess we can give it a try."

"OK," said Elodie. Alex pulled himself into position on the support bar below the hatch. Elodie made no move to help him. Alex turned the crank to unlatch the hatch, grabbed the lower handle and tugged gently upwards. There was no motion. He pulled harder until he was straining. There was still no motion. He relaxed and gave a forceful pull as hard as he could. He grunted at the strain, but nothing happened.

"Maybe we could try together?" Alex suggested. Elodie looked slightly annoyed, but she positioned herself next to Alex.

"On three," Alex said. "One...two...three!" They both

pulled and grunted and strained. The hatch wouldn't move even a little.

"OK," said Alex, panting. "Let it go. We must have lost all air pressure in the node, which means we'll never get it opened. And even if we did, our air would leak out and we'd be dead in a few minutes."

Elodie released the hatch and turned slowly towards Alex. Her mouth was closed tightly, and she looked like she was fighting back tears. She blinked a few times quickly before asking in a voice that was almost a whisper, "So does that mean that my dad is..." Her voice trailed off and she covered her face with her hands.

"No, no," said Alex. He grabbed her in his arms and wrapped them tightly around her. "They are probably safe in the crew quarters with the hatch closed, just like us." Alex wanted to believe this as much as Elodie.

They are safe in crew quarters. They are going to come rescue us. My dad knows what to do in every situation. He'll fix this.

Elodie was sobbing, but trying not to show it. With his arms tightly around her, Alex could feel every one of her short breaths and the muffled whines coming from her throat as she exhaled. Her brown hair was still in a tight bun in the back of her head, but some strands had come loose and danced around Alex's face, tickling his skin. The warmth of Elodie's body brought some comfort and hope to Alex, like feeling the heat of a fire on a cold winter day.

After several minutes, Elodie's breathing slowed to a regular rhythm and Alex loosened his grip.

"Look, Elodie," said Alex. "It's...well, it's going to be OK. My dad will figure something out. If we were able to survive this explosion or whatever it was, he definitely did. We just need to figure out how to keep everything working until they can come rescue us."

"But how will they rescue us? We can't open the hatch and there's no other way out of here."

"I don't know yet," said Alex. "We need to find a way to communicate with them. Or with mission control."

"I have my phone but it stopped working after all this happened," Elodie said.

"Yeah, it was using the station's communication system which is down. There must be some other way to establish communications," Alex muttered, mostly to himself. He tried to remember if there were any other radios onboard besides the ones in the wall communication panels. The Venturer used radios and so did the spacesuits. Maybe there was some way to set up the system to use a radio instead of a wired link through the server.

"I think we have some reading to do," said Alex.

"What kind of reading?" Elodie asked.

"Probably not the type you're going to like."

Alex pushed off the ceiling and propelled himself Superman-style towards the Commons hatchway. Elodie followed close behind. Jennifer was near the window, staring out at the earth with her back to them.

"No luck with the hatch," he said to her. She didn't respond. Alex didn't bother wasting any more time with her. He pulled out two computer tablets from storage and tossed one to Elodie.

"These are the space station procedures and manuals," he said. "We need to see if there's any backup radio system that we can use. The main communication uses the station's computer server, which I think might have been destroyed. Ever read a technical manual before?"

"I don't usually do reading."

"Well, time to start."

Jennifer let out a deep sigh. Alex thought he heard her mumble something about this being the end, before she said, "I need to go lay down for a few minutes." She left the Commons for the hotel.

Alex flicked on his tablet and clicked on the NewStar Technical Manual. He directed Elodie to do the same. Soon the two of them were floating around the Commons in all kinds of orientations, their noses buried in their tablets, reading silently as if they were lounging in a local library.

CHAPTER 25

Scott Weber whistled as he exited his convertible BMW and strode towards the glass office building that housed NewStar One's mission control. It was a sticky July afternoon in southeast Houston. The windows were dripping with condensation as the thick summer air met the cold glass of the air-conditioned building.

Scott loved his job as a mission director. He led a small team of engineers that monitored and controlled the NewStar One space station, home to astronauts doing important scientific work as well as world-famous hotel guests. Tonight he was on the "swing" shift, from 3 PM - 12 AM. These were the coveted rock-star hours, where you could sleep in late and then get off work with just enough time to hit the bars for an hour or two before last call. As a single thirty-one year old who liked to drive fast, party hard and pick up girls, it was the ideal shift in an ideal job.

Despite a few issues at the start, Scott felt like the space station had been functioning well. There were enough minor glitches to keep things interesting, but not so many that the team's nerves began to fray. Scott and his fellow mission controllers could even spare a few hours here and there to watch sports on one of their numerous workstation monitors.

Scott strutted down the hallway to the double doors marked "Mission Operations: Authorized Personnel Only." He flicked his badge against the card reader in the wall and pulled open the door to the large room. He knew instantly that something was wrong.

The operations staff usually consisted of a mission director, a space station systems operator and a ground systems operator. Other specialist engineers would come and go as needed, but they generally spent most of their time at their desks and would come into the control room only for specific events like software uploads, maintenance activities, or to answer questions from the astronauts onboard. Today, however, the room was packed with nearly every engineer they had on staff.

Scott spotted Stewart Sanders, the company CEO, in the back row. He was leaning back in a chair and was white-faced. The man was usually animated and most of the time angry at something. Scott then looked up at the center screen where the overall space station status was continuously displayed. His trained eye immediately noticed the "Loss of Signal" icon in the upper-right corner. Below it was a timer that read "+02:48:21." That would mean they had been out of contact with the space station for nearly three hours!

Scott looked around the room and prepared himself for a very busy night.

*****

"Alex, take a look at this!" Elodie said excitedly. She showed him a drawing she was looking at on her tablet. "This shows an air duct that goes from here out into the

Node and all the way out to the docking compartment. Maybe we can crawl through this!"

Alex looked at the drawing on the screen. He wondered if maybe he would be better off without Elodie's "help" on this project.

"That's a good idea," Alex said. "But look here - the pipe diameter is only three inches. And this symbol here is a valve, which automatically shuts off in the event of an air leak."

"Oh."

Well, at least she keeps me from falling asleep reading. This is the most boring book I've ever seen.

Alex and Elodie had been searching the manuals for nearly two hours. From what Alex could tell, Elodie was mostly looking at the drawings. Not that the words had been that much more helpful to him. Alex had learned that their air supply, normally provided from tanks located outside the airlock, would have been automatically shut off in the leak. They were probably going to run out of air at some point. The power lines all ran on the outside of the space station to each module, and surprisingly seemed to be undamaged since the lights and fans were still running in the hotel section. The hotel had a dedicated water storage tank and recycling system, so water shouldn't be a problem for them. There had been no mention of any radio system besides the one outside the space station used to contact Houston. That radio could only be accessed from the central computer, which was either dead or disconnected from the hotel and commons.

"I wonder if we should check on Jennifer," Alex suggested.

"Why? She was acting like a lunatic. I wish she wasn't

even here," said Elodie. Alex shrugged.

"I don't know. She seemed pretty upset, and maybe she is in shock or depression or something."

"She's just super dramatic. I mean, you and I are here trying to figure this whole thing out and she - the ADULT in the situation - just acts all crazy like she's the only one having problems right now."

Alex didn't feel like arguing. Jennifer had been stubborn and petulant, but she was still a person who was stuck in the same bad situation as them and besides, she might have some ideas. Alex left for the hotel. Elodie trailed him reluctantly. Alex knocked on the door and when there was no answer, he slid it open. Jennifer was laying in the bed against the wall, the elastic straps holding her against the mattress. She was awake and looked over as Alex entered.

"How are you doing?" Alex asked.

"I'm fine, I just have a headache," said Jennifer flatly.

"Why don't you come out and get something to eat with us? We're trying to figure a way out of this and we could use your help."

"I think we should wait for someone who knows what they're doing to rescue us. No offense, but you and little miss pretty over there are not going to figure out a way to save us. We need to wait for the real astronauts to come and help us. Or those mission control guys to send a rescue ship. So I'm going to wait until I hear from one of them."

Alex couldn't stand this woman who was older than him acting like a child in the middle of a serious situation. He let out an audible groan and left the room quickly before he started arguing, which would have been pointless. Elodie closed the door and gave him a look that so much as said, *I told you so.*

They returned to the Commons. Alex made some dinner - macaroni and cheese for both of them, with hot sauce. They ate in silence. Alex wanted to return to the technical manuals, but Elodie suggested they take a break and watch a movie to lighten the mood. Reluctantly, Alex agreed. His mind was shot, and he wasn't going to get anything useful done if he burned himself out completely.

He set up the projector and they watched an old pirate movie while floating freely in space, feeling as though they were in the most comfortable movie lounge chairs on or off the earth. At the end of the movie, when the main characters came together and kissed, Elodie wrapped her arm around Alex's waist. He didn't move at all, but just let her float near him with her arm around him as the credits began to roll.

"I'm exhausted," Elodie said. Alex felt tired too. His head still ached from the earlier exertion, and watching the movie had cleaned the adrenaline out of his system, leaving him feeling drained. He knew that they had a limited air supply and should do something, but he didn't have any better idea what to do besides read manuals, which in his current state was a recipe for a fast trip to the land of nod.

"Maybe we should sleep for a couple hours. But not long. I don't know how much oxygen is left in the air. We need to keep looking for a way out of here, but I think I need a little rest before I can keep going."

"Me too," said Elodie. She paused for a few seconds and then added, "I don't really want to sleep alone though."

"I can't..." Alex started, but Elodie interrupted him by saying, "Not like that. I know you have a girlfriend, but I just don't want to be alone."

Alex didn't really want to be alone either. He was afraid he might never wake up again. "OK," he said.

Alex turned off the projector and the two of them went to Elodie's room. They didn't even bother to change clothes. Elodie wiped her face with a wet washcloth while Alex slid beneath the elastic straps on the wall-mounted bed.

Elodie climbed in next to Alex a few minutes later. Beneath the covers, he felt her hand wrap around his. The two of them floated against the wall-bed, held down by a few elastic straps. Alex had never slept this close to another person. He felt uncomfortable and daring doing something that only grown adults normally do. He also felt unsure about what he should do, but his exhaustion was too strong to allow the awkwardness of the encounter to keep him awake. They both fell asleep within minutes, their fingers still entwined.

CHAPTER 26

WHEN HE WOKE UP, ALEX'S HEAD WAS THROBBING. HE CHECKED his watch. It was one o'clock in the morning. Elodie was still sleeping, her breathing slow and steady in his ear. As quietly as he could, Alex slipped out of the bed and checked the computer terminal on the opposite wall. The environmental display showed the oxygen level in the atmosphere as 17%. Alex remembered that it was usually around 21%. They were using up the oxygen.

Luckily, the carbon dioxide level remained normal for the space station at 815 parts per million. That meant the scrubbers were cleaning it out of the air as they were designed. But with their oxygen supply line cut off, it was only a matter of time before the lack of oxygen would render them useless.

Alex's headache reminded him of the one he had experienced in the hyperbaric chamber training right before he had passed out. At least this time he wasn't hyperventilating - yet. The situation certainly warranted a panicked response, but somehow Alex was calm. He tried to think of something they could do to get more oxygen. Was there anything in storage that could be turned into oxygen? Maybe with some kind of chemical reaction? He racked his brain, but the chemistry eluded him and anyway, there weren't many chemicals available in the hotel area besides food products and toiletries.

The only other hope was to find a way out of the hotel. If they could just get to Venturer or Destiny, they would be safe. The ships had their own power sources, their own life support systems and communication with the ground.

The problem, of course, was that to get there, they needed to go through a module that had been depressurized and was probably still exposed to space. The air pressure in the hotel was keeping them alive but was also keeping the hatch forced shut. In order to open the hatch, they would have to depressurize the hotel corridor, which meant they would die unless they were wearing spacesuits.

If only we had spacesuits here. They were all in the airlock and were probably destroyed by the fire.

Alex looked around the room. He just needed something big enough to hold a person and strong enough to withstand around 8 pounds of pressure per square inch, the current pressure left in the hotel. They needed something that wouldn't leak air out. Or would at least leak it out slowly enough that they could make it to the ships before all the air escaped. It didn't have to be perfect. Just good enough to last ten or maybe fifteen minutes.

Then it hit him. Alex rushed out of the hotel room and towards the Commons.

*****

Stewart slumped in the chair at the head of the table in the modern mission control conference room. It was nearly two in the morning, but the building was buzzing with more activity than ever, even more than during their first launch.

Scott Weber opened the door and entered the room. He walked confidently to the front and whispered something to a young man sitting at a computer terminal in the corner of the room. A few seconds later, a graphic appeared on the screen showing the orbit of NewStar One. The space station was surrounded by several red dots on the screen.

Scott stepped to the front of the room next to the projector screen and began talking.

"This is the NewStar One orbital data we received from Space Force Command. You can see unidentified objects that were detected in its orbit shortly after we lost contact. This is consistent with an explosion event, which Space Command has observed on several occasions with older unmanned satellites."

The graphic changed to a series of line charts, most of which showed steady lines that jumped up near the end of the chart.

"The data we did receive before losing contact indicated smoke or other particulates in the interior atmosphere and a sharp spike in air pressure before it began to quickly fall. What little data we have seems to indicate the issue originated in the airlock. If there was an explosion, it would take a great deal of force to rupture the hull, but the airlock hatch window is one of the weakest structural points in the spacecraft. It is still designed to withstand more than double the normal station pressure, but a direct impact by debris from an explosion could cause a rupture. This would have resulted in depressurization and debris in space. The trajectory of the debris seems consistent with this kind of an event."

Stewart looked at the data, most of which he had

already seen. A sense of horror and panic filled his gut for what seemed like the tenth time today. He had been able to shake it for a few brief moments but it always returned.

Scott continued, "We still do not know the cause of the explosion, but we are looking in more detail at the atmospheric data and may have an answer on that soon. At this time, we have been unable to establish contact with NewStar or the crew despite multiple attempts on normal and emergency frequencies. Per procedure, we would have expected them to evacuate the space station; however, there has been no communication with Venturer or Destiny, which indicates they are still not activated." Scott paused and swallowed hard. His voice choked a little as he said, "At this time, sir, we have to assume that all crew and guests have been lost."

Scott had worked closely with Mike Stone for the past several years. He had never met his boy, Alex. Of course he knew of the tragic death of Barbara Stone. Scott tried not to think about it. He did his best to maintain his professional demeanor, as he had been trained in his former career with the Air Force. He looked across the table at Stewart who was pale and speechless.

"OK, everyone out," Stewart said. A few people at the table looked puzzled. Nobody moved. "I said OUT!"

The room cleared quickly. Stewart buried his face in his hands. After several minutes in silence, he walked out of the room, down the hallway and exited the glass doors into the humid night. He found his car, climbed into the driver's seat, and sped out of the parking lot.

*****

Alex rocketed into the Commons only to be met by a

jungle of debris. Kitchen trays, utensils, sports equipment, tools, empty bags, food and paper were bobbing around like garbage in the ocean. Alex looked through it and saw Jennifer on the other side of the module, near the window. She was grasping a handrail and banging her fist against the wall. A stream of profanities flowed screechingly out of her mouth.

Embarrassed to watch this display of an adult tantrum, Alex turned to slink away before he remembered the whole reason he had come in the first place. He moved towards the supply cabinet, but it had been mostly emptied. Jennifer noticed him and suddenly went silent.

Feeling awkward, Alex turned to face her.

"What are you looking at," she muttered.

Alex moved towards her, unsure of what to say. "Is everything OK?" he finally asked. She turned away from him, but Alex could hear small whimpers emanating from her throat.

"I can't do this...John's dead." Her voice was barely a whisper.

"He might not be dead," Alex offered.

"We're going to die. I can't take it anymore. I just want it to be over...now." She paused. "It's just too much." Alex looked her over. He was annoyed at her childish attitude, but he also knew how it felt to lose someone. She was worried about John. Feeling sympathetic, Alex reached out his arm to touch her shoulder. When he did, she pulled towards him and soon Alex found himself holding her in an awkward embrace as she curled her body into a ball against his as her shoulders heaved with quiet sobs.

"Jennifer," he said quietly. "We're not going to die. I think I know a way to get us to Venturer. But I need your help. Elodie needs your help too."

"No she doesn't, she hates me," Jennifer said through sniffles.

"I'm sure she doesn't hate you," Alex lied. "Our oxygen levels are getting low. That makes you not think clearly. Please, Jennifer, just help me and we can get out of here."

There was a long pause. Finally, Jennifer took a deep breath. "What do I need to do?"

CHAPTER 27

ELODIE WOKE UP ALONE IN THE HOTEL ROOM. IT WAS ORBITAL night, so even when she clicked the button to turn the window glass transparent, there was not much additional light. She turned the room lights to the dimmest setting and tried to rub the sleepiness out of her eyes. The clock on the wall read 4 AM.

Her body felt heavy and slow, despite the weightless environment. She wanted her dad there to rub her hair and tell her to wake up and get moving. She tried not to think about the fact that she might never feel his hand against her head again or hear his jubilant voice.

Slowly, she made her way out of the bed. She undid the ponytail she had formed before sleeping and her hair exploded around her head. Taking a brush from its Velcro nest against the wall by the mirror, she tried to straighten the wild strands. After only a little progress, she gave up and twisted the hair into a bun and fastened it firmly with an elastic.

Why am I so tired?

Elodie took a big pull from the straw of a water pouch velcroed to the wall and then left the room, struggling to find enough energy to slide the door open. She entered the commons and her eyes widened. The place was a mess, with all sorts of stuff haphazardly strapped or velcroed to the walls. Alex was in the middle of the room using scissors to cut a hole into a large equipment bag. Jennifer was rummaging through a storage closet.

"What's going on?" Elodie asked, her voice raspy with sleep.

"Oh, hey," said Alex, turning to her with a smile. "Just doing a little arts and crafts project."

"Huh?"

"I'm working on a way to get us out of here." Alex stopped what he was doing, pushed off the floor and met Elodie at the entrance to the Commons.

"Listen," he said in a low whisper. "Jennifer is in bad shape."

"What do you mean?"

Alex looked back at Jennifer, who was still busy picking through a cabinet. "Come with me," he said. He led Elodie into the hotel corridor on the other side of the hatch.

"When I woke up she had emptied half of our storage all around the room and was screaming curses and banging the window," Alex said, his voice still low. "I think the low oxygen levels and the stress are getting to her."

"Oh, she's such a drama queen! Alex, she can get so crazy sometimes." Elodie started to feel her throat choking up. She had always hated how needy Jennifer was and how she always found ways to steal her dad's attention away from her. "I wish my dad had never met her."

"Elodie!" Alex sounded surprised. "She's still your family. Anyway, it doesn't matter. I have an idea to get us to the ships and I need your help."

"What is it?"

"It's easier to show you. Follow me."

*****

The NewStar engineering team was fading rapidly. Most had been at work the entire day and then stayed on through the night. The sun would be rising in about an hour. Scott had pushed them to review and re-review all the data from just before they lost contact, but no new information was discovered. By now, almost all shreds of hope had vanished, and when some individuals approached asking if they could go home to get some sleep, Scott had reluctantly agreed to let them go.

He sat at the mission director's chair, staring at his screen and willing the red boxes that indicated loss of signal to turn green. By now, he had pretty much given up hope too. When the sun rose on a new day, the company would need to reveal to the news media what had happened. John Fritzer was dead, along with his family and all the crew aboard NewStar One. The company was finished.

Melanie Howell came bursting into the room wearing a crisp suit with her hair perfectly coiffed. She marched straight over to Scott.

"Have you seen Stewart?" she asked. Her voice was strained.

"Not since the briefing a few hours ago. He kicked us out. Did you check the conference room?"

"Yes, of course I did. How could he not even answer his phone in a situation like this?"

"He didn't look too good."

"Well, nobody is looking too good right now," Melanie shot back. "I've arranged for a press briefing at 10 AM.

They have no idea what's about to hit them."

"Better to get it over with than try to hide it. The last thing we need is to be accused of covering things up."

"I need Stewart to agree before we say anything. So let me know if you find him. Oh, and you're going to be at the press conference so put on something that makes it look like you didn't just roll out of bed. Be at the auditorium at 9:45 sharp."

Scott cringed. He normally had no problem being on camera or talking about a mission, but the last thing he wanted was to be the face that the world saw when this news was delivered. Melanie didn't wait for a response and turned to march out of NewStar's now useless mission control as quickly as she had entered.

*****

"What is it?" Elodie asked.

"It's going to be a spacesuit," Alex replied, beaming.

"Are you kidding me? A bag?"

"Not just any bag. It's a bag that will be lined on the inside with duct tape."

"OK, Alex. I think the lack of oxygen or whatever is getting to you too. This is not a spacesuit."

"Look, all we need is something to hold pressure around our bodies for about five minutes while we get from the hotel to the ships. We don't even need any extra oxygen, what's in the bag around us will be enough."

"How do you know that?"

"Well, I don't for sure, but it makes sense. I mean most people can hold their breath for like a minute. We only need five breaths of air each."

"I definitely can't hold my breath for a minute."

"You can have some of my oxygen then."

"Why are you cutting holes in the bag if it's going to be a spacesuit?"

"That's the tricky part. We need some kind of arms to move ourselves along. I'm going to cut some other fabric into a tube and attach it to the holes. We can put our arms in them and push off the handrails and walls. We'll have to make those really tight so they don't come off. Lots of duct tape."

Elodie shook her head. Jennifer came over, bringing some rolls of duct tape she had found. After calming down and getting to work, she had become much more helpful.

"So we need to make three of these spacesuits?" Elodie asked.

"Well, about that," Alex said. "We only have two of the really large equipment bags that will fit a whole person. We're going to have to double up in one of the bags."

"I'm really not so sure about this, Alex."

"Don't worry. I have a plan to test them before we use them. We can inflate them using the hand pump that we use for the sports equipment. That way we'll make sure they hold pressure before we try to use them. Besides, do you have any better ideas?"

"Not really," Elodie admitted.

"I think we should try it," Jennifer said meekly. At least she was on Alex's side now, even if she was crazy.

"Alright, let's get to work," said Alex. The three of them began cutting fabric and laying out duct tape against the inner walls of the bags. As they worked, Alex glanced up at the wall panel and noticed the oxygen level reading had turned red. It was at a dangerously low level of 12%. He shut off the display before anyone else could see it.

CHAPTER 28

THE BAG SPACESUITS LOOKED UGLY, BUT ALL THAT MATTERED WAS whether they would work. Alex had closed one of them up and was now vigorously pumping air into a small hole with a hand pump. The hole around the pump needle had been sealed with duct tape, just like everything else in this homemade contraption. According to the label, duct tape was supposed to be able to seal up air ducts that were running at high pressure. Hopefully they weren't over-hyping the capabilities of the famous gray fix-it-all.

As the air filled the bag's interior, it began to balloon out and the walls became firm. Alex kept pumping and watching the small pressure gauge attached to the pump. When it reached 10 psi, he stopped. The gauge began to fall slowly.

"Darn it," Alex said. "There's a leak somewhere."

"Let me see if I can find it," Elodie said. She began orbiting the ugly gray and white beast they had created. There were two fabric tubes for arms that now jutted out of the bottom of the bag. The front of the bag had a squarish hole that had been replaced with a piece of clear plastic they had found in storage. This would let them see where they were going, although the visibility was very limited.

Elodie traced the edges of the plastic with her palm, but she felt nothing. Then she moved on to the arms. When her fingers passed over the mass of duct tape that formed the joint between the duffel-bag shaped arm and the larger bag that would house their bodies, she could feel air blowing against her skin.

"There's a bit of a leak here," she said. "Let me try to tape it up a little more."

Alex pumped some more air into the bag to keep it from deflating too quickly while Elodie wrapped more tape around the arms.

"All done," she said. Alex stopped pumping and watched the gauge. After about a minute, he began to feel a sense of relief. The pressure was holding!

"This might actually work," said Alex.

"Yeah, that's totally the confidence I'm looking for in something that my life is going to depend on," replied Elodie. Alex turned and stuck out his tongue at her. She smiled back at him.

"Now we just have to test the other one and we'll be ready to go," Alex said. He removed the needle from the bag and covered the tiny hole with several layers of duct tape on both sides. He went to work on the other bag suit while Elodie and Jennifer heated up some lunch.

"So if there are only two suits, who's riding together?" Elodie asked as she placed several food containers into the rehydrator.

"Maybe you and Jennifer should go together in one and I'll take the other. That way you can help each other out," Alex suggested.

The two women were silent. *Or maybe not,* thought Alex.

"Maybe I should be the one to go alone," said Jennifer solemnly.

"I think that's fine," said Elodie in an upbeat voice.

"Well, I don't know," said Alex. "We won't have any radios to talk to each other. Could you handle anything that might go wrong alone?"

"Are you saying that I can't handle myself?" Jennifer asked, glaring at Alex.

OK, OK. Sorry I asked.

Alex went back to work on the bag suit without saying anything else. He had created the pinhole and placed the needle inside it. He began to pump the hand pump furiously. His arms were burning from the day's exertions. He would be glad when this whole thing was over.

Alex pumped harder and harder as the bag began to firm up. The pressure gauge read 7 psi. Just a little more air to go and this one would be done. Alex kept pumping. Suddenly, he heard the sound of a tear. He looked up just in time to see the right arm swing to the side as it popped off the bag and opened like a door on a hinge. The bag deflated instantly, along with Alex's face. All of his work to pump up the bag would have to be repeated after he fixed the arm.

To make matters worse, the alarm tone began to ring in the module's speakers. Alex rushed to a wall panel and found, as he expected, that the oxygen levels were critically low.

*****

Scott ignored the third phone call coming from the Australian ground site. He knew they were calling to tell him that they couldn't make contact with NewStar on the latest scheduled track. His manager had told him to cancel all of their antenna passes. It cost money to lease the huge satellite dishes that tracked NewStar One across the sky, and the antenna operators were starting to become suspicious of the many scheduled tracks where no signal was received and no data was passed back to Houston. Scott knew he should cancel the service, but it felt like putting a final nail into NewStar One's coffin. He let the phone go until the ringing finally stopped.

The control center had emptied, the final engineer having left about 30 minutes earlier. Scott sat in the mission director chair and stared in disbelief at the dark and empty computer monitors lined up in neat rows. What could possibly have happened up there? What little information they had certainly pointed to some sort of explosion, but how was that even possible? Mike was one of the most careful and talented astronauts Scott had ever met, and he had met quite a few. It seemed unthinkable that Mike would have let something happen.

There had been a lot of little problems discovered with the station. Maybe there had been a larger problem lurking somewhere deep in the guts of the metallic beast, just waiting to lurch out at an unsuspecting crew. Like on Apollo 13 when faulty electronics had led to an oxygen tank explosion.

Scott shook his head. He was going to be without a job very soon, but that was nothing compared to the sacrifice the crew had made for this experiment in commercializing outer space.

The phone rang again. It was Melanie Howell. This time Scott picked it up.

"Scott, have you seen Stewart?"

"No, I still haven't seen or heard from him."

"Damn. Nobody's seen him. What the hell is he thinking? Scott, this is starting to leak out. Someone found out from space command that there was debris in our orbit, and I'm starting to get questions. We're going to have to go public with this soon, before it gets out other ways and it looks like we're covering it up."

"What does it matter, Melanie? The company is done either way."

"Yeah, well I'm hoping to be able to find another job after this. Stewart can go into hiding and look like a royal asshole, but I'm not going down with him!"

The phone line went dead and Scott placed the handset back in the cradle. There was no way to handle this situation gracefully with the press, even for an expert like Melanie. They were in it deep. He might as well admit it. And so he picked up the phone and dialed Australia to start canceling communication attempts with NewStar One.

*****

Alex's cheeks felt flush. He knew they didn't have much time left. Repairing the second suit could take another hour. Would they even be conscious by then? He looked over at Elodie. Her wide brown eyes were filled with worry. She looked vulnerable, which actually enhanced her natural beauty.

"We don't have a lot of air left," Alex said, stating the obvious. "I think we should give up on the second suit and see if we can all fit in the working one."

"All three of us?" Jennifer asked incredulously.

"Yes, it will be tight, but we're running out of time."

"Tight? It's impossible! That gym bag will not hold

three people."

"We have to try," said Alex.

"No way," said Jennifer. "Why don't you two go and then Alex can come back and get me?"

"That won't work. To exit the hotel, we have to depressurize the entire module. The only air left will be inside the bag."

Jennifer's eyes widened. "Oh," she said. "You're going to let all the air out?"

"We have to," said Alex. "The air is pushing against the hatch to hold it shut. Unless we evacuate it to space, the hatch will never open."

Jennifer was silent. The sobering reality of their situation seemed to be finally sinking into her.

Alex continued, "Look, I know this bag spacesuit doesn't look like much, but it should work. Once we depressurize the module, though, there's no turning back."

Then he added, "If we do nothing, we are going to be out of oxygen and unconscious in just a few short hours, or less."

With a look of genuine fear, Jennifer said, "OK, let's try to fit in."

"Alright," Alex said. "I'll go in first so that I can reach the arm holes and push us along. Elodie should be able to fit in next to me. Jennifer, I want you to come in back-to-back with me. Then you'll zipper the bag shut and seal it with duct tape. After that I'll open the hatch valve. The bag will seem to inflate but really all the air around it is going away. Then we open the hatch and make a quick trip down the corridor to Venturer. Easy, right?"

Alex hoped his voice sounded confident, but all he could think about was what would happen if the bag didn't hold the air pressure. They would be dead in minutes as the blood literally boiled inside of them.

Don't think about that. Don't think about that.

Alex looked over at Elodie and Jennifer. Both looked terrified, their skin pale and their eyes wide. Alex floated over and gave them each a hug. With Jennifer, it was an awkward embrace. However, Elodie fell easily into his arms and held him tightly, burying her head in his shoulder. Then she looked up at him and put her hand up to his cheek. Without warning, she pulled him close and kissed him deeply. Alex felt lightheaded, and he wasn't sure if it was from the kiss or the lack of oxygen. When Elodie released him, she just smiled. He smiled back. It could be his last kiss ever. There was no use in feeling guilty at this point.

Alex took a deep breath. "Here we go," he said. They carried the spacesuit bag solemnly through the hotel corridor to the front of the hatch that led to the node. Alex took two computer tablets and velcroed them to the inside of the bag. He would use them to remotely actuate the depressurization valves and close Venturer's motorized hatch once they arrived. Then he pulled the bag over himself and stuck his arms through the tiny arm holes they had made. It was an awkward fit as the holes only covered half of his arms. His elbows jutted out into the bag volume.

Elodie came in next, sliding up against Alex's side and wrapping her arms around his waist. As she came in, the entire bag tumbled backwards away from the hatch. Alex hadn't considered how they would control themselves if they weren't near a handhold.

"Jennifer," he shouted. "Can you push us up against the hatch before you get in? I want to try and grab the handle." Jennifer pushed the bag up to the hatch. Alex tried to move the stiff arm tubes up to the hatch, but with no gloves at the end, the stubby tubes could not easily grasp anything. After a few minutes of struggling, Alex asked Jennifer to put the bottom of the bag where Alex's feet were located against a handrail that was bolted to the floor. Then he had her position the arm tubes underneath the hatch handle. By pushing against the handrail with his feet and up against the hatch handle with his arms, Alex was able to keep the bag wedged in place. However, if he slipped off of this location after they were depressurized, Alex realized they might have no way to make it back. He closed his eyes and said a silent prayer before asking Jennifer to come into the bag.

Jennifer was the tallest of the three of them. The bag was already stuffed with Alex and Elodie, and it seemed impossible to think she would be able to fit. She first tried to stuff her feet into the bottom of the bag, but nearly knocked Alex's feet off the handrail. Her upper body tumbled out of the bag.

She tried again, this time using her arms to pull the bag around her shoulders. She curled her legs into the bag, being careful not to knock Alex. With a deep breath, she reached up and pulled the zipper down past her head. It felt like they were being shut into a coffin.

When the zipper reached just below her waistline, Jennifer found that she couldn't reach any lower. The bag was pressed against her face and her back was firmly against Alex's back. Elodie was sideways against Alex's right side.

"I can't reach down to close the zipper the rest of the way," she said.

"Elodie, can you reach it?" asked Alex.

"I'm not sure," said Elodie. She reached between her stepmother's legs. She couldn't see what she was doing but eventually her hand was able to find the zipper. She tugged at it, inching it down slowly from an awkward angle where she had little leverage. Finally, the zipper reached its base.

"I think it's closed all the way."

"Great," said Alex. "Now cover it all with duct tape. Overlap each piece with the tape that's already on the bag next to the zipper. We want to make sure no air leaks out." Alex floated a roll of tape over to Elodie. She tore off a long piece and covered the lower part of the zipper as best she could. Then she passed the roll to Jennifer who did the same with the top half of the zipper.

Alex took a deep breath. This was his last chance to change his mind. Keeping his right arm in place, he pulled his left arm in and tapped the computer tablet a few times. His finger hovered above the button that, once pushed, would open valves and release all the air in the hotel and commons. After that, they would have only the little air in the bag to keep them alive. If they couldn't make it to Venturer and repressurize, they would run out of air and suffocate. It would be his fault if this didn't work. Elodie and Jennifer could die because of his choice. Of course, they would all die anyway if he did nothing.

Alex's head hurt. He had loved the idea of having an adventure in space. Now, his dad might be dead and he could very well follow both of his parents in a few minutes unless things went perfectly with his crazy long-shot plan. His mind turned to Mackenzie. He could see her blond hair, her smile. Would she be upset if she knew that Elodie had kissed him? Surely, she would understand, given the circumstances.

"Now what?" Elodie asked. Alex realized he had been lost in thought and floating motionless for a while.

"I guess we give this a try," Alex said.

"So, if this doesn't work...then..."

"Yeah."

"But it will work, right?"

"I'm pretty sure."

"OK, I'm ready."

"Jennifer?"

"Yes," Jennifer squeaked. "Do it."

Alex took another deep breath. He looked at his own hand, with his index finger pointing at the glowing tablet.

Should I really do this?

He took another breath.

You have to do this. It's the only way. Just do it. Do it!

Another breath.

Then in a swift motion, Alex pushed down. The tablet read, "Command Accepted" and deep inside the space station, a series of valves popped open.

CHAPTER 29

THE AIR EXITING THE HOTEL SOUNDED LIKE A HURRICANE. ALEX could feel the air pressure pulling at their "spacesuit," and he stiffened his arms in the tubes to keep the suit from being pulled away from the hatch. Jennifer let out a little scream as the noise increased around them. Elodie squeezed Alex so tight around his middle that he could barely breathe.

The suit seemed to grow and balloon out, just as Alex had anticipated. The air around them was disappearing and the air inside their bag was trying to escape but meeting the resistance of the tape-coated walls.

The sound of wind began to die out, and soon there was only the sound of three people breathing. All the other sounds of the space station were gone. There was no more hum of fans, no sound of alarms or computers or radio calls. The silence was more complete than Alex had ever experienced.

"Did we make it?" Elodie asked quietly.

"Well, the depress is done," said Alex. He found himself breathing quickly, which he knew was a bad idea. There was only a little air inside the bag. He tried to calm his nerves and focus.

"OK, OK, so now we open the hatch," said Alex. If this didn't work, they were dead for sure. He pushed his feet against the bottom of the bag. It was harder to feel the handrail through the duct tape and fabric now that the bag walls were so stiff. With the added stiffness, it took Alex a lot of effort to bend the arms slightly and straighten his legs in an attempt to slide the hatch up along its rails. It moved slowly at first, and then more quickly until it was about halfway open. Alex couldn't bend the arm tubes any more at that point.

"I think this is as far as I can get the hatch opened," said Alex.

"Is it enough?" asked Elodie.

"I'm sure we can fit through."

"OK."

Alex moved his arms down and tried to push off with his feet towards the open part of the hatch. He expected the suit to follow him, but instead he moved inside the suit and his head pushed against the top of the bag. The suit began to move away from the handrail, but they were too high to make it through the opening. Alex looked through the small strip of clear plastic they had installed near the "head" of their spacesuit and saw the gray metal of the hatch just before they crashed into it and tumbled off into the open space of the hotel corridor.

The three of them tumbled inside the bag, arms and legs becoming entangled as they bounced off the hatch and then hit the ceiling. Alex tried desperately to right himself and gain control of their motion. He finally was able to slide his arms back into the tubes. Looking through the plastic, he saw they were moving towards the door to hotel room 4.

Alex strained against the stiffness of the pressurized armhole, trying to bend it so that he could catch the large door handle and push back towards the hatch. He grunted as his arm struggled, and miraculously he caught his target. He felt them stop as his arm caught the door handle. He pushed against the door and they reversed direction, heading back towards the hatch.

When they approached the hatch this time, Alex stopped them by using the end of the arm tube like a mitten and clutching the handrail by squeezing his hand. It took much more effort than he would have expected, and his hand squeezed hard until it hurt. He put his other arm forward and pulled along the next handrail until their spacesuit bag was being pulled into the Node.

Inside the Node, there were no lights or computers. Slivers of sunlight cut through from the airlock windows above them. Some of the walls seemed charred, but it was hard to tell for certain in the dim and uneven light. As Alex moved through the Node, he was able to get a brief glance at the airlock. It was nearly devoid of the usual equipment and papers. Then he noticed the windows inside the pressurized changing area. Only jagged edges of thick glass remained in the windowpane. The rest of the glass was gone, exposing the entire module - and in fact all the modules of the station that did not have closed hatches - to space.

For a brief moment, he panicked, picturing the three of them being sucked out the window and into space, lost forever in their suit. His already sore hand gripped the handrail even harder through layers of duct tape and Nomex. But then he remembered there was no air left to suck them away.

Alex could only see what was directly in front of him.

As he gripped one handrail, he had to feel for the next one by memory, often unable to see it before his arm made contact. With Elodie and Jennifer attached to him, everything moved slowly and awkwardly, like trying to do an obstacle course with someone riding piggy-back on your body.

"You're doing great, Alex," said Elodie. Her voice was quiet and small, nothing like the exuberant girl he had been introduced to only a week ago. Alex guided their inflated suit through the next hatch into the corridor that led to the docking port.

He was turning down the corridor when the lab came into view of his plastic window. He noticed the lights were still on in the lab. There were a few items floating freely in the module. Alex was about to turn away when he saw a dark red sock float into view from behind a lab table. Then the rest of a blue flight-suited leg appeared.

Alex let go of the handrail and sucked in air. The blue flight suit was spattered with blood. Alex looked away.

"Alex, we're falling!" Elodie said. The three of them tumbled backwards as Alex lost control of the arm tubes.

"No, no," said Alex. He covered his face with his hands. The tears came instantly, before he could even fully understand what was happening. The shock of knowing that one of the crew had died in the lab was almost too much for him to bear. Who was it? Erica Reid? Doug Williams? Or could it even be his father? His dad had no reason to have been in the lab, but who knows what could have happened right before the explosion.

Jennifer was yelling now. Elodie grabbed Alex, asking what happened, if he was hurt. He could only barely manage to say, "Someone's dead in there."

"Oh God, oh God," Jennifer was saying. They had hit a

wall, and the gentle impact banged Jennifer's elbow before they bounced off and tumbled slowly.

"Alex, we can't stop," Elodie said. "We can't, we have to keep going. You said there isn't much air in here. We have to go."

Alex tried to shake off what he had seen, but he had an almost primal fear of looking out the window. He blinked away tears welling in his eyes and tried to feel anything with his hands.

"Oh God, Alex, you have to keep going," said Jennifer, her voice nearly an octave higher than normal.

Alex was lost now, unsure of where they were floating and unwilling to look out the window to see what might be in front of them. His back made contact with some surface. He pulled his arms from the tubes and tried to push the back of the bag away from the wall. He was so tired. He felt movement around him and twisted his head to find Elodie sliding up to the arm tubes.

"Push us away," she said. Alex pushed against the wall and his back pushed against Elodie's back and they all began to move somewhere. Alex wasn't sure where they were facing, but Elodie must have been able to grab something because the bag moved again and Alex felt himself dragged along like a potato in a sack. Then there was another jolt. She must be pushing off the handrails now.

Elodie grunted with each exertion, and she was breathing heavily. Alex's mind was thickening with fog. He remembered oxygen starvation from class. You start to breathe more heavily because your body wants air. He was feeling starved, even more than he had been in the chamber. His body wanted more air. He kept breathing but it wasn't enough so he tried again and again. It still wasn't enough and he was feeling dizzy.

The bag kept jolting around, like ocean waves. He wanted more air, but there wasn't enough. It was a thirst he couldn't quench. Elodie was panting.

"Alex...," she said, then breathed a few times. "We're...at...Venturer."

Alex wanted more air now. Maybe he could have it.

"Get...the tablet," he said between breaths.

Elodie reached for the tablet velcroed to the inner wall of the bag. Alex dared to turn his eyes towards their tiny plastic window and could see a glimpse of Venturer's interior.

Elodie handed the tablet to Alex. He looked at the display. It was confusing. He tapped the Venturer icon.

The display said, "Connecting..."

"Alex," said Elodie. "You..." She didn't finish. Alex realized that he hadn't heard Jennifer say anything in a while. Was she still breathing?

The display blurred in front of him, as if it were suddenly underwater. He tried to remember what to do. Initialize, that was it. He pushed the button.

Elodie had stopped moving. Alex tried to remember what to do next. He just couldn't think of it.

He dropped the tablet. He watched curiously as it floated away from his hand and bounced off the side of the bag. He decided to close his eyes for just a minute to regain his strength.

CHAPTER 30

MACKENZIE WAS DOING HER HOMEWORK WHEN HER MOTHER knocked on her door.

"Come in," Mackenzie said. She looked up and saw her mother's red eyes and knew instantly that something was wrong. "What's the matter?"

"Sweetie...I just saw on the news. There was an accident on NewStar One. He's..." Her voice trailed off. Mackenzie jumped up, knocking over her computer and a stack of papers.

"No." She searched her mother's face for answers. Her mother just shook her head.

Mackenzie covered her mouth with her hands. She could see Alex in front of her, the last time they had done a video chat. The tears began to flow as her mother wrapped her arms around her.

*****

"Yes, sir, that's correct, we would like to cancel all antenna tracks," Scott said into the phone. He was talking with an antenna operator in Peru that was one of NewStar's contracted communication providers. This was his fourth phone call to an antenna field, and they had all gone pretty much the same way.

"So when you will resume the service?" asked the man on the other end of the line in a heavy accent.

"We will inform you if and when we are ready to resume service."

"You not happy with the service? Maybe we make a mistake that causing you to have no contact?"

"No, it's not that. I'm sorry but I can't discuss our reasons for canceling at this time."

"OK, boss. We cancel service. But you want me to stop the data you getting now?"

"We don't have any data coming at the moment, so you can cancel right away."

"You not have the data? We see some started just a few minutes ago."

Scott looked up at his display and immediately dropped the phone. There was a signal coming, but it wasn't from NewStar One. The signal was from Venturer. He grabbed the mouse and clicked through several displays. Somehow Venturer had been initialized out of its dormant state, causing its radios to come on.

He grabbed the phone from the desk and shouted into it, "We changed our mind. Do not cancel the service. We are very happy with it. OK, do not cancel it!"

"Yeah, yeah, OK, boss. You got it, we keep the schedule then?"

"Yes, keep the schedule. Thank you." Scott slammed down the phone and looked at the data on his screen. Venturer was depressurized and at vacuum. Scott issued a command to retrieve data logs. Messages shot across his screen. Towards the bottom, he saw the last event that had occurred - "Initialize command received from tablet X5321:

Wireless"

Someone had sent a command to initialize the vehicle! The wireless control system had very limited range, so that someone would have to be nearby. But how was that possible if the vehicle had no air pressure? Scott looked up at the wall. A timer indicated that he had only two minutes left before they would be out of visibility with the Peru gateway antenna.

Damn, I already canceled Brazil and Africa.

He issued another command to power on the internal video camera. They were normally forbidden from doing this without the crew's permission in order to respect privacy, but as the lead Mission Director, Scott knew the override codes. It took about thirty seconds for the video to initialize and come to the ground.

Scott almost lost his mind when he saw the inflated cargo bag floating in the Venturer. There were two stubby cylinders sticking out of the bottom that were covered in duct tape. The entire bag was covered in a LOT of duct tape.

Scott looked up at the wall. Thirty seconds left in the contact and then NewStar One would be below the horizon at Peru. Scott grabbed the keyboard and began furiously typing commands.

*****

Alex felt himself being shaken and his first thought was that his mother was trying to wake him up.

"No, stop," he mumbled.

"Alex..please." The voice was tired but sweet and definitely not his mother's. He opened his eyes and Elodie's face slowly came into focus. He could feel another body against his back. Jennifer.

They were still inside the bag spacesuit. The gray walls seemed like they were closing in on them. And there was a sound coming from outside the bag. A hissing sound. Air!

Alex turned his head to look out the Plexiglas. His head throbbed and protested every movement. Just this small turn made him so dizzy that he reached his hand out to steady himself but there was nothing to hold onto except the smooth duct-taped walls of the bag.

Outside, he saw the hatch was closed. He must have been able to issue the command. If Venturer was repressurizing, they were saved! They just had to get out of this airtight bag before they suffocated. Alex reached down to the leg of his jumpsuit. His hand fumbled around but he was finally able to find his pocket knife, the one his dad had given him when he was in fourth grade.

Alex took the knife in his hand and opened the largest blade. He was so dizzy now that even this simple task seemed difficult. With a lethargic arm, he tried to stab at the duct tape around them. It wouldn't pierce. He needed to push harder. With a grunt, Alex stabbed as hard as he could at the walls, which by now had lost their rigor as air pressure filled the module around them. This time the knife went through. Alex dragged it down until there was a large hole. He could feel the cool air rush into the bag and he took a deep breath, which filled him with relief.

They crawled out of the bag and Elodie wrapped her arms around him instantly. She was sobbing as she squeezed Alex and kissed his neck and cheeks with unabashed adoration. Alex had never felt anything like the elation that filled him. He had saved himself, but even more importantly, he had been able to save two other people's lives. He hugged Elodie and never wanted to let go. He felt tears coming to his eyes.

That's when Alex realized Jennifer had never come out of the bag. He pushed Elodie aside and rushed back into the hole that his knife had opened in the bag's side.

"Jennifer! Are you OK?" Jennifer was not moving and her back was facing him. Alex dragged her out, or rather, he pulled the bag off of her motionless floating body. She wasn't breathing. CPR was all Alex could think of. He had been told to strap the body to a wall or bulkhead if CPR was necessary. *There isn't time for that.*

Alex grabbed Jennifer's head and tilted it back. As best he could with both of them floating in space, he placed his mouth over hers and exhaled strongly. He could feel her chest expand only slightly. She needed more. Alex tried again with a deeper breath. Still no response. He took another deep breath and exhaled into her mouth. This time her body twitched when he did it.

Then Alex noticed Jennifer take a shallow breath. Had she been breathing the whole time? Jennifer's body twitched again, and she let out a groan. Alex looked over at Elodie, who was watching with wide eyes.

Jennifer moved again and then finally opened her eyes. "Where are we?" she asked in a raspy voice. To Alex's surprise, Elodie came over and hugged Jennifer.

That's when the memories of the body in the lab came flooding back to Alex. They hit him with the force of a bulldozer, causing his stomach to churn. He covered his face with his hands and began to cry, not caring what Elodie or Jennifer thought of him at that moment.

Just then a speaker crackled to life. "Venturer, this is NewStar Control. Do you read me?"

CHAPTER 31

ALEX'S HAND WAS TREMBLING WHEN HE REACHED FOR THE microphone. He felt overwhelmed physically and emotionally. He took a few breaths, but his voice still cracked when he said into the microphone, "This is Venturer. I read you."

"Alex, is that you?" said the voice. Alex vaguely recognized it as someone he had met on the ground. He couldn't remember the name.

"Yes, it's me."

"You're alive, thank God! Nice work with the spacesuit bag. We picked it up on video and I sent up commands to shut the hatch and repressurize Venturer. We switched ground stations though and I've lost my video feed now. Is anyone else with you?"

"Yes, Elodie and Jennifer are here. They're OK."

"How about the rest of the crew?"

"I don't know about all of them. But I saw at least one dead body in the lab." There was silence for a few seconds.

"Alex, I'm sorry to hear that. What happened up there?"

"I don't really know. We were in the Commons exercising when there was some kind of explosion. It was bad and we couldn't make it to the ships in time. We had to shut the hatch to the Node. When we came through in the bag, I could see the airlock windows and they were broken."

Silence again.

"Copy that, Alex. We lost all contact with the station over 24 hours ago. If the explosion was as bad as you say, it might have taken out all three central computers in the Node. The engineers are on their way in. We're going to figure out a plan for you. Are you guys OK in Venturer?"

Alex looked at Elodie and Jennifer. They looked beaten down. "Yes, we're fine here. Is there any way we can find out if anyone else survived?"

"We're going to think about that, just give us a little time. Like I said, we lost all communication with NewStar One. But we'll try to get creative. No matter what, though, we will make sure we can get you home safely in Venturer. Just hang tight for a little while."

"OK, copy that NewStar Control."

"And Alex."

"Yes?"

"You did a good job."

Alex clicked off the microphone and stuck it back on the wall. Jennifer and Elodie's faces were a mixture of relief and worry. Alex shared their conflicted emotions. His body was physically tired and he was glad to be safe, but not knowing what had happened to the rest of the crew, including his father, gnawed at his insides in a way that made him feel like he would burst.

In order to distract himself, Alex suggested they find something to eat. Most of the supplies had been transferred out of Venturer, so they searched the remaining bags and lockers for food. Elodie found some food packages stuffed into a small bag near the bottom of the capsule. She smiled and held one up for Alex to see. Macaroni and cheese.

Alex heated the food and the three of them ate in silence, each lost in thought and hope. Just as they were finishing, a radio call came in. "Venturer, this is NewStar Control."

Alex grabbed the microphone. "Go ahead."

"We have a few engineers in here taking a look at the situation. They wanted to ask that you do them a favor and be absolutely still for a couple of minutes. Don't touch the walls or floor of the capsule at all. In fact, it would be best if you don't touch any structure."

Elodie looked at Alex with a puzzled look. He shrugged his shoulders.

"OK, I think we can manage that. When do you want us to do it?"

"Starting now would be great."

"Alright, just let us get away from the walls." After he turned off the microphone, he added aloud, "And I hope you crazy scientists know what you're doing." The three of them pulled themselves into the center of the capsule away from the walls. They locked their arms together for stability and then Alex picked up the microphone again.

"OK, NewStar Control. We're in the middle of the module and we'll try to be still."

"Great, thanks, Alex. I know this is a funny request, but trust us that it may help tremendously."

Alex just shook his head. He kept the microphone in his hand as the three of them floated freely in the center of Venturer. Their arms were interlocked as they hovered in place, and Alex felt comforted by the warmth of Elodie and Jennifer's bodies up against his. He silently mouthed a prayer that they would find his father and the rest of the crew alive.

"Venturer crew, you can resume your normal activities," said the voice on the radio. "And we have some news for you."

"Thanks, what's the news?" Alex replied after they had all grabbed onto handrails and Alex had retrieved the microphone.

"We asked you to remain still because Venturer has some extremely sensitive accelerometers and rate sensors onboard. Our engineers watched the data from those sensors and detected erratic vibrations that we see often onboard NewStar...whenever there are crew members awake and moving around."

"Are you saying that someone else is moving around?"

"That's exactly what we're saying."

"Like in another module?"

"The vibrations usually propagate throughout the entire structure. Remember, in zero gravity there is nothing to stabilize the station. Every time you push off a wall, the entire station gets a little jolt."

"You're sure it's from people?"

"I would bet my car on it. And I love my car."

"Where are they? Maybe I can rescue them with the bag suit."

"Hold on just a second there, cowboy. Remember, you'd have to depressurize the Venturer again, so all of you would have to go. And once you got to where they are, it wouldn't help because you wouldn't be able to open up a pressurized hatch."

"Oh, yeah."

"We don't know exactly where the vibrations are coming from either. But from what you've said, the hotel, Node and labs are all depressurized. So they would most likely be in crew quarters."

"That's what I was thinking too. I'm pretty sure my dad was in there when this happened." He looked over at Elodie. "And John too." Alex paused and thought for a moment. "So if they are in crew quarters, how can we get to them?"

"We have an idea on that too, but it's going to take us a little while to see if it's possible. We need to do some research on how the station was assembled."

"Well, how long will it take?" If anyone else was left alive, they would be running out of oxygen just like he had been in the hotel. They had to act fast, and Alex couldn't stand being helpless and safe while his father might be slowly asphyxiating.

"We are working as fast as we can. We'll call you back soon."

CHAPTER 32

ALEX TRIED TO BUSY HIMSELF AROUND THE CAPSULE. IN ORDER to leave NewStar One and re-enter the atmosphere, everything would have to be securely strapped down at the bottom of the capsule. Anything left elsewhere could come falling down on them when gravity returned. Alex moved bags and used Velcro straps to secure items, as he thought about what it would take to get back home. He didn't know if he would be able to pilot Venturer back to earth. He'd practiced a few times on the simulator for fun, but those few games hardly qualified him to operate the vehicle in real life, even with the help of mission control. On top of his lack of qualification was the fact that he couldn't stop thinking about the body floating lifelessly in the lab. He tried to tell himself it wasn't his father, but he had some nagging doubts. And there may have been more people in the lab he couldn't see. He knew Jennifer and Elodie were probably thinking the same thing.

After an hour, Alex was growing impatient. He wanted to do something, anything. If his dad and John and some of the other crew were still alive, it felt wrong to just be sitting around waiting for mission control. Elodie and Jennifer seemed impatient too. They had started out helping Alex put things away and searching the supply bags for useful items. But they had given that up, and both of them were now up against the windows, silently watching the earth below.

Alex took the microphone and squeezed down the button with his thumb. "NewStar control, do you have any updates yet on what we can do to rescue the others?"

There was a pause. Alex waited for a minute, then threw the microphone against the wall. "Come on!" he shouted.

As if in response, the radio beeped and a new voice said, "Sorry, Venturer. No update yet. We're still working on the plan."

"Oh, for crying out loud!" Alex said, without depressing the microphone's push-to-talk button. Elodie floated over and put her arm on his shoulder.

"It's OK," she said. "They'll figure it out. They're all like genius engineers, right?"

"I guess," said Alex, a little bit calmer. "They're not even telling us anything, though. Do you really think they have a plan or are they just trying to make us feel better?"

Elodie shrugged. Then, with no warning, she snatched the microphone out of Alex's hand and pressed the button to talk. "Um, mission control guys? This is Elodie Fritzer. I think my dad might be trapped in the crew quarters, and probably Alex's dad and hopefully a bunch of other people. So it would really be awesome if you guys could stop screwing around down there and figure out a plan so we can go save them. Um, thanks." She released the push-to-talk button.

The reply came almost instantly, and it came from a voice they recognized from their first call. "Elodie, this is

Scott, the lead mission director. I'm sorry for the delay. Trust me, we're just as eager as you to rescue the other crew. Do you want to at least hear the idea we have right now?" Alex looked at Elodie in amazement.

"That would be great, Scott," she said sweetly into the microphone, looking at Alex and smiling.

"Do you always get what you want this easily?" Alex asked.

"Pretty much," she said.

"OK, guys," said Scott's voice from the speaker. "Here's our idea. The crew quarters does not have a docking port, but it does have what we call a berthing port at the end. In case of future expansion, the berthing port allows us to attach a new module to the front of the crew quarters. We're trying to figure out if there's a way Venturer can fly to that berthing port and attach.

"The engineers down here think they have found a way. Right now, Venturer is docked to a docking port that was attached to the space station with the same bolting mechanism that berthing ports use to attach new modules. If we can detach the entire docking port and leave it stuck on the nose of Venturer, you'd be able to fly over to the crew quarters and reattach. The only problem is the docking port was never meant to come off after the space station was built. The mechanisms were shut down. We are trying to figure out a way to apply power to them from inside Venturer, without making any of you go back into the unpressurized section of the space station. That is turning out to be a little trickier than we thought."

Alex suddenly got very excited. "Wait a minute," he said to the microphone. "I think I know what mechanism you're talking about! When we docked to NewStar One, the latches didn't tighten all the way. My dad had to open a panel to tighten it. There were some connectors that he said used to feed power to things when the station was being assembled."

"Connectors inside Venturer?"

"Yes, they were behind a panel up near the hatch. Where the manual latching mechanism is."

"OK, let me look into that. I don't remember seeing that on the drawings."

"I know they were there. I'll go find them."

"Well, Alex, let us check the design drawings first and then we'll let you know if we need you to look at something." It was too late, though. Alex had already pulled a screwdriver out of the tool kit. He began working on the panel. Elodie decided to help and grabbed another screwdriver. Eventually, Jennifer joined in and the panel was off within minutes.

Alex grabbed a headlamp and stuck his head up in the panel.

"Hand me a camera," he said. Jennifer retrieved one that was velcroed to the wall and handed it up to Alex. In a few minutes, Alex had snapped twelve pictures of the empty connectors up in the hull.

"Did you find it?" Elodie asked when Alex pulled his upper body out of the panel.

"Oh yeah," Alex said. "There's a bunch of connectors up there. I'm sure one of them is the one we need."

"How do we figure out which one?"

"We need to send these pictures to mission control, so they can tell us."

Alex drifted over to the portable desk and opened the lid of the laptop computer sitting there. His e-mail had been left open and came up on the screen immediately. Since Venturer had a direct satellite link, his inbox had been updated. There was a message from Mackenzie at the top. Alex forgot all about the pictures and opened the message.

Alex, I know you'll never even get this message but I'm writing it anyway. I can't stop crying. You were the best thing that's happened to me in my life. I wanted to know you forever, to be a part of your life. Maybe you're up there in heaven right now, up in the stars reading this. I hope so.
I miss you. And always will.

"Did you send them?" Elodie was right behind him. He turned to face her with tears balling in the corners of his eyes. "What's the matter?"

"It's my girlfriend," said Alex. "She wrote me an e-mail even though she thinks I'm dead. It's just...I don't know. I'm just happy to be alive. And to know how much she really cares about me." Elodie looked away.

"Yeah, she definitely must," she said softly. Silence hung in the air for a few moments. "Well, come on, Alex, we have to get those pictures sent. Our dads are waiting, right?"

"Right, right," said Alex, visibly shaking his head to clear his mind. He connected the camera to the computer and transferred the files.

"NewStar Control, this is Venturer. There are some pictures for you in the downlink folder."

"Copy that. We'll take a look at them."

Alex and Elodie waited. After a while, she said, "You know, your girlfriend is pretty lucky to have you. You're a good guy, Alex." Then she floated up and kissed him on the cheek. Alex blushed and watched as Elodie turned away to join her stepmother at the window of Venturer.

After a few minutes, mission control called them back.

"Venturer, we've taken a look at the photos. Two of those connectors will in fact power the bolting mechanism for the docking port. They actually aren't on our drawings here since they were only supposed to be included on Genesis, which was the ship that did most of the heavy lifting during construction. But I guess it was easier to include them on all the ships than to make different versions. Nice job finding that."

"Thanks," said Alex. "So what do we need to do?"

"I'm sending up instructions. Check the uplink folder. We can talk you through any parts you don't understand."

"OK," said Alex. "I'll go look at them."

Jennifer and Elodie joined Alex as he opened the file that mission control had sent up. It was a massive document and half of it could have been written in Russian for all Alex knew.

"Do you understand all of that?" Elodie asked.

"Well, some of it," Alex said. "We may have to ask for a little help."

Jennifer moaned softly, but Alex ignored her.

"Alright, let's call up the smart engineers and figure this out," he said.

With the help of the ground team and Elodie, Alex was able to shut down power from one battery bank and reroute cables to the empty connectors. Elodie did most of the connector work since the area was small and she could fit back behind the panels the easiest. She didn't seem to mind the work or complain at all. Everyone understood what was on the line.

When they were done, NewStar Control explained what they would do next. The mission control team would send commands to drive out the bolts. Once that was done, they would be floating free and need to back away from the space station slowly and carefully. Using the manual controls, they would have to fly around the station and try to reconnect with the crew quarters at the empty berthing port.

The piloting, they explained, would be very difficult. Since they would be approaching from in front of the space station, every movement back towards the station would slow their orbit, causing them to fall down and away from NewStar One a little bit. So Alex would have to compensate with thrusters using upward motion at the same time he moved them closer to the station. The berthing port had some alignment guides that would allow for a little bit of error, but not much.

"Do you think you're ready?" the voice in the radio asked.

Alex swallowed. His palms already felt clammy. Why did they have to make it sound so difficult?

"OK, yeah, I guess I'm ready," he said into the microphone. Jennifer and Elodie were staring at him silently. Alex didn't get the impression they were very confident in his ability to pull this off.

"Don't worry, we'll talk you through this as much as we can. Are you in the pilot's seat?"

"Just a second." Alex replaced the microphone they had been using on the wall. Before he pushed himself down to the seats near the bottom of the capsule, he pulled out the laser ranger. He gave Jennifer a quick lesson on taking measurements and told her to stay by the window.

"Elodie, I'd like you to sit with me and talk to mission control and double-check that I do everything they say correctly."

Elodie nodded and the two of them dove to the bottom of the capsule. Sitting in the commander's seat that his dad usually occupied felt like the first time he had sat in the driver's seat of his grandmother's Honda. His parents had been working late, and it was the day after his sixteenth birthday, so his grandmother offered to teach him. She had patiently explained how to place the car in gear and press the gas to accelerate. Alex had followed her instructions exactly, but had pressed the gas pedal too hard. The car had lurched forward, and in a panic he had turned the wheel. They had ended up on the sidewalk with their neighbor's mailbox destroyed. He had done chores for his neighbor for a month to pay off the damage.

Alex hoped his first attempt at flying went better than his first attempt at driving. He pulled a communication headset over his ear, the microphone jutting out by the side of his cheek. He looked over at Elodie who had copied Alex and put on a headset herself. "Here we go," he said.

The rotational control joystick had a convenient push-to-talk button mounted on the top. That let him queue his microphone without taking his hands off the controls. He wrapped his right hand around the joystick and reached for the square translational motion controller on the left, which he held with a claw-like grip he'd seen his dad use.

"NewStar control, Venturer," he said, depressing the button under his right finger. "We're in position and ready."

"OK, Venturer. First we need to start the unbolting sequence. We can do that remotely from ground command.

You may hear some motors turning within the structure
while we do this. Don't be alarmed."

"Copy, control."

A few seconds later, the ship began to rumble. It sounded like ten power drills were going at once. It seemed like
no time at all before Houston called them back.

"Venturer, Control. We are at the last stage of unbolting. About 30 seconds after our next command, you'll be
floating free. Before we do that, you need to activate the
thruster system. At the top of the panel switch Rotational
Thrusters and Translational Thrusters to Active."

Alex scanned the panel. It wasn't very large but he
wasn't familiar with the switches. Elodie found it first and
reached over to point to the switch.

"Thanks," he said as he flipped the two switches.

"It's done," Alex told the ground.

"Great, standby for final unbolting." Alex realized he
had a death grip on the controls. He tried to loosen his
hands up. He didn't want to go too fast like he had with
grandma's car.

Just slow and steady...slow and steady.

"We're drifting away!" Jennifer called from up front.
Alex glanced past the panel and out the window where he
saw the edge of the station moving slightly away from
them.

"Venturer, you're clear to back away from the port,"
said the radio voice.

Alex took a deep breath and pulled back on the square
joystick. He could hear thrusters pulse with each motion of
his hand. He watched the range on his display increase and
pulled back again to fire more jet pulses. This was just like
the simulator. A small but blurry video on his right screen

showed the view out the front. The docking port that was attached to them blocked most of the view, but Alex was able to see a little of the station behind it. He was shocked when they backed far enough away to clearly see what was left in the docking compartment. Since they had never shut the inner hatch, there was a wide opening right into the space station. Alex watched as a closed laptop computer drifted lazily out of the hatch and into space.

As carefully as he could, Alex twisted the rotation joystick in his right hand. The ship responded by yawing according to his command. The real vehicle seemed even more responsive than the simulator. Just the slightest hand motion would cause jets to pulse and the images on his screen to change accordingly.

When the ship was far enough away from the docking port, Alex began to bring it down and below the space station. Once in a lower orbit, they began to naturally move towards the front of the space station.

In what seemed like no time, they were past the front end of the labs. Alex twisted the joystick on his right hard and Venturer began to yaw around quickly. He was trying to face the nose back towards the space station. After a few minutes, Alex could see the station above and behind them. It was growing smaller quicker than he'd expected.

The yaw was continuing and Alex knew he needed to counter it with jet pulses against the direction of their rotation to stop them. He twisted the joystick left, but they had already rotated more than a hundred and eighty degrees. He twisted some more and jet pulses sent the nose quickly towards NewStar One. The nose swung too far and the station was already off to the right before Alex was able to stop the rotation.

Alex felt panic rising inside him. He needed to point the nose at the crew quarters module and fire the aft thrusters to counter their motion away from the station and start them on a course back. Why couldn't he get this?

He started another yaw back towards the station. At the same time he began to pitch the nose up to point towards the crew quarters. By now, the station was far enough away that he could no longer make out details like the wires that ran alongside the hull. Venturer's nose was coming past the space station again. Alex tried desperately to stop it, but he couldn't seem to find the right combination of movements to stop their momentum without over-correcting. The nose danced around the target, but didn't seem to find it.

"Dammit," said Alex. He could almost feel Elodie and Jennifer's eyes on him. They said nothing as they watched him with furrowed brows.

The station was getting too far away. In a few minutes, it would just be another bright star in the sky. Alex needed to stop their motion away from it. He used the square joystick on the left to fire the aft engines a few times, hoping that would be enough to slow or at least stop their backwards movement, even if the nose wasn't pointing exactly at NewStar One.

"Venturer, this is control. If you need, use the rotation hold button on the bottom row of the right-hand panel. That will stop all rotation and then you can start over."

"Wish they'd told me that earlier," Alex said aloud, the frustration evident in his voice. When he pushed the button, he could feel jets firing and then NewStar One stopped moving from side to side. However, it was still getting smaller.

Alex tried to focus. His dad needed him. He could not

mess this up. He took the rotation joystick and made just a few small twists. The movement was agonizingly slow, but when NewStar approached the center of the circle on his video screen, it took only a few equally small twists to stop the motion. Alex jammed the thrust control forward. Finally, it started to seem like the station was increasing in size. The display in front of him read +0.3 m/s approach speed. They were nearly a kilometer away now, but finally they were heading in the right direction.

They approached to within 300 meters, and Alex slowed down the ship with careful jet pulses. He was just starting to line the nose up for a final approach, when Jennifer yelled, "Alex, watch out!"

Alex looked up at the window where Jennifer was floating. One of NewStar's solar arrays next to the airlock was bent at an impossible angle. Wait, it wasn't just bent. It was entirely detached from the station. And it was heading right for their ship!

CHAPTER 33

"VENTURER, ABORT YOUR APPROACH," SAID THE NEWSTAR mission control voice on the radio. "I repeat, abort now!"

Alex reached for the red abort button at the top of the panel. It was protected with a plastic cover. Alex lifted the cover and put his thumb on the button. Then he hesitated.

"NewStar control, if we do an abort burn, will we have enough fuel to come back?"

"That is unknown, Venturer. But you need to abort now. Less than 30 seconds to impact with the array. Abort!"

Alex looked up. He saw the array tumbling slowly towards them, but his eyes focused on the space station behind it. His father might still be alive in there. And Elodie's father and the rest of the crew.

"Alex," said Elodie, "what are you doing? That giant flappy thing is getting close!"

Alex pulled his finger away from the abort button. He looked up at the array coming at them on his screen. With a decisive motion, he grabbed the translational joystick and pushed it down hard, holding it as far as it would go. The jets fired fiercely and everything in the capsule started to fly to the ceiling. Alex was pulled upward as well but his harness restrained him.

The center of the array consisted of a metal truss and now that they were so close to the array, Alex could see how bulky it was. The beams looked massive and while the array seemed to be tumbling slowly, Alex could see now that because of its size, the ends were slicing through space with damaging speed. The end of the beam shot past the front of the window, missing them by a few feet.

They were under the array as it tumbled sideways overhead. Another ninety degrees of rotation and it would hit them unless they got out of the way quickly enough. Alex pressed as hard as he could on the controller, his hand hurting as the plastic dug into his skin.

They lost sight of the array as it rotated out of their view in the window.

Everything was silent except for the whoosh of the jets, and Alex smiled, sure that his actions had avoided disaster.

Then a jolt hit the capsule, sending Elodie and Jennifer flying against the bulkhead, while Alex was thrown back against his seat. His hand slipped off the controls and the capsule began to rotate.

Alex shut his eyes. His mind flooded with memories of the air leak during their launch. He waited for the telltale signs - a pop in his ears and the sound of alarms. But nothing happened. After twenty seconds of silence, Alex opened his eyes again.

The capsule was still tumbling, but there were no alarms. Everything seemed OK. Elodie was clutching the back of her head, but she seemed more annoyed than hurt. Jennifer had peeled herself off the wall and was checking herself.

Alex reached up and hit the rotation hold button, his

new best friend in the cockpit. The capsule stopped its tumble with the nose pointing to deep space and the space station visible at the edge of the port window.

"Are you OK?" Alex asked Elodie.

"Ugh, yeah, I'm fine. Stupid head cushions in these seats are not very soft." Alex smiled. She would be okay.

"Venturer, Control. Do you copy? Do you copy?"

Alex pushed the button to activate his headset microphone.

"Control, we're here. Just got a little fender bender but no damage."

"That was a really stupid thing to do." These people were sounding like his father.

"Well, not as stupid as living the rest of my life knowing I could have saved my dad's life but didn't," Alex retorted. "I'm going to continue the approach."

"Standby, Venturer. Just slow down. You need to do a visual inspection to make sure there's no more debris. We have radar and other assets looking, but they can't detect everything. And you won't hear it coming." Alex wrinkled his nose at the radio. He wanted to tell them to shut up, but they made a good point.

"We'll take care of it," he said, and then he tore the headset away from his face and let it float freely, its cord acting as a leash to keep it near the control panel. Alex unbuckled and joined Jennifer and Elodie by the windows.

"How does it look out there?" Alex asked.

"Um, not that great," Elodie said, pointing out the port window. Alex pulled himself closer to her. They were at an awkward angle and the station was barely visible at the edge of the window. It didn't take more than a quick glance, though, to see they were in trouble. The entire port side array was twisted and looked like it might come loose at any minute. The array consisted of three panels, each one further from the center. The last panel was missing, which is what had come free and hit them. The remaining two were attached by a large metal truss with four beams that were bolted to the station just aft of the airlock. Three of the beams had broken off and looked blackened and scarred. The explosion in the airlock must have damaged them.

"Wow, that looks like it might come off at any moment," said Alex.

"Yeah, duh," said Elodie. She grabbed Alex's arm and looked at him directly, with her beautiful puppy brown eyes fixed on his. "But Alex, I don't even care. We have to go back for them."

"I agree," Jennifer piped up. "We can't leave John or the others to die."

Alex nodded in agreement. He would never give up as long as he thought his dad was alive.

Alex returned to his seat and strapped in. He snatched the headset out of the air, brought the microphone to his mouth and said, "Control, Venturer. We have visually confirmed no more debris or damage in the area. We'll be approaching now. Over." Without even waiting for a response, he grabbed the controls.

The first order of business was to reorient the nose towards the space station. Alex was getting the hang of things by now, and he was able to perform the maneuver smoothly. Next, he began thrusting towards the space station. This was a bit more tricky. By now, they had drifted far below the space station. As Alex tried to force them back up, the physics of orbital mechanics fought his inputs, trying to pull the ship further below the space station.

Then Alex remembered what his dad had told him. To raise your orbit and go higher, you need to speed up. And to do that, Alex had to fire jets to push him further in front of NewStar One. It seemed counter-intuitive, thrusting away from the station to get closer. But when he tried it, he saw that his rate of motion, at least in the up/down direction was reversing.

Once they were up at the same height as the space station, Alex began a series of thruster pulses to move them closer. This also had the effect of slowing their orbit slightly and causing them to drop down, but now that they were up higher, Alex was able to counter that downward motion with upward jet pulses.

They approached to one hundred meters. Alex pulled back on the controls to slow them down.

"Whoa!" said Elodie.

"What's happening?" Alex asked.

"The array just moved a little."

"Shoot, it must be getting knocked by the thruster pulses. I'll have to keep those to a minimum."

"You mean, like, not steer us very much?"

"Unfortunately, yeah."

"I hope you're a good driver."

"Come on, you don't think I can drive this thing?"

"No, no. That's not what I meant."

Alex smiled but kept on with the approach, trying hard not to pulse any jets that were facing towards NewStar One. Unfortunately, those were the jets he needed to use to slow down, so he wouldn't be able to avoid them forever.

When they got to 50 meters, Alex was approaching at 0.5 m/s, way too fast to successfully dock. Crossing his fingers on one hand, he pulled back on the controller to slow them down. He heard the jets pulse and then immediately heard Jennifer and Elodie gasp.

"It's really bouncing!" Elodie said. Alex released the controller right away. They were down to 0.4 m/s. He knew they were supposed to be below 0.1 m/s to successfully capture. It didn't seem possible without blowing off part of the solar array.

They reached 40 meters distance. Alex hesitated. Should he slow them down? The closer they got, the worse the damage would probably be. They would be at the port in less than two minutes. He might as well try now.

"I've got to slow us down more," Alex yelled to Jennifer and Elodie. "Watch the array!"

He pulled back again. The speed decreased to 0.35. Alex kept pulling. The jets exhaled their combustion products right at the station.

"Oh, Alex, it's moving like it's in a hurricane!"

"Just a few more seconds!" Alex said.

They were now at 25 meters, but the speed was still 0.3 m/s.

"It's coming off!" Elodie said. Alex stopped thrusting and looked up at the window. The array had broken loose and was tumbling backwards towards the hotel module in slow motion. Then he looked down at his display. 10 meters away and 0.25 m/s. Doing quick math, Alex realized they had 40 seconds to contact.

Well, it's already gone. I guess it can't hurt us anymore.

Alex pulled back on the thruster controller as the station's berthing port filled the camera. He got the speed to 0.12 m/s before he heard the mechanism make contact with the outside of the station. He released the thruster controls and everything was still for a moment.

"Venturer, NewStar Control," squawked the radio. "We see you as soft captured. We are initiating the bolting sequence now."

Alex wanted to scream and jump up and down. He grabbed the radio microphone and copied the call joyfully. Then he unbuckled and joined Elodie and Jennifer at the window. Elodie smiled at him and gave him a hug. But then she looked out again and her face became concerned.

"Alex, it looks like the array is about to hit..." Elodie began. But she was interrupted by a jolt of sparks inside the module that seemed to come from every piece of electronics they had. Then everything went dark.

CHAPTER 34

THE SUN WAS SETTING AS THEY HEADED INTO THE NIGHT SIDE OF the earth, leaving just a faint glow of light coming through the window, which would soon fade to black. Alex rushed to the tool kit and pulled out a headlamp, which he promptly strapped on. At least they would have some light.

"What just happened?" Jennifer asked.

"I think when the array hit the station, it must have made electrical contact," said Alex. "It would have surged power to the hull. Everything gets grounded to the hull, so that surge might have knocked out the electronics. Since our hull is now connected to NewStar's, we got hit as well."

"So the ship is dead?" Jennifer asked, her voice trembling.

"I don't know if it's completely dead or not." Alex tried punching buttons on the control panel nearby. Nothing happened. He looked up at the hatch. Had the bolting of the docking port to NewStar One been completed? He pulled himself up to the hatch using the handrails.

"Let's see if we can pressurize the docking port," said Alex. "My dad will know what to do if we can get to him."

"So we can get into the crew quarters now?" Elodie asked excitedly.

"Um, probably."

"What do you mean probably?"

"If your ears start to pop too much, let me know."

"Wait, Alex, what are you doing?"

Alex didn't reply. If the bolting wasn't completed, the pressure seal might be bad and whatever air he let into the docking port might just leak overboard. But he couldn't leave the others behind, even if it meant taking a risk with all of their lives. Alex closed his eyes for a moment. He thought about Mackenzie, about his life back home. He had made it this far. Time to finish the job. He grabbed the manual pressure equalization valve and twisted it open in a swift motion before he could change his mind.

The stream of air hissed as it left the module. Alex felt his ears pop. With the instruments and displays dead, he had no idea what the pressure was. His ears popped again. Then the whooshing sound slowed. It seemed to be holding. Alex pulled the manual override on the hatch and swung it open.

The hissing sound of air was still there, although it was not as loud as before. They must still be leaking some air. His ears popped again.

"Alex, what's happening?" Elodie was screaming.

"It's fine. We just have to get to the others!"

Alex banged his hand hard against the cold hatch that led to somewhere in the crew quarters. He had never noticed a hatch there before. Then he remembered...at the front of the module was a soft-sided rack where they kept towels, wipes, cleaners and other household-type goods. This hatch must be behind that!

Alex tried pushing on the hatch but it wouldn't open. The pressure in the crew quarters must be higher than what they had in Venturer. Or maybe the rack in front of it was blocking the way.

Alex's ears popped again. Their air was still leaking out. Like when they were in the bag, Alex could feel the air growing thinner as he breathed.

Alex looked around desperately for something that he could use to open the hatch. Nothing came into his view or his mind. He was starting to feel lightheaded. He would have to give up and shut the hatch or they would run out of air and die.

Alex pulled back into Venturer. There would be nobody to save them this time if he didn't get the hatch shut. He slid it along the rails and was about to lock it into place when he thought he heard a banging noise from the other side. He peeked through the narrow gap left between the hatch and the bulkhead. The NewStar hatch was opening!

Alex slid back the hatch into Venturer. Elodie and Jennifer were suddenly around him, and they watched in wonder as the NewStar One hatch slid aside. Alex felt a breeze against his cheeks and then he was staring directly into the eyes of his father.

With tears welling up, he rocketed forward. His dad met him in the middle of the hatch and they embraced tighter than they had since Alex was a child.

"Alex," his dad said hoarsely. "Oh thank God." Alex could feel his father's chest heaving against his, and he knew his dad was sobbing. Alex smiled and cried at the same time. It felt like their embrace lasted forever, but in reality it could only have been a few seconds.

His father pulled back and his demeanor snapped instantly back to seriousness. Alex realized that his dad hadn't shaved and looked nothing like the crisp and clean man he was used to seeing. Even with his rough facial stubble, his father emanated control of the situation.

"We have an air leak," he said, suddenly noticing the sound of whooshing air. The burst of air from the crew quarters had helped raise the pressure back up slightly, but it was beginning to decrease again.

"Yes," said Alex. "We lost power before the bolting was complete."

Alex's father shook his head. "I don't know how you were able to do this, Alex. Amazing. But now we need to get everyone into the ship fast and shut the hatch."

Before he knew what was happening, Alex was being pushed back into Venturer. His father helped the crew down into the capsule one at a time. First came Jim, with disheveled hair and a stained flight suit. A moment later John entered the capsule. He was swarmed instantly by Elodie and Jennifer, who burst into tears as John laughed with joy.

In no time at all, the capsule designed to hold six people was filled with eight bodies, floating around and on top of each other, as beams from headlamps danced around the darkened walls. Alex watched as the shadowy form of his father closed the hatch to NewStar One before pulling himself back inside Venturer where he quickly slid the hatch closed.

In the darkness of the capsule, his father's booming voice soared over the chattering crowd. "Jim, can you check the mains and see if there's any way to restart from battery?"

"Already checking it." Alex spotted Jim tucked into a corner working on a panel with a screwdriver, his headlamp beam reflecting brightly off the polished white. Alex's father wormed his way through the crowd towards Alex.

"Alex, I need to know. Where were you when the explosion happened? How did you make it out?" His father's voice suddenly sounded desperate.

"We were in the hotel. I shut the hatches, but we knew we had to make it to Venturer." Alex swelled with pride as he next said, "So I made a kind of spacesuit out of bags and duct tape."

His father's eyes widened. "You did that?"

"Yes, and we made it to Venturer...barely. Then we activated the capsule and mission control helped us get here."

"So, in the hotel, it was just you and Jennifer and Elodie?"

"Yes."

Alex's father's eyes dodged around the capsule. He grabbed Alex by the shoulders and suddenly Alex was frightened. "Do you have any idea where Erica was?"

Nausea rose in Alex's belly. His father looked desperate. Alex tried to say something but the words caught in his throat. The images of a limp red leg came flying back at him. He tried to them out of his mind but he could not and tears fogged his vision.

"What is it?" his father pleaded.

"I saw...someone..." Alex's breaths were gasps. "...in the lab."

"Was she OK? Was she safe in the lab?" Alex was being shaken by his father's strong arms.

Alex shook his head, flinging tears away. "The hatch was open."

"No." His father's voice was less than a whisper. "No." Then louder. "No!" The horrible wail that came next rushed

Alex back suddenly seven years. Standing on a metal bench at the Kennedy Space Center. His grandmother pulls him into her arms. And he heard that same wailing, desperate scream.

Now in Venturer, his father's scream silenced the capsule, and as Alex watched, his imperturbable father, the great and heroic Mike Stone, buried his face in his hands and began to cry uncontrollably. Alex knew then that his father had been in love. He had suspected it since the start of the mission, and he had hated the idea that someone could replace his mother, but now with Erica gone he could feel only anger that fate would take away such a person and deal his father a piercing blow like this.

He suddenly found himself angry at everything. Angry at NewStar for doubting his ability and designing a crappy space station, angry at God for taking away his mother and Dr. Reid when they were just trying to make the world a better place, angry at himself for not being able to do more to stop their deaths, angry even at his father for hiding his relationship with Dr. Reid. Alex screamed with his father, and banged his fists against the metal back of a nearby seat.

He knew everyone was watching him and he didn't even care. Screw all of them! Let them judge me! He pummeled his fists against the seat, shouting profanities, while his father hid his face and tried to shut the world out. The rest of the crew watched uncomfortably - a sea of faces twisted in sympathy and grief and embarrassment. Finally, Alex had spent his anger, and he stopped moving, and a hand touched his shoulder. He didn't have to look up to know it was Elodie, and as her arms engulfed him, he melted into a ball and sobbed. After a short moment, he broke free and moved to his father and hugged him tightly.

"I'm so sorry, Dad."

Just then the capsule lights came on. Jim popped up from his corner of the capsule.

"Reset the main breakers," he said matter-of-factly, ignoring that spectacle he had clearly just heard. Alex's father nodded, his face still flushed red. Alex released him from his hug, and he watched as his dad, with tears still gathered in his eyes, moved to the commander's seat and began punching buttons on the console.

"Jim, let's get everyone strapped down," he said in a voice cracking with emotion.

Jim began to herd people into the six seats. There were eight people total, and with only six seats, there was a quick debate on what to do. John offered to sit unrestrained on the floor, but Jim would not allow a guest to do something so dangerous.

"You don't understand," Jim explained. "The re-entry forces can be 2G or more and if you go flying, you will be seriously injured."

"Well, what if I just strap in on top of some bags?" John asked.

Other crew offered to do the same, and in the end, a couple of improvised seats were made out of storage bags, extra clothing and cargo straps. After a fierce debate, it was decided that Doug Williams and Megan Sanford, the two scientists, would occupy the "cheap seats." Jim and Alex's father needed to take the commander and pilot seats, and Jim insisted that all of the hotel guests have seats. Alex offered to give up his seat, but his father steadfastly refused.

With the crew finally settled, Alex's father began to work the controls robotically, his face and voice an impenetrable mask of business.

"Begin comm system powerup," his dad said.

"Roger, in work," Jim replied.

"Prepare re-entry targets."

"Copy."

This back-and-forth went on for a while, and soon a deep rumbling emanated from the hatch. It took only three minutes before they were free and the battered NewStar One began to fall away from them. The capsule rotated in response to the joystick movements of Alex's father's hand, and Alex took one final look through the window at a place he knew would never be seen again. Broken fragments of the hull, and twisted, sheared metal truss segments shone in the bright light of the sun. Scattered glass and debris still danced lazily in the space around the outpost. Though this space station had nearly killed him, it looked peaceful, quiet now, a sad and desolate outpost surrounded by nothingness yet flying over the endless beauty of the Earth. Alex hated this place for what it had done to Dr. Reid and what it had almost done to him and his father. But he also couldn't forget that here was where he had first learned to live in space, where he had been kissed by a celebrity, and most importantly where he had made a scientific break-through that validated and completed his mother's life's work.

As he watched the station slowly drift to the edge of the window, he thought about what would happen to it next. Thin atmospheric drag and solar winds would gradually slow its orbit until eventually it would plummet into the thickening atmosphere, heating up as it sped faster and faster into molecules of oxygen and nitrogen. It would be shredded, in many cases down to its individual atomic elements which would rain down invisibly on the planet like the detritus of any meteoroid. Perhaps one day those elements would be taken up by plant or ocean life, or maybe even some larger chunks that survived would be found and melted down to be used in some kind of ship or machine in the distant future. Some bits of NewStar One would become part of future life, like almost everything else that currently existed or had ever existed on planet Earth.

NewStar One reached the edge of the window, and just before disappearing, the sun hit one of the remaining solar arrays so that it reflected right into Alex's eye. The bright glint forced him to close his eyes for a moment and when he opened them again, NewStar One was gone.

CHAPTER 35

THE ENGINES BEGAN TO FIRE, AND EVERYONE GREW QUIET. THE reentry into the atmosphere was normally the second most dangerous part of a mission, after the launch. Today, the violent meeting of the spacecraft's heat shield with the thick atmosphere at 15,000 miles per hour seemed like a welcome relief to everyone onboard. It couldn't be any worse than what they'd already endured.

From his seat, Alex could see out the window. He watched the blackness of space give way to an orange glow. A hot flame surrounded their capsule. The ship shook more violently than it had during launch.

As the atmosphere slowed the capsule, the crew began to feel their weight coming back and then more than that. They were in a 2G deceleration, feeling twice the normal force of gravity on earth. If they hadn't been in a laying down position, they would have passed out as the blood drained from their heads.

Before long, the forces eased and the sky out the window turned blue. Alex spotted a cloud whipping past. They were falling fast, but there was not much of a sensation of it.

Suddenly, the entire capsule jolted like a bucking

horse.

"Parachutes deployed!" Jim announced excitedly. Alex felt a wave of relief, and he looked over at his father with a big smile. They had made it! But when he looked at the taught lines of his father's mouth, he knew that his dad was still thinking about Erica Reid. Alex reached out his hand and touched his father's leg. His dad looked over at him and his eyes were deep pits of sorrow.

The ship continued to fall and Jim began to call out their altitude as they approached the surface of the water.

1 kilometer...

500 meters...

250...

100...

"Brace for impact!"

The capsule hit hard, but the seat cushions absorbed most of the impact. The scientists who were strapped to the improvised seats both let out loud grunts. Alex looked over and saw Dr. Williams clutching the side of his head.

"I'm OK," he announced.

Jim removed his harness and stood up shakily. They had only been in orbit a relatively short time, but the effect on Jim's muscles and balance were obvious from his attempts to pull out the rope ladder and climb it to reach the hatch which was now overhead. Jim opened the pressure equalization valve on the hatch. Air hissed in and the atmosphere around them changed almost instantly from the sterile conditioned air of their life support system to the warm and steamy tropical environment of the Florida coast. Jim opened the hatch, climbed out of the capsule and sat up on the rim of the docking ring.

"I can see the recovery ship," he called down. "It's not

far, probably about 10 minutes out."

In slow motion, everyone removed their harnesses and tried to stand or sit up. Alex dangled his legs over the side of his seat into the capsule center. He felt chained to his chair, already missing the freedom that zero gravity had given him to float anywhere effortlessly.

The capsule was evacuated one person at a time, until only Alex and his father were left. Silence hung heavy in the air, as Alex tried to think of something...anything....to say.

Finally his father broke the silence, keeping his eyes focused on the panel in front of him. "Son, I owe you my life. We all do. And I know..." He turned to face Alex now and his eyes were glistening. "I know...your mother...would be so...so proud of you." Alex grabbed his father around the torso. He sobbed in big, loud, heaving breaths. His father held the back of his head and Alex was momentarily transported back to his childhood, feeling a closeness that had been missing for years. He hung on to his father tightly until the rescue boat crew appeared at the hatch. It was their turn to leave. But Alex needed to hear one more thing.

"Dad, were you and Dr. Reid..." Alex wasn't sure how to finish, but his father was already nodding.

"We had a relationship," he said simply. "I was going to tell you, but I knew it would be hard for you."

"She was a good person." His father only nodded silently. And then the rescue crew was in the capsule, and it was time to go.

CHAPTER 36

ALEX SQUINTED IN THE BRIGHT LIGHTS, AND THEN REMEMBERED the instructions to keep his face relaxed and calm. He tried to see out beyond the edge of the stage, but to his eyes everything was complete darkness surrounded by a bright white halo coming from the multitude of overhead beams.

The announcer spoke in a deep voice. "Our final award recipient of the Worldwide Spaceflight Congress exceptional achievement medal, the highest award given by this organization, and only available to those who have achieved astronaut status by flying above 65 km altitude, is presented to Alexander Stone, for exceptional bravery..." The rest of the man's words were drowned out by an uproar of applause and cheers. Even in this invitation-only event, there were over 800 people plus a large press corps.

Alex smiled and walked to the front of the stage to accept the award, his heart beating quickly with excitement. He tried to appear calm and walk with a swagger, but halfway across the stage, he tripped on his own feet and stumbled forward, catching himself before he fell completely down onto the stage. A chuckle emerged from the darkness and Alex winced.

When the award ceremony was over, Alex returned to

the darkness behind the stage. The awards ceremony was being held at the Space Center Houston complex, just down the street from NASA's Johnson Space Center and only a few blocks away from NewStar's old headquarters. That building was vacant now, awaiting a new lease after NewStar had formally declared bankruptcy.

Alex's father approached him first and embraced him warmly. They were hugging more now, and since his father was temporarily out of work, they were spending a lot more time together. Alex knew how badly his dad wanted to get back to work. It was his crutch in hard times - his way of dealing with things like death. But for now, Alex was happy to have a little bit more of his time. He had even taught him to play *Star Crusader*. As expected from an astronaut/pilot, he had picked it up quickly and was already beating Alex regularly in battles.

"I had a chance to talk to the computer guys out in the auditorium," his father said. Alex's heart skipped a beat. Since their return to earth, he had been trying to retrieve the logs from his experiments. Unfortunately, the computer downloads from the day of the explosion had been corrupted in transmission, and computer experts were trying to see if they could unscramble the data. After Alex had explained his discovery, his father had even arranged for some NASA grant money to help pay for the effort, arguing that the information might help lead to a cure for cystic fibrosis. Alex was hoping this last-ditch effort would help prove that his mother had been correct.

"And?" Alex asked.

His father shook his head. "They said they tried, but there was just too much corruption. The data was lost with NewStar One."

Alex hung his head.

"Don't look so down," his dad said. "This is just a bump in the road for you. I have seen you do amazing things over these past few months, Alex. You'll just have to get up there and do it again. I know you will."

Alex looked up and smiled. His father's newfound confidence in him was inspiring.

"You ready to head home?" his dad asked.

"Actually, I'm going out with Tyler and Mackenzie for a little bit." His father looked a bit disappointed, but Alex promised to be home soon and let his dad beat him in *Star Crusader*.

As soon as his father left, Alex turned to find the Fritzer women coming his way. Elodie walked straight over to Alex, and without warning, grabbed his face in her hands and planted a kiss directly on his lips. Alex's eyes opened wide with surprise.

"Nice to see you again, space hero," she said when she was done. This was the first time they'd been together since their return to earth. Alex had seen two sides of Elodie in space - there was a sweet and kind girl inside her, but it seemed often hidden beneath a showy persona she inhabited around most others. Alex's eye caught Tyler and Mackenzie coming around the corner, wearing their backstage passes and escorted by a guard in a suit.

"How have you been?" Alex asked Elodie politely.

"Really well, except I realized I was missing somebody's number in my phone," she said, pulling out an expensive-looking model from her elegant purse. "Think I could get a famous astronaut's digits?"

Alex looked over at Mackenzie who was watching from the shadows a few yards away.

"Sure," Alex said and rattled off the numbers.

"Elodie, we have to go," said Jennifer, tugging at Elodie's arm. "Alex, darling, you were wonderful, and we can't thank you enough. So sorry to have to rush out on you. I'm sure we'll be in touch." She sounded polite but her mind seemed elsewhere.

"I'll definitely be in touch, cutie," Elodie said with a wink. She gave him a kiss on the cheek and left with her stepmother.

Mackenzie walked over with Tyler behind her. "You know, I should punch you in the face for even talking to that whore."

Alex shrugged. "What can I say? All these famous people can't keep their hands off me."

"She's not even pretty," said Mackenzie. Alex disagreed, but didn't say anything. "Anyway, thanks for giving her the wrong phone number."

"Well, she's not really my type," Alex said. "Way too high maintenance." Mackenzie wrapped her arms around his midsection and kissed him on the lips. Her kiss was so much more gentle and caring than the aggressive, almost desperate lips of Elodie. Alex felt a surge of warmth and happiness inside of him.

"Yeah, well, you could have at least done your best friend a favor and given her my number instead. Man, you're so thoughtless sometimes," Tyler piped up.

"I'm pretty sure she's looking for someone at least over five feet," Alex retorted.

"Hey, man, I'm five-four, and I'll have you know in Hollywood, short men are sexy!" Tyler tried to look offended, but he was smiling. "Anyway, I think this astronaut thing is going to your head. Since when did you get big boy pants and start fighting back?"

Alex grabbed Tyler into a headlock. Tyler struggled but eventually broke free.

Mackenzie wedged herself between them. "Boys, boys. There's no need to fight. If you really need, Tyler, I can find you a nice girl who will be much less work than Elodie Fritzer. I know a lot of short girls." Tyler knocked his elbow into Mackenzie's ribs gently as she wrapped her arms around both of them.

The trio ambled out the back door into the warm air of the Houston night, talking and laughing loudly, as the stars shone brightly above them.

ACKNOWLEDGMENTS

As a first-time writer with a full-time job, I would never have been able to reach the point of publication without the help and encouragement of many people.

Christina Lin provided invaluable guidance that helped transform my flat early first drafts into a story with much deeper nuance and meaning. Both my Mom and Dad gave a plethora of encouragement and feedback on the characters and storyline, which was rocket fuel to keep my writing moving forward. My siblings Laura and Joel remained supportive and encouraging of this and my many other projects, and I can't thank you enough. To my brother-in-law Jon, I will always remember finally getting some quiet time at the coffee house in Minnesota where we were both able to sit together and write.

Thanks to Judy Leane for her encouraging feedback on the story. I would also like to thank all of the members of the Bull Run writer's group who listened and commented on readings of several chapters before the pandemic interrupted our cadence. Richard Barr's persistence and dedication to keeping the group running is inspirational.

Many others along the way have given me encouragement and ideas, and while my life is full of too many good people to name, you all know who you are.

Finally, to Sonia, Alex, Eliana and Brayden - thank you from the bottom of my heart for always being there for me, sharing adventures, making me laugh and helping me through hard times. I couldn't ask for a better family to come home to every day.

ABOUT THE AUTHOR

Paul Brower is an aerospace engineer who has worked in spacecraft operations for NASA and several commercial aerospace companies. He has led teams in mission control centers supporting the shuttle, space station and commercial satellite flights, but unlike the characters in his book does not drive a convertible (anymore) or pick up girls at bars following his shifts. While he has not yet flown to space, Paul has experienced zero-gravity during two flights conducting experiments aboard NASA's reduced gravity "vomit comet" aircraft. In 2022, Paul was the recipient of a Rotary National Award for Space Achievement.

Paul has a wide variety of interests and hobbies including writing, hiking, cooking, skiing and sailing. He resides in Virginia with his wife and children. *NewStar One* is his first novel.

9 798986 186306